THIS IS A LIE

THIS IS A LIE

A NOVEL

CLEO BALLARD

NEW YORK

Books should be disposed of and recycled according to local requirements. All paper materials used are FSC compliant.

Published in the United States by Crooked Lane Books, an imprint of The Quick Brown Fox & Company LLC.

Crooked Lane Books and its logo are trademarks of The Quick Brown Fox & Company LLC.

Library of Congress Catalog-in-Publication data available upon request.

ISBN (hardcover): 979-8-89242-586-5
ISBN (paperback): 979-8-89242-587-2
ISBN (ebook): 979-8-89242-588-9

Cover design by Emily Mahar

Printed in the United States.

www.crookedlanebooks.com

Crooked Lane Books
34 West 27th St., 10th Floor
New York, NY 10001

First Edition: June 2026

The authorized representative in the EU for product safety and compliance is eucomply OÜPärnu mnt 139b-14, 11317 Tallinn, Estonia, hello@eucompliancepartner.com, +33757690241

10 9 8 7 6 5 4 3 2 1

This Book is dedicated to Henry

Sometimes you find an adventure buddy always game
to discover new places, challenges and sports.
Now and then, you are gifted with a true friend,
rain or shine. If luck allows, life might even bring
you a devoted life partner. Henry is all those things,
and I am grateful beyond measure.
Love you forever, H.

“Beware; I am fearless and therefore powerful.”

— Mary Shelley

Near the end . . .

THE GIRL'S HAIR is plastered to her skull. Her jeans and hoodie are soaked through and untied black Converse sneakers balance on a slick railing. One hand hovers in the cold air. The other is wrapped around a light post.

A hundred feet below, cars race by, oblivious to the teen perched above and ready to take flight. My headlights slice through the rain, but she doesn't register the beams, or my driver's door as it rasps open.

I whisper, "Please." More loudly, "Please, don't jump."

She glances over her shoulder. "You can't understand."

I know when she lost her first tooth, advanced from crawling to walking, learned to ride a bike . . . "I do."

Cautiously, I take a step forward. Her left hand releases the steel post. She sways, then steadies, but the storm's wind kicks up and her back arches, arms flutter . . . *like wings?* One of her sneakers slips, and she grabs the post, rights herself, a single breath from oblivion.

There's a taste to terror—bitter, salty, metallic. "Let me tell you a story."

"Don't come any closer," she warns.

I hold up my hands, like I'm the victim and she's the one with the gun. But that's not true. I don't have a gun, would never shoot anyone, but what I've done is far worse. "I promise I won't. But will you listen?"

"Why should I?" she demands.

"Because this is my fault. Let me tell you why. Then you can decide what to do next."

She shifts on the top rail. Her knees tremble. Breath catches in my throat . . .

"If I listen, you won't try to stop me?"

She used to love tea parties, sleepovers, and every dog she met . . . I wedge my hands in my jacket pockets to prove I'm no threat. Another lie. "I won't, if you listen to the whole story." *But if you jump, I will, too.*

"Tell me."

"It all began when the phone rang. The caller ID said Potential Spam . . ."

Part I

CHAPTER

1

"DINNER OUT TONIGHT?" I ask. It's our anniversary and we always go to Oscar's for Italian, followed by the best tiramisu in the city.

Bruce adjusts his tie. He's a partner at Crosby & Stone Insurance, believes if he doesn't dress seriously, why would their clients trust him. "Can't tonight. Partner meeting with Hal. We're opening a new office in Chicago."

He forgot? This is the first time, and it lands like a sucker punch. Bruce is under a lot of stress. *But he wouldn't forget. Would he?* Uneasy, I tap the icon I recently created and installed on my phone. "Are you sure you don't want to go out?" I repeat.

My husband gives his head a quick shake, the way he does when he thinks I've missed the obvious. "Penn, hello?" he jokes. "Work meeting. New office in Chicago."

"Got it. Sorry."

"No worries. Your head was in the clouds."

Irritation chafes. I don't like it when he makes me sound like a space cadet. Bruce's phone rings, he glances at the screen—Potential Spam—declines the call. His screensaver, a photo of him with our daughter, Circe, at Alpine Meadows, reappears. The setting sun casts them and the mountain in alpenglow. That shot got 4,500 views on LivLoud and earned three gold medals, meaning more than three thousand people actively engaged to like it.

"I can make a late meal."

"Up to you, hon."

"I don't mind." I could remind him it's our anniversary, but don't want flowers or a gift out of guilt. Plus, if he does have something planned, I'd be ruining the surprise.

I sip my coffee. "You get so much spam."

"'Tis always the season for scams," he replies, then downs the last of his cappuccino, pushes back from the breakfast table, leaving half the caramelized onion, roasted red pepper, and Havarti cheese omelet I made uneaten.

Bruce grabs keys to his new BMW, hanging on a hook by the back door. "Can you pick up the dry cleaning? I'm running low on shirts."

"Sure."

"You're the best." He slips out to our garage.

I flick on the TV to fill the silence. A self-help show plays, though it's a repeat. "You can't change what you don't admit," Dr. Bob tells Bill and his wife, Shelly, who are fighting nonstop.

Circe lopes into the kitchen, a long-legged gazelle dressed in ripped jeans and an oversized black hoodie. Yesterday it was a short skirt, high socks, and a white blouse tied at the waist that showed a peek of her midriff. My daughter is trying to find her style—all part of being fourteen. I'm glad she has choices.

She passes a wall hung with yellow-and-white painted disks of tiny hand- and footprints, a framed paint-by-number of a sailboat that we made when she was eight, and a glass shelf lined with some of the mother-daughter art projects we've done over the years. There are decorated Easter eggs set on silver stands and coffee filter butterflies, along with Circe's first Popsicle-stick bird feeder, painted a shocking pink that stained our hands for days.

"You should throw all that crap out," Circe says, then plops onto a kitchen chair, takes a sip of OJ, squeezed fresh, bites into the sunflower spelt bread I learned to make from Ken Bianco's *Best Bread Ever* book.

"Never," I reply. "They remind me of all my favorite times." Circe rolls her eyes but can't help a half smile.

On TV, Dr. Bob listens to Shelly talk about how insensitive Bill is, how she does everything and it's never enough, then remarks, "No matter how flat you make an omelet, it's still got two sides."

"FYI, that guy you're watching is a has-been."

Fact? Teenage girls believe they know everything, and that their mothers are fools. I study my only child. Her blond hair is shoulder-length, and she has her father's light-green eyes, something I'd hoped for when I was pregnant. Mine are a muddy greenish-brown. I'm not sure when Circe turned from a little girl who loved craft projects, bike rides, and snuggling to a tween with braces and now an opinionated young woman. But I'm glad she's found her voice early on.

The has-been, according to Circe, tells Bill and Shelly their problem is that they don't like each other. "You can glue feathers on a dog," he explains, "but it still doesn't make him an eagle."

"Seriously ridiculous," Circe commentates.

I turn off the show and pivot. "Did you finish your computer science homework?" Two weeks ago, one of her teachers called to say Circe was handing in half-completed assignments.

Circe makes a face. "Done. But I still don't get why I need C-Sharp."

"Once you have a handle on it, you'll be able to learn other computer programming languages more easily."

"But I have no interest in coding, and—news flash—I'm not you."

She's right, programming does come easily for me, even after all these years. It just makes sense. For fun, I visit sites like HackerRank and Codewars to see if I can solve their challenges. I don't know all the newest languages but always figure out a creative solution. "You'll get the hang of it," I say with encouragement.

"What are you two lovebirds doing for your anniversary?" Circe asks to change the subject.

She remembered. But there's a good chance Bruce has something up his sleeve. He's always been a surprise kind of guy—hand-drawn coupons for foot rubs, ice cream sundaes, breakfast in bed. Uncertainty stresses me out, though. I'd gladly trade a romantic surprise to know the truth about Bruce's plans for tonight. A muscle twinges in my low back. Lately there have been moments between us, slightly off-key notes that pass quickly enough that I'm not sure I've heard them at all. Maybe I should talk to Bruce about it, but I don't want to rock the boat when it's probably my own insecurities and childish paranoia.

"Mom?" Circe prods.

"Your dad needs to work late."

"No Oscar's?" Circe arches one brow. "But you do that every year."

I focus on scrubbing a pan. "No big deal. We'll celebrate another night."

"I was supposed to go to Emi's, but I could have dinner with you and watch one of those old movies you like?"

The gesture catches me off guard. That's the way it is with teens. One minute you're radioactive, the next they shock you with kindness. "That's okay," I say with a sunny smile. "Just call when you get to Emi's house, make sure you do all of your homework, and curfew is nine thirty tonight."

"If it was up to Dad, he'd let me stay out later," she wheedles.

"Nine thirty," I repeat. Even though it'd be nice to be the easier parent.

Circe shoulders her backpack, then grumbles, "Sometimes it's hard to like you."

It's one of those offhand remarks teenagers make, especially girls, to their mothers. But it still leaves an invisible bruise. "I love you, too!" I call after my daughter as the quiet of our home, far beyond my wildest childhood dreams, brings on a wave of claustrophobia.

Button Bridge Underpass, San Francisco

The Past

I HOLD DADDY, MY stuffed kitty, tight. "Was she scared?"

Mama J looks out the tiny tent's flap. "Who?"

"Persephone." Sometimes she loses track of the story.

Mama J glances over her shoulder at me, fiddles with the blue-green feather earring dangling beneath wavy brown hair. "Persephone was just picking flowers. Why would she be scared?"

"Because the God of the Dead saw her, fell in love."

"Yeah, but Persephone didn't know Hades was gonna kidnap her."

I scoot closer. "Why did he?"

"You already know."

"Because she was so pretty."

"Fat lotta good that did Persephone. Hades dragged her to the Underworld. Then, she was terrified. But there wasn't nothing she could do. Men."

I nod even though I'm not sure what Mama J means. "What did her mama do?"

"Demeter? She called for Persephone but only found scattered flower petals. Then she scoured the world looking for her kid. Punished anyone who didn't help find her—"

Mama J abruptly switches gears, tears through her backpack, tosses the tattered book of Greek myths she sometimes still reads me, cracked makeup tubes found behind a CVS, a few pairs of underwear, and her *Do not ever touch!* plastic baggy onto the floor of the tent.

Goosebumps dot my arms. "What are you looking for?"

"Medicine."

If anything happens to Mama J, I'll be alone. "Are you sick?"

She scratches her neck, nails rasping on pale flesh and crusty scabs. "Not yet."

It's cold tonight and I burrow deeper in my sleeping bag. It has daisies on it and sometimes I imagine them in the same breeze as the flowers Persephone picked. *Mama J would come find me.*

"How did Demeter get Persephone back?"

Mama J rocks onto her heels. She coughs and the sound is thick, wet. "She traveled to the Underworld and demanded that Hades free her daughter or else."

"And he did!"

"I don't know why you love this story so much." She sighs.

"'Cause Demeter saved Persephone!"

Mama J scowls. "The truth is that Demeter was forced by Zeus to have Persephone."

Her tone is sharp. That happens when I'm being dim. I'm only five and three-quarters. I really, really want to understand the truth part, but don't. I can tell, though, that Mama J thinks Demeter didn't really love Persephone. But she went to the Underworld, a very scary place, and rescued her.

Headlights flash on orange tent walls held together with gray tape. Mama J, dressed in a T-shirt with a lightning bolt on the front that shows her belly button and tight jeans she calls her moneymakers, looks out the flap, then sprays her body with perfume that clogs my nose like a cold.

"Did you name me Penny after Persephone?" I can sing the alphabet and know that both of our names begin with the letter *P*. I'm hoping the answer will take a long time and the driver of the car will move on.

"I saw an old penny on the sidewalk. Thought naming you Penny would bring me luck. Joke's on me. Go to sleep." She scooches forward.

"When are you coming back?"

"Two minutes."

I can never tell if she's lying but do know it'll be longer if she gets in the stranger's car for a ride. "Stay. Please."

Before Mama J ducks out of the tent, she says, "Don't go anywhere."

She doesn't want me to end up like Persephone. "Never ever," I reply, but she's already gone. I hear gravel crunch under heavy footsteps, a man's low voice, Mama J's laugh, then rustles, zippers, a ripping sound, lots of moans and words I'm not allowed to say. It's now pitch-black. I'm afraid of the dark.

Headlights sweep, illuminate Cerberus, the watchdog of the Underworld, and throw his shadow on our tent. He keeps the dead from leaving hell and now he's outside. Shaking, I watch Cerberus's two heads, double back, eight legs, and serpent's spiked tail writhe each time a car goes by. Sharp cries cut through the night. My heart hammers. No one in the other tents stirs. *I want Mama J!*

With shaking fingers, I count the sewn-on cherries dotting my favorite sweatshirt again and again and again. Finally, the beast runs off and Mama J slides back into our tent. She smells of roses, dirt, and a sharp funk that makes my stomach clench. As a truck rumbles past, I see that the neck of her shirt is torn and there are red marks on her arms.

"Mama J's gonna take her medicine now."

I roll away like I'm supposed to, squeeze my eyes tight, and hear the tin foil crinkle. Her lighter hisses like a snake.

"Cerberus was outside," I whisper.

Mama J slides onto her blanket, kisses my cheek, then says dreamily, "That wasn't the beast. The only real monsters are the ones inside us."

CHAPTER

2

OUT THE LARGE window over the kitchen sink, San Francisco Bay sparkles and cars stream across the Golden Gate Bridge. Our house is on a steep street in Pacific Heights. The exterior white, the style Victorian. Bruce's father was a gardener for homes like ours, his mother a housekeeper for the place two doors down, and I grew up with Mama J. This house is meaningful for both of us.

When we purchased the home ten years ago, it was run-down but still an enormous stretch, the mortgage massive. Bruce believed that if we created the illusion of the life we wanted, our dreams would come true. And he was right. We restored the place ourselves using how-to books checked out from the library and home improvement videos, scrimped and saved to renovate, bought secondhand furniture.

Now everything in our home is custom—velvet upholstery, Turkish carpets, artwork picked for its future value, all chosen by an interior designer. Sometimes it feels like I've been plopped down in someone else's life. Occasionally, I still have nightmares that my family, our house, was a beautiful dream and that I really live alone in a roach-infested apartment with peeling ceilings, clanking pipes, and a cracked tub with rust stains that look like dried blood.

Banishing that thought, I make another cup of coffee, finish Bruce's cold omelet, then open my computer and click on Liv-Loud. It's a social media site with endless free creative filters and super easy video options that have made it popular with both middle-aged women and teenagers. Teens employ the disappearing DMs to get into all sorts of trouble.

I pull up a photo of this morning's breakfast. The sun streams onto our maple table, glances off a blue hydrangea centerpiece I cut from outside the front door early this morning, the omelet, sprinkled with home-grown chives, and a cut crystal glass of orange juice. Steam from Bruce's cappuccino spirals upward. Beneath the photo I type: *Another perfect breakfast with the family! Try lightly browning the butter when you make an omelet to add a caramelized flavor. #breakfasttip.* I click the green button and hear the satisfying bell chime.

Val has posted a new shot. It's a black-and-white of her daughter Emi's blond hair in a perfect French braid. My best friend was once primarily a stylist. I leave a star on Val's post and a private DM: *#jealous.* Val knows that Circe thinks I'm totally uncool these days.

My phone rings. It's Magnolia High School. "Hello?"

"Hey Penn, it's Lindy from the school office. We have another computer problem I can't solve. Could you stop by?"

"Sure thing. I'll swing over before lunch."

"I'm not sure what we'd do without you. Thanks a million!"

Her palpable relief makes me smile. School networks have private personal information on students, staff, and teachers, including their Social Security numbers. There was a hacking incident last year, and ever since I set up a firewall to protect Magnolia's confidential data from malware, ransomware, and phishing attacks, Lindy thinks I can solve any IT problem. It's nice to feel productive.

I return to LivLoud. Kiki, my other best friend, has posted a photo of Charlotte, also fourteen, in her winter-white cheerleading uniform. My phone rings again; the tone is a fox giggling. Kiki picked it herself.

"Hey there! I was just thinking about you. That picture of Charlotte is gorgeous."

"Too gorgeous?" Kiki asks.

Her daughter filled out this past year, and she worries that Char will now attract boys like bees to flowers. "It's fine, promise." We're like Rachel and Monica on the *Friends* reruns I still watch. We talk each other off the ledges.

"I also have two boys, Penn. I know how they think." She sighs dramatically. "What are you up to?"

"Right now, I'm going through Circe's posts."

"You are such a better mom than me," she laments. "I can't stay current with it all."

"It makes me feel like a stalker," I admit. Even though Circe knows I occasionally check her feed. Social media can be a cesspool—there's bullying and predators. I scroll on as Kiki rattles off her morning plans—SoulCycle and acupuncture. Circe's most current posts include selfies with Emi and Charlotte. The three went to the same Montessori school pre-K and have been friends ever since. I notice a new guy—tall, brown hair, lacrosse jersey, a cocky smile that hits like a wrong note. Beneath his photo is *#topscorer #winnerwinner*. I click on the boy's face and the name Wess Morehead appears.

"Have you heard of a kid named Wess?" I ask.

Kiki giggles, sounding like her ringtone. "Char is seeing Wess, but they're not official yet."

I don't ask what it takes to be considered official. Our daughter hasn't brought up dating. I'm relieved that she's a late bloomer. Dr. Beth, a psychologist podcaster I sometimes listen to, says that kids shouldn't date one-on-one until they're eighteen. That's over-the-top, but I do want Circe to enjoy childhood for as long as possible.

"We still on for lunch?" Kiki asks.

Her voice is higher pitched than usual, but getting three kids off to school is mayhem. "I'll be there."

I continue scrolling as she shares the new word Char taught her—*karmaquences.*

"It means if you do something good, you'll attract good things," Kiki explains.

"And if you're bad?" I ask.

"Karma will kick your butt."

"I like it!"

Hal Crosby's wife, Heather, has posted on her LivLoud feed a photo of a shiny black Range Rover with a yellow bow on the hood. Underneath it she's written: *Who knew another trip around the sun would bring this baby! #besthusbandever.* I swipe right to a shot of Heather's tall, handsome sons and Hal, who is short and bald, around a birthday cake. Below the picture I add *#youdeserveitall!*

Kiki asks, "Weekend plans?"

I stretch arms over my head, yawn despite two cups of coffee. "Let's see . . . Bruce and Circe are going skiing with Hal and the boys at their house in Tahoe."

"You're not going with them?" Kiki sounds worried.

"I like them to have father-daughter adventures." *And I never learned to ski well.* Kiki doesn't say anything, and the silence feels freighted. *Why am I so on edge?* "Anyway, I plan to be a slug, read a Stephen King novel."

"It's impossible for you to be a slug, and no one would ever guess that you're a horror fan."

"Why not?"

"Because you're you. Former Girl Scout leader, PTA member, computer whiz, and consummate corporate wife."

Perception is reality. "Stephen King's stories aren't just about horror. They shine a light on the human condition."

"Okay smarty-pants," Kiki says with a chuckle. "See you in a few hours?"

"Yup." I hang up, then open a flagged folder on my desktop for the project that I resurrected in earnest six months ago. Once it sank in that Circe is now a full-fledged teenager with a busy schedule that rarely includes me, unless she needs a ride. Bruce works all day and has more and more late meetings, so I've been left with way too much time on my hands.

I pull up the computer program begun the first year of my PhD program. The idea was to create a different kind of lie detector that, instead of recording pulse, blood pressure, and perspiration, used word choices, cadence, enunciation, and rate of speech to detect lies. I interviewed and recorded thousands of people reading declarative statements that could be true or false, like "I have never urinated in a public swimming pool," or "I once stole a candy bar," then had them truthfully answer those questions on a corresponding form with the goal of creating a computer program that could determine with 99.9 percent certainty—nothing is 100 percent but death—if they were lying.

Why tackle lying? Dr. Edmunds, my PhD Applied Language Sciences doctoral adviser, had asked when I first proposed my thesis project.

I'm not high.
I'll be home in an hour.
We won't have to live back on the street.
He's a good guy.
Just one hit.
You can stay in this school.
He loves little kids.
I'll keep you safe . . .

By my teens, I'd learned all of Mama J's tells. But experience had also shown me that the world was full of liars. I wanted a way to weed them out. But instead of the truth—the irony didn't escape me—I told Dr. Edmunds that a new kind of lie detector could have fascinating, real-world applications.

Penn, you have a hunger to learn that's rare, Dr. Edmunds said. He leaned back in his leather office chair, a pipe clenched between back molars. *You can achieve greatness.*

I blushed from my head to my toes, unused to compliments, especially from this professor, but also because Luc, his teaching assistant, was in the doctoral meeting. Anytime Luc was near, my stomach filled with butterflies, despite having a boyfriend. Part of that was Luc's intellect, the other part, his intense eyes . . . and dimples.

But there is a danger to the program you're proposing, Dr. Edmunds continued. *To quote Marvin Minsky, the 1970s computer scientist, "Once the computers get control, we might never get it back."* He paused for emphasis. *We would survive at their sufferance. If we're lucky, they might decide to keep us as pets.*

I laughed. *My computer program will just identify lies.*

He took a puff of his pipe. *What if that program developed a mind of its own?*

In the 1950s, Luc said, *Alan Turing proposed a test to see if a human evaluator could tell the difference between a conversation with a human and one with a machine. But far as I know, no computer has passed it.*

A resigned look settled on Dr. Edmund's face. *Yet. But when one does, how will you know what to believe?*

There was a knock on the closed door. *Come in,* Luc called.

Bruce stepped into the wood-paneled office. He knew I had a meeting with my thesis adviser; we'd agreed I'd call him when it was finished.

Ready to go? Bruce said.

Could you give us a few more minutes? Luc asked. *We're finishing up a discussion about the future of artificial intelligence.*

Bruce chuckled. *That fad? It'll be great for playing checkers, maybe chess.* He shifted the leather briefcase he always carried to his business school classes. *It's Larry, right?*

Luc smiled. *Luc.*

I blushed again. They'd met several times. Bruce had taken an instant dislike to my TA.

Sorry, but we have lunch reservations, Bruce said.

Dr. Edmunds set down his pipe. *Then let's wrap this up.*

Bruce held out his hand and I took it.

Turns out, we didn't have a reservation anywhere, but Bruce had made us peanut butter and jelly sandwiches. We had a romantic lunch on the university's lawn. It only bothered me a little that he'd been able to lie so easily.

CHAPTER

3

A WAVE OF MELANCHOLY descends. I never had the chance to finish compiling the data, prove my thesis. But I've gone back to it over the years, picked it up now and then. It's a touchstone that reminds me of a time when I was finally turning into the person I wanted to be. For the past six months, I've been focused on developing a framework for growing the program. The idea is to make it not only able to detect lies, but eventually capable of giving advice. I have no idea how to do this, but I'm sifting through the options.

Bruce would say it's a rabbit hole and I'm Alice, chasing a white bunny. He's probably right. I mean, my doctoral ship sailed almost fifteen years ago. I'm so far behind the newest advances it's laughable. I do wonder, though, what Dr. Edmunds would say if he knew my current plan. He'd probably ask me to consider the AI implications, but he'd also want to know, why a program that gives advice, too?

The answer is embarrassing. Over the years, my confidence has deteriorated. It makes no sense—Girl Scout leader, PTA member, computer whiz, and consummate corporate wife . . . All true. But the world I inhabit is sometimes so foreign to me, even now, it's like living on a different planet. I've heard it can take a lifetime abroad to master a new culture and language. That even when you're fluent, it's still difficult to fit in. I want a safeguard in order to avoid missteps. A guaranteed way to be the best wife (lately it feels like I'm somehow failing, though I can't pinpoint how), mother (a constant minefield, more so as the years go by), and friend (I can never lose Val and Kiki, who are both best friends and guides).

Pushing the past aside, I pull up the recording made of Bruce this morning, load it. My old thesis is far from done. I still have reams of data to parse. Basically, I need to teach my program how to most accurately detect lies *and* understand the social nuances of infinite situations. A few months ago, I finally began phase one, testing a skeletal program that uses previous recordings. For fun, I'm now adding Bruce to that mix. If he knew I'd taped him this morning, he'd be annoyed. Not because he has anything to hide. Bruce would just think it was a colossal waste of energy. If it doesn't have a bottom line, can't be monetized, my husband isn't interested. When you grow up like him, feeling like you're behind in the race to succeed, you don't want to waste a moment. Bruce can't possibly understand that when you're raised the way I was, always afraid of losing what little you have, unsure who to trust and how to navigate the world, the need for truth and advice is ever-present.

Once my husband's voice has downloaded, the icon I created—an image of a woman in a white off-the-shoulder gown, with wide blue eyes and long blond hair topped with a crown of roses—spins as the program does its thing. It took me weeks to make that likeness, but it adds a flare.

My body tenses. *What am I worried about?* Lately a sense of unease has permeated through me, like a low-level chronic illness. Maybe it's my age—is thirty-eight too early for a midlife crisis? Am I regretting past decisions, or wishing for the road not taken? That's silly. Circe is my world.

My thoughts drift back to breakfast. Bruce's patience with me has been decreasing in direct proportion to his success. Other things have declined, too. We've been married fifteen years.

Familiarity can sometimes breed disinterest, but that doesn't mean our commitment to each other has changed. Still, sex used to be so important to us. Is that why things are feeling off?

As I wait for my program to tell me whether Bruce was lying, my stomach seesaws. I hope he was, and that he's planned a special night. Fifteen is a big number. It seems wrong to complain, though. All I ever wished for was love and stability, and I got so much more.

Finally, the icon slows, then stops. Her hair settles back on polished shoulders. A message appears.

Can't tonight. Work meeting. New office in Chicago.

That is a lie.

Relief rains down and I release the breath stacked like sandbags in my lungs. Disaster averted. Midlife crisis ten years off. Bruce has been distracted lately; who wouldn't be, running a huge company with offices in San Francisco, LA, Portland, and Seattle, and another one about to open in Chicago? *But he didn't forget.*

Of course, I could've told him or taken it upon myself to surprise Bruce. I have done that in the past. But come on! No matter how long you've been married, sometimes you just need your man to, well, sweep you off your feet.

The icon spins again, a glitch. They abound at this early stage of a program. It revolves two, three, four more times, then abruptly stops.

I don't mind.

That is a lie.

I must've forgotten to stop recording. "Of course it's a lie," I say with a laugh. "What woman wouldn't mind?" I wish my program could already respond, tell me I'm normal, then drop the perfect morsel to see me through and settle nerves that are still twitching.

Again, the icon resumes spinning. Her blond hair whips sideways as she turns in tight circles, then comes to a halt.

'Tis always the season for scams.

That is a lie.

The icon remains still. Her eyes, the color of the Pacific Ocean, the darkest of blues, regard me. It doesn't *mean* anything, just another error in the code I've written. So why do I imagine sharks lurking beneath the calm of her irises?

An old-fashioned ringtone cuts through the quiet. It's Bruce's. He left for work fifteen minutes ago. If he doesn't realize he forgot his phone before he gets to the office, I'll drive the half hour and drop it off for him. Now I search for his iPhone and find it under the *San Francisco Times*. The screen says Potential Spam. I hesitate—Bruce doesn't like me to engage with spammers—then pick up anyway.

"Hello . . . Hello?" The line is silent, but I hear someone breathing . . .

Pacific Heights, San Francisco

The Past

"CLOSE YOUR MOUTH. You look like a fish tossed out of water."

Mama J yanks my hand, and I stumble. We're not anywhere near home—the Tenderloin, sometimes the Mission if the police decide to clean up the neighborhood, which just means pushing us to a different underpass. "That house," I say, looking back over my shoulder at the white castle with turrets and windows filled with blue, yellow, and green glass, "is where I'll live when I grow up."

"Places like these," Mama J says, gesturing at the three-story homes with balconies, trimmed hedges, and gardens filled with perfect blooms, before hawking up phlegm and spitting a yellow-green gob on the smooth sidewalk, "aren't for people like us."

"Why not?"

"Penny, there are stories and there's real life. In real life, happily ever after doesn't happen the way you think."

"But it could."

Mama J sighs. "You'll get it, eventually."

A man in a suit and tie walks to his car. It's a white one with a Mercedes symbol on the front. He glances at us, frowns. My skin burns. I'm dressed in my favorite cherry sweatshirt and the overalls

Mama J found at the Salvation House that have cartoon characters sewn above the pockets—a mouse, a duck, and a grinning pig. I loved the overalls but now I don't as much.

"Fake it," Mama J says, then squares her shoulders, lowers the sunglasses she swiped from the Dollar Store, and struts like she owns this street. I stand up straighter. "That's my girl."

We near a mother, yellow dress, low heels, putting her baby in the back of a shiny silver minivan. When we pass, she glances at us, waves. Maybe Mama J is right about pretending.

"Keep up," she instructs.

We fall in behind three teenage girls in matching gray-and-blue plaid skirts. Snow-white collars peek from cabled sweaters, shiny loafers make tappity-taps. They must be best friends. If I found a magic lantern on the beach and a genie came out of it, granted me one wish, I'd ask to be them. The tallest girl, her hair in a blond ponytail, giggles as they race up the wide steps of a columned stone building. I can't read the sign, I'm only six, but bet it's a school. Jealousy is like the cough syrup Mama J once made me take when my skin was on fire, throat too sore to swallow.

"Can we go home?" I ask, longing for the familiar orange walls of our tent; desperate not to see a world that's like the chocolate in a store window we can never taste.

Mama J nods at the plastic blue cans lining the street. "Rich folks throw out good food, nice clothes, and new shoes, sometimes even jewelry. It's garbage day, and who better to take out the trash than us?"

"I don't want to," I whine, embarrassed.

"Damn it, kid, sometimes you're hard to like." Mama J drags me over to the trash bins. "Get used to it. This is life."

CHAPTER

4

"HELLO? IS ANYONE there?" More breathing. I hang up just as the front door opens.

"Forgot my phone," Bruce calls, his Italian leather shoes clopping down the front hall.

"You got another spam call," I say as he rounds the corner.

"Did you answer it?"

Invisible fingers pluck at the back of my neck. "Yes."

Bruce grimaces. "Penny."

I hate when he uses my full name instead of the shortened version I chose when I left for college. It's like being shoved in the chest, stumbling back into the past. He knows that. He's the sole person in my life who does. But he still calls me Penny when he's annoyed. I sneeze three times in a row. Bruce is wearing a new cologne with hints of patchouli. "Sorry. Thought I could ask them to stop calling you. But the line dropped."

He takes his phone. "Never answer. That just spawns a dozen more calls from different numbers."

"So, how do you stop the calls?"

Bruce pockets his phone. "I block the number."

It's not worth telling him that his plan doesn't make sense. He no longer thinks of me as the promising PhD candidate he met at grad school, head stuck in books, parsing data as I battled through my thesis.

What are you working on? Bruce had asked when he neared my library carrel late one night.

An interactive program that allows the user to detect lies.

Impressive, Bruce said. . . . *but am I lying?*

I laughed. Bruce was geeky—oversized glasses balanced on a narrow nose, outdated jeans, and no-brand sneakers. I recognized a fellow traveler. Plus he had beautiful green eyes.

A few weeks later, he left a scavenger hunt in my carrel on paper burned at the corners to look like old parchment, rolled into a scroll and tied with a gold ribbon. I followed the hunt all over campus, picking up prizes along the way—a plastic snow globe with sailboats that rocked in waves of glitter, a pair of navy-blue socks dotted with white rabbits, a small box of chocolates, a dozen cherry lollipops wrapped like roses in green tissue paper, vouchers for the local laundromat, a bottle of Chianti, and a pen that, when tipped, went from the SF skyline at night to dawn breaking over the Golden Gate Bridge. The final stop was the student union where Bruce was waiting with two hot chocolates and gingersnap cookies. I'd never been pursued before. It felt like standing in a sunbeam.

Now Bruce pecks my forehead with chapped lips. "Sorry for being short, hon. Lots on my mind. Have a good day."

I can't recall the last time he kissed me like he meant it and wish we could wind back time. "No worries. See you tonight," I call out as the door slams.

The memory of our first conversation in the library fades and my mood slips. I'm Penn Stone, not Penn Roberts, who was once on a full-ride scholarship, both undergraduate and grad school at San Francisco Polytechnical Institute. I've been a wife and mother almost half my life. And my husband has long forgotten that I was anonymously nominated for the Henry Johnson Fellowship only six months into my PhD work, given to students in financial need, for exceptional creativity, promise, and the belief that the nominee's work will lead to future advances important to the world at large. Sometimes, I do wonder what I could've accomplished with the no-strings-attached award. But I dropped out of the PhD program before I had the chance to find out.

When the kitchen is clean, I head upstairs for a quick shower and shampoo with the citrus blend Kiki gifted me this past Christmas. After toweling off, I study my reflection in the mirror—something I rarely do. My breasts are small, legs long, middle a little soft. I do Pilates, spin, and hot yoga when Kiki drags me to the classes, but lately I've begged off. In college I owned a pair of Hoka running sneakers, a castoff from my freshman-year roommate, and loved to jog in Golden Gate Park, listen to the pound of my heart until I was carved-out. A nameless anxiety pinches. *Maybe I need to start running again?*

Turning away from the mirror, I pull up Dr. Beth's podcast. She always makes me feel better. She's talking with a married lady embarrassed to have sex with the lights on after gaining weight during pregnancy. Her husband is frustrated, and she's worried he might leave her.

"Go for morning walks or bike rides," Dr. Beth advises. "That will provide endorphins. Then buy a new dress, cook your husband's favorite meal, and act like his girlfriend. He loves you, not the number on a scale. Tonight, leave those lights on and blow his mind!"

While Dr. Beth sounds like a 1950s housewife—out of date and politically incorrect—some of her advice is pragmatic. It doesn't hurt to remind your husband how he felt when you first started dating.

I focus on the present. My program might be wrong—it's not foolproof yet. Bruce still could've forgotten our anniversary. Last week I recorded the statement "I have four children," and the program told me that was true. Just in case it's mistaken now, I'll plan a late candlelit dinner, cook all Bruce's favorite foods, have the freshly ironed sheets on the bed that he's loved ever since he was delighted by them at a small family-run hotel on a vacation we took to Greece. Then I'll do my best to blow his mind.

I spin through my photo album, pull up a nice shot of us from a fundraising dinner at Circe's school. Bruce's arm loosely circles my waist. I upload the photo to LivLoud and write beneath it: *15 years today!!! Happy Anniversary to my best friend, soulmate, and darling husband.*

Now I feel better. *I really do.* But my nerves still rustle like an intruder creeping up the back stairs.

CHAPTER

5

Val and Kiki already have a table in the corner when I arrive at Le Pain Quotidien. I left my Tesla in doggy mode—even though Bruce's allergies won't allow us to have a dog—to make sure the lamb I picked up from the butcher doesn't spoil in an overheated car. The café is busy, a friendly buzz punctuated by the grinding of coffee beans and clatter of plates and cutlery. My friends have ordered. A steaming double cappuccino and an almond croissant dusted with confectioners' sugar wait for me at a linen-covered table. *They know me so well.*

Kiki wears a matching Lululemon yoga outfit and Val's gleaming brunette tresses brush the top of her checkered dress. I'm in my usual uniform: a perfectly pressed baby-blue button-down from Frank & Eileen paired with linen khakis and Cole Haan leather slides, my navy-blue blazer at the ready in case I get cold.

A lock of highlighted brown hair slips from a neat bun and I tuck it behind an ear decorated with a tasteful diamond stud. "Sorry I'm late." I slip onto the woven chair. "The high school called, hardware malfunction. Their system was freezing because of a faulty RAM combined with a failing hard drive."

"In English?" Kiki jokes.

I laugh. "It's fixed."

Val takes a sip of her latte. "They really should pay you."

"They don't have the funds." Once the principal, Dr. Boone, learned at a school event that I have some IT skills, he asked if I'd volunteer to get their systems up to date. My croissant crumbles as I take a big bite, sends pastry flakes down the front of my shirt. Quickly, I brush them away.

"We're lucky to have you helping out," Kiki notes.

"Thanks." Magnolia is a public school—Bruce wanted private, but I dug in. Like Val and Kiki, I don't want my daughter to live in a bubble, though neither of my friends know I didn't grow up in one. I've told them that I spent my childhood in a suburb outside Chicago, Dad was a CFO, mom volunteered; that they're still happily married but don't like to travel so we Zoom a lot. My best friends might find my real past fascinating, lean into stories about Mama J, living under a bridge, scrounging food from dumpsters. But ultimately those things would paint me as other, leave an invisible stain. Sometimes I do feel guilty lying about my past. Real friends tell each other everything, just like the characters on *Friends*. But who I am now is what matters most.

You'll get it, eventually, Mama J whispers.

Lately, I've been flashing back to my childhood and hearing her voice more and more. *What is going on with me?* I take a quick photo of my croissant and coffee and post it on LivLoud: *#besties-coffeebreak*. As Val munches a tofu lettuce wrap and Kiki nibbles her Cobb salad, I ask "So, what'd I miss?"

"Sara Curry has a new petition," Val says. "She wants to have Madame Gault, the high school French teacher, fired because she'd once appeared in a swimsuit calendar. In a one-piece."

Kiki leans in. "I heard Caroline Gold has a boyfriend. He's twenty-four!"

Caroline is one of the older moms. Her daughter, Sophia, is the same age as our girls, but Caroline is fifty-two while the rest of us are late thirties to mid-forties.

A few years ago, Caroline's husband cheated on her. She caught him in the act, in their bed, then sent an email to all their friends, acquaintances, and Roger Gold's business partners telling them about her discovery with a photo that showcased Roger's hairy ass.

"Good for her," I say.

Kiki gives me a startled look. "Okay," she says, drawing out the word.

"What?" I ask.

"It's nothing. I'm being judgey." She glances at my empty mug. "Do you want more coffee?"

"Sure. You can never be too caffeinated, right?"

Kiki signals the busy waiter for a refresh when he gets the chance, then sighs. "Christopher wants us to go to St. John's, scuba dive for spring break."

"And that's a problem?" Val asks with a snort.

"Topher has lacrosse practice during vacation and Haynes is desperate to go skiing in Utah with his best friend's family. Charlotte wants to attend cheer camp in Texas."

"Topher can stay with a friend, send Haynes skiing and Char to cheer camp, then you and Christopher could go alone," I suggest.

"You're right." Kiki grins. "I'll buy the tickets today."

Those tickets will be first class. Christopher Hunt is one of *the* Hunts, a mining family originally from Nevada, though they sold the business a generation ago. Kiki and Chris met in San Francisco, at a bowling alley of all places. He saw her dark-blond curls, heart-shaped face, and sexy curves and threw a ball into her lane, said it was love at first sight. Because it's Kiki, I believe him.

Val notices a man at the next table staring at us—or more probably the two of them. "What are you looking at?" she demands. He blanches and moves his coffee and croissant to a table inside.

Kiki chides, "Don't be a hater. In ten years, we'll wish a guy would check us out."

Val makes a face. "He seemed like a creep."

Unlike Kiki, there was never a Christopher in her life. Val's Prince Charming bailed after learning she was pregnant. *Good riddance*, Val always says, *I'd never want to share my kid.* The three of us have watched many divorces play out over the years and all agree that a fifty-fifty custody split would break our hearts.

"Did I mention I'm opening another salon?" Val asks, then takes a sip of her cold brew. She already owns three, plus a med spa.

Kiki hugs her, which Val hates but allows. "You're flipping amazing!"

"No biggie," Val replies with a wave of her hand.

She's being humble. She's successful and totally independent. I feel a twist of envy. I don't want her life, but it'd be nice to know I'm capable of success.

Val adds, "Helps that I only have one kid."

Heat dusts my cheeks. I only have one kid. "Congratulations," I say and raise my coffee mug to toast her. A hand darts over my left shoulder. There's a tattoo—

Fingers curl over the ripped fabric of the station wagon's front seat, nails ragged, a black skull tattoo on the back of a meaty hand. The skull's eyes are red pits, and a snake with fangs slithers from an open mouth. Before I can scream, the man launches over the seat. He smells like a wet, dirty dog, grips a serrated knife, and holds it to my neck. There's a sharp bite and then blood dribbles down my sweaty skin. The man puts his finger to his lips and says shhhhh, then unbuttons my jeans and yanks them down . . .

C H A P T E R

6

PETRIFIED, I DROP my mug, sweep my arm up, twist and grapple for the knife. The waiter's narrow silver coffee carafe goes flying. Hot brown liquid spills when it crashes on the sidewalk.

"Penn, what are you doing?" Val asks.

As the past recedes, sickness rises like the tide followed by a hot flush. "Oh! Sorry. You snuck up on me," I feebly explain to the waiter, then see it's not a skull on the back of his hand. It's a yin-yang symbol.

"Clearly, she's had too much coffee already," Kiki says with an ingratiating smile that the waiter instantly returns. Everyone loves Kiki.

The waiter wipes up the spilled coffee. And after only a couple of moments of awkward silence, Val says, "I've never understood why you didn't go back to grad school" to cover for my strange overreaction.

The adrenaline charging through my body eases. What are friends for . . .

"You know that I considered it—"

"No," Val says. "You've never mentioned that."

Her stare is intense. *She's the one who's had too much caffeine.* "Oh. Well, I did, once Circe was in school full time. But Bruce pointed out that we didn't need dual incomes, and Circe would spend afternoons home alone since I'd be required to work as a teaching assistant as part of my program."

"You live in Pacific Heights," Kiki says. "It's not the Tenderloin."

I explain, "Bruce was a latchkey kid and didn't love it." I, too, had spent afternoons and too many nights alone once Mama J and I had our own place, scared, watching sitcoms to drown out the fights on the other side of too-thin walls and the blare of police sirens.

Val frowns. "So, Bruce was against it."

Yes. Despite our plans when he proposed. "We both wanted what was best for Circe. And anyway, there was no guarantee I would've gotten into a new PhD program."

"But are you ever sorry that you didn't even try?" Val presses.

There's an intensity to her question and I'm starting to feel ganged up on. Usually, Val and Kiki are content to talk about themselves or our girls. The truth is that I *was* sorry over the years, especially once Circe needed me less, and broached the subject multiple times to Bruce until he finally put an end to it.

I appreciate all you do for Circe, me, our family. We're so lucky. But sometimes, Penny, I worry that subconsciously you want to sabotage our lives; that you're drawn to the chaos of your youth.

Horrified at the idea Mama J had buried a secret grenade inside of me, set to detonate if I followed my desires, I never brought up grad school again.

"There are always little regrets," I now admit. "It would've been exciting to see what I could've accomplished."

My friends share a look, and my scalp tightens the way it used to when Mama J lied. That pesky lock of hair escapes and again I push it back into place.

'Tis always the season . . .

I dig nails into my palm to refocus. My program's glitches have just made me jumpy.

"Big plans for your anniversary tonight?" Kiki asks.

"I'm pretty sure Bruce has something in store." But when was the last coupon book for foot rubs? At least ten years ago. And ice cream sundae surprises, or breakfast in bed? Three years, maybe more. I can't even remember our last date night. "He might've forgotten," I concede, keeping my tone light. "It's not a big deal. Bruce is swamped at work. If it did slip his mind, we'll have lamb lollipops, braised veggies, homemade gnocchi, and tiramisu for dessert." I smile, but salt water still pools. It's mortifying. I don't ever cry in public.

Kiki reaches for my hand. "What's going on?"

A rush of gratitude that I have two best friends who care hits. *They're the answer to my childhood wish.* "Bruce is very busy with work—"

"But . . . ?" Val prods. She's the protective one, quick to defend, and always on a friend's side.

My cheeks warm, but friends share things. I know that Kiki had an eating disorder, still struggles with it, and constantly worries that Charlotte might follow in her footsteps; that Val's mostly estranged from her parents because at nineteen, she decided to keep Emi instead of putting her up for adoption like they wished. She's also afraid that her inability to have lasting relationships will affect Emi's future choices. They both know about my miscarriage, were there to pick up the pieces when I didn't even want to get out of bed. They don't know about the following two, but who wants to be that friend?

I take a deep breath and spill. "Lately, Bruce has been more impatient, and we haven't . . . We haven't had sex in ages."

"What's ages?" Val asks.

"Two months." *It's more.* Val puffs out air in a breathy whistle and looks away. Embarrassment hits. *Is it my fault?* I blow my nose into a cloth napkin, rude in a public restaurant but necessary.

Our table falls into an uncomfortable silence, and I want to disappear. Abruptly, Val says, "Let's go."

"Where?"

She jerks her head at Celeste's, a high-end lingerie boutique across the street. "Sometimes men need to be reminded of what they're missing."

I dutifully follow Val across the street, Kiki in tow. They make me try on various silk and lace outfits. We settle on a whisper-thin chemise and robe in pale pink.

"You will look so sexy Bruce's eyes will fall out of their sockets," Val says at the register. "I'll do your makeup before dinner. A glamorous chignon will finish off the look."

Be your husband's girlfriend, Dr. Beth whispers.

"Penn . . . ?" Kiki asks.

She and Val watch me, concerned. I can't admit that I'm thinking about Dr. Beth's counsel. They both believe she's a pop shrink whose views are regressive. They could never understand that she's one of the people who has helped me have a good marriage, raise Circe, along with lifestyle guru Maddie Stuart, twenty-minute-meal chef Bonnie Roy, therapist Dr. Bob, hip talk show host Olivia, motivational speaker Tanya Decker, blogs, LivLoud, and stacks of self-help books.

"How about I swing by the salon for glam after I get dinner prepped?" I ask.

"Promise you'll show?" Val demands.

She's so serious that again, my nerves scrape. The dirty hand with its skull tattoo flashes like a nauseating strobe in a dance club. As a child, that man wanted my innocence, maybe my life. The remembered taste of terror and impotence curdles on my tongue. *Why has that long-buried memory suddenly resurfaced?*

"Penn?" Val prods.

"Promise," I say and smile so wide it makes the muscle under my right eye twitch.

C H A P T E R

7

ON THE WAY home, my phone buzzes. It's Oscar's Restaurant. My heart lets out a celebratory whoop. *He didn't forget!* I pick up on the Tesla's speaker.

"Hello, is this Mrs. Bruce Stone?"

"It is," I say with a grin, wait for the man to confirm we have a reservation for tonight. Maybe I'll wear the black sling-back high heels Bruce says make my legs look longer. They're hard to walk in, but tonight I'll be his girlfriend. When we get home, I'll slip into the negligee, pull my hair from its chignon, pretend I'm a hot librarian. Bruce and I have never role-played but it might spice things up, set us on a new course.

"Mrs. Stone? Are you there?"

"Oh. Sorry. Yes, I'm here."

"Your husband left his credit card."

"Pardon?"

"Yes. He left it after lunch."

Can't tonight. We're opening a new office in Chicago . . .

"Mrs. Stone?"

"How did you get my number?"

"Our bookkeeper, Claudia Weeks, recognized the name."

Claudia's daughter is on Circe's cheer squad. "I'll swing by and pick it up."

Oscar's is on Nob Hill with a gorgeous view of the Bay. The parking lot is almost empty when I arrive. A flagstone path leads down a tree-lined walkway that twinkles with tiny white lights at night. I push through the ornate iron-and-glass door. Inside, chairs are stacked on tables and a young guy with a ponytail mops the wood floors. Plush red-velvet banquettes and wooden tables set beneath crystal chandeliers look garish in the bright light of day, but at night there's no place more romantic.

Bruce took me to Oscar's the day we married at city hall. It was way too expensive back then, but we splurged to mark the occasion, ate shrimp cocktail and fettuccini alfredo, and shared a tiramisu for dessert. We've only missed one anniversary since—the year he had an emergency appendectomy.

I head to the polished bar where a gray-haired man in a white button-down and black trousers washes out glasses at a small sink, his back to me. "Excuse me, I'm Mrs. Stone. My husband left his credit card?"

"Ah," he says, drying his hands. "Yes, I'm the one who called." He reaches into a drawer and pulls out the card and a gray cashmere cardigan. Turning, he hesitates for a split second, or maybe just straightens up after being bent over the sink, before handing both over.

I glance at the black credit card. It's Bruce's. But the sweater isn't. The floor beneath my practical leather shoes shifts and rolls.

"Did you feel that?" I ask the bartender. *Tiny earthquakes happen all the time in San Francisco.*

"What?"

"Nothing. Thank you."

Once in the car, I check the sweater's tag: Zara—cheap chic—size extra small. I smell it and recognize Sweet Nothings from a recent shopping trip with Circe. My daughter wanted to pick out her first bottle of perfume—Emi and Charlotte already had theirs. I gave her a forty-dollar price limit, and she picked the light, woodsy scent. My hands grip the steering wheel as worries flutter like moths to a flame. But Dr. Bob says that *past behavior is the best indicator of future behavior.* Bruce has always been a devoted husband and father.

Carelessly, I toss the cardigan onto the passenger seat, put Bruce's card in my wallet for safekeeping, and drive away. But the past nips at my heels . . .

Tell me the one about Icarus, I begged Mama J.

She made shadow birds on the wall of our tent using her hand and a cigarette lighter, then began . . .

Daedalus, Icarus's dad, was an inventor held captive by King Minos on the island of Crete. To escape, Daedalus made two sets of wings out of feathers and wax. Before they jumped out of a window and left the island behind, he warned Icarus not to fly too close to the sun. But the kid did anyway.

Why? I asked.

Arrogance.

What's that?

Believing the rules of this world don't apply to you. Anyway, Icarus's wings fell apart, and he plummeted to the earth and died.

If you made me wings, I'd listen to you, I promised.

That's BS, Penny. You think you're special, too. One day it'll bite you in the ass.

"That's BS," I now tell Mama J, then pull into the garage of our home and carry the sweater and groceries inside.

Before starting on dinner—it never hurts to have a fallback—I work a bit more on my computer program. Parsing data always settles my nerves. After an hour, I'm ready to prep the backup meal and make tiramisu. *Just in case.* After putting the potatoes in the oven for the gnocchi, I mix a spice rub and slather it on the raw lamb, then wash my hands at the kitchen sink. Outside, the sun has begun her descent, and the Bay is a sparkling obsidian blanket. *I have so much to be thankful for and tonight will be perfect, no matter where we have dinner.*

Something dark flutters in the corner of my eye. It grows larger and larger as it hurtles toward me. I leap back, shocked, as it smashes into the window like a bullet. The kitchen is filled with sharp crackles as fractures in the glass spread, then radiate out in a spiderweb pattern. At its center is an ugly blot of bright-red blood and torn black feathers.

"Will you walk into my parlor?" said a spider to a fly. Mama J cackles.

The line is from an old poem she'd memorized as a child, about a cunning spider who used flattery to trick a silly fly into landing on his web, then trapped her in silk threads and ate her alive. Clearly, the angst I'm feeling about my marriage is resurrecting unsettling memories. Mama J only repeated that poem when she was high.

I head out the kitchen's back door. A large crow lies in the grass, neck broken. Its claws twitch, and the bird's beak opens and closes, like it's trying to tell me something. One beady eye watches me for a few seconds, rolls, then glazes over.

"Poor thing," I say.

A crow means bad luck, Mama J reminds me.

The weight of a shadow lands on my shoulder. Heart thudding, I whirl. But there's no one there. I take a few slow breaths to ground myself. "Birds fly into windows all the time."

Using a kitchen towel, I gently pick up the broken bird and bury it below my garden, then head back inside to finish making Bruce's favorite dessert. More than ever, I'm determined to set my marriage back on track and return the memories of Mama J to the deep waters where she's buried.

CHAPTER

8

I HEAR THE FRONT door open at nine forty-five. No rumble of a garage door, so it's Circe. She's close enough to curfew that I won't mention it. This is not a hill to die on, according to the parenting accounts on LivLoud that I follow. Rolling over in bed, my eyes trace the crown molding around the ceiling of our bedroom. Clockwise. Counterclockwise. Clockwise . . .

When we first bought the house, half the molding was missing. It was challenging to find matches, but I discovered a small shop beneath an overpass in the Mission. The owner, an old builder named Ike, had worked in San Francisco for half a century and saved glass windows, parquet flooring, and crown moldings from heritage homes when clients gutted them. After he retired, he opened his shop to help people who wanted to preserve their houses.

We shape our buildings; thereafter, our buildings shape us, Ike told me as we dug through piles to find the perfect match to the molding I'd presented. *Winston Churchill said that,* Ike explained.

So how has our house shaped me?

I keep it immaculate. Throw cocktail and Christmas parties to support Bruce's company, making them unique by following party planning influencers like Lory Parson's, Brittany Young's, and Camille Styles's blogs. I spend countless hours on the landscaping.

Research the *right* ornamentals, balance them with the hardscape, make sure gutters are cleaned along with exterior windows and that the paint is always touched up. Our house has given me something, other than Bruce's success, our marriage, and Circe, to do and be proud of. No one would ever guess that the woman inside it is frequently riddled with self-doubt.

I glance at the gray sweater slumped on a brown velvet chair in the corner of our bedroom and try to imagine the woman who wore it. She's two sizes smaller than me. Blond? Brunette? Redhead? Did she wear a skirt, and heels that accentuated long legs? Did they sit across from each other at Oscar's or side by side in a cozy banquette? Where were my husband's hands? Where were hers?

There is a simple explanation. I turn over, but still feel the sweater's presence behind me. *Stop it.* We have a good marriage. A solid marriage. We're devoted to being a family.

Are you happy? Kiki asked me that, out of the blue, last week. She's been a little off lately and I make a mental note to check that everything is okay. Sometimes we forget our most beautiful friends might need some time and attention, too.

I finally hear the rumble of the garage door at 1:04, the latest Bruce has ever come home. At a little after nine, I gave up waiting, ate dinner, even lit the candles beside a fresh flower arrangement picked from the greenhouse behind our garage. That was a bit dramatic. Anyway, my program was wrong. Bruce didn't lie. He did have a late meeting.

Mama J's voice pipes up. *Do I smell melting wax?*

Maybe I'll shelve my thesis again, use the time to learn French or take another cooking class, Vietnamese this time. I can throw a themed dinner party. And I'll plan a vacation, just Bruce and me, when Circe goes to summer cheer camp. We'll go back to that little hotel in Greece.

My head feels wobbly. There's a half bottle of wine in the fridge. Bruce's partner Hal Crosby once said it's a sin to eat lamb without a hearty cabernet, and I agree. Though now there's a bitter taste in my mouth and the beginnings of a headache from the tannins. A plate waits in the fridge for Bruce with perfectly seared lamb lollipops and homemade gnocchi drizzled with jus. I tossed out the veggies—carrots, zucchini, and eggplant, julienned the way he likes. They never hold up. And the half-eaten tiramisu is on the counter—it's best when fresh.

Bruce drops his clothes on the floor and carefully slides into bed. He reeks of cigars, Hal's favorite pastime, and scotch. I don't move, feign sleep in the lingerie I put on to entice my husband. Within minutes, he's snoring loudly. When he falls asleep first, it's always hard to drift off.

I stare at the chair in the corner. I can't ignore the gray cardigan. I should wait until morning, talk to my husband, but instead slide out of bed, tiptoe across refinished wood floors to his crumpled slacks, feel for his phone.

In the bathroom, I quietly close the door, sit on the toilet and put in his security code. It's the same as mine—Circe's birthday. But access is denied. I try again. Denied. *When did he change his code?*

With careful steps, I walk to Bruce's side of the bed and hold the phone close, so he's captured in the glow of the screen. Facial recognition kicks in and it opens with a soft ping. I hold my breath, but he doesn't stir, then pad down a wide hall with the original wainscoting to the walk-in closet.

I slide to the floor, back against a set of drawers that hold Bruce's ties, socks, and boxers, sorted by color, and scan his recent calls. There's the usual—Circe, his partner Hal Crosby, me—and some employees' names I recognize. Does one of them shop at Zara and own a gray sweater in size extra small?

Mama J whispers, *Happily ever after doesn't happen the way you think.*

How would you know?

I pull in my legs to stand, go back to bed, and inch close enough to feel the reassuring heat of my husband's body. But instead, I stay seated, return to Bruce's phone and the multiple outgoing calls to Potential Spam. My finger hovers, then I tap the number while simultaneously telling myself no one will pick up, but also that I'm crossing a line that can never be uncrossed.

The phone rings once . . .

A woman answers. "I'm touching myself and thinking very dirty thoughts about you," she says, her voice breathless. "Bruce? Baby? Can you come over? I need you—"

I hang up. The world spins and when it stops everything is the same. Bruce's clothes hang neatly, the bespoke suits and shirts fitted by the most expensive tailor in the city perfectly pressed. My side is filled with linen, crisp Egyptian cotton, understated dresses for events, stylish shoes with kitten heels and classic leather slides.

Robotically, I slip off the lingerie that Val and Kiki thought would remind Bruce that I'm some sort of prize, unpin my elegant chignon and pull on an oversized T-shirt. My bare feet pad on polished parquet floors; the swivel chair sits in the corner of our bedroom, same gray sweater resting on its velvet; drapes rustle as I pass and slide into bed.

Everything is the same . . . and nothing will ever be again.

The Dee-Light Motel, Oakland, California

The Past

THERE ARE TWENTY rooms with doors that open on a big parking lot. Ours has orange shag carpet and purple flowers printed on a tan bedspread. The walls are painted yellow, and the ceiling has a water stain that looks like an elephant. I trace the flowers on the bedspread, fingers running over the stiff material as I watch a movie. I only get to watch TV when one of Mama J's special men spring for a room, so this is a treat.

The movie is called *The River Wild*. It's about Gail, a teacher who used to be a river guide. Her family isn't getting along so she decides to take her husband, son, and their dog on a whitewater river trip. They meet some guys rafting, and when Gail realizes that they're in over their head, she offers to guide them for the rest of the trip. The guys are super grateful, but soon, Gail discovers they have a gun, robbed a bank, and killed one of their friends. Gail's husband and the dog escape but she and her son are left behind.

Lots of scary stuff happens, and the bad men threaten to kill Gail and her son unless she guides them down a dangerous section of the river called the Gauntlet. She makes it through the big waves and her husband is waiting and flips the raft to rescue his family. But it's Gail who gets the gun and kills the bad guys. Her family is reunited, including the dog, and they love each other more. That's a happily ever after in my book. Plus, I love Gail's voice and courage. When I grow up, I want to be just like her.

While I watch the movie, noises and bad words come from the bathroom, but I don't go to the thin door. Mama J told me to *stay put*. Eventually, her special friend comes out and pulls a stained undershirt over a flabby chest carpeted with black hair.

"You gonna be just like your mama?" he asks.

When he grins, two of his teeth are gold. I don't answer. Mama J says not to talk to strangers, and especially men.

"Call me Uncle Jordie," he says. "You like candy or chips? I can go to the vending machine and get you some."

This man has narrow-set eyes like one of the bad men in the movie. When he sits down on the edge of the bed, I push backward until I'm pressed into the headboard.

"Uncle Jordie's gonna tell you the secret to life," he says with a smirk. "You can always get what you want, if you're willing to pay for it."

Mama J stumbles out of the bathroom. "Leave my kid alone."

"We were just getting know each other. She's gonna be a beauty."

"Shut the fuck up," Mama J slurs.

"Don't be a bitch," the man says and heads out the door. Halfway gone, he turns and winks. "See you next week."

"Not if I see you first," Mama J replies with a laugh that sounds like she doesn't think what she said was funny. She falls onto our shared bed and squints at the TV as the movie begins again. "That actress is Meryl Streep."

"No, her name is Gail." I can tell that Mama J has taken her medicine. I'll stay up all night to make sure she doesn't throw up in her sleep. She had a friend who died that way. She's just in a thin T-shirt and gray undies, the jut of her hips poking out. I pull up the bedspread so she's warm enough, and notice Mama J's neck is red and purple. Worry nibbles at my insides. "What happened?" I ask. But I know it was the man. They always leave a mark.

CHAPTER

9

There's noise coming from the bathroom—plink, plink, plink. Slowly, I approach the sliding door and ease it open. Cracked tiles are cold beneath my bare feet. On the far side of the room, the window is open. A plastic cord from the metal blinds blows against peeling wallpaper covered in red, yellow, and blue fish. Plink, plink, plink. Standing on tippy-toes, I pull the window shut, then turn to go back to our shared bed. But Mama J is in the empty bathtub, her scrawny body naked, a syringe in her arm, eyes fixed. A rope of yellow vomit is dried to her lips and chest . . .

BRUCE IS ALREADY in the shower when I wake, gasping from an old nightmare. My head throbs. All I want to do is pull up the covers, push away what comes next. Life will now forever be divided—the day before I knew about Bruce's affair, and the day after.

How did I get here?

I was twenty-one. Six months into my graduate program. Beginning to believe I might do something with my life after being nominated for the Henry Johnson Fellowship. Then Bruce ran out of condoms from the school's health clinic. We'd split a bottle of cheap wine, took the risk. I should've been on birth control, but I didn't want to take any pills. One month later, I barfed three mornings in a row and bought a test. Two blue lines.

I didn't tell Bruce. Instead, I climbed onto a bus headed to a free women's clinic down on the Peninsula. I'd finally earned a real chance at a different life, couldn't throw it away. A well-dressed lady beside me was listening to a small radio on her lap. The host of the program on air was a psychologist named Dr. Beth. The way she spoke, tough but kind, drew me in, and one call changed the trajectory of my life.

My name is Henrietta and I'm calling to thank you. When I was in my early twenties, I was lost, had no parents for guidance, and you gave me great direction that set me on the right track.

That's wonderful to hear, Dr. Beth said. *How are things now?*

Well, I went to community college, found meaningful work, eventually met a great guy, got married, and we have wonderful kids. I still listen to your show most days—you're the mom I never had.

When I reached the clinic, I sat on the curb, dialed the station, talked to a screener who tried to help me formulate my mess of a life into a coherent question. A few minutes later, Dr. Beth took my call. She listened to my family history, asked insightful questions, then inquired what I really wanted.

This baby, I replied, shocking myself. *But I can't lose what I've worked so hard to get.*

No one can have it all, Dr. Beth said. *Life is about making hard choices, living with the consequences. What was your dream when you were a little girl?*

I wanted to live in a real house with a loving mom and dad who never yelled, have enough food, and feel safe.

And then?

To someday create my own family, give a child everything I never had. But now isn't the right time.

Life doesn't unfold on a calendar, Dr. Beth explained. *This is your choice, but talk to the father before you make any decisions, okay? That's only fair, right?*

I took the bus back to campus and told Bruce. We'd only been dating about three months, and a week prior I'd shared that I didn't want to be exclusive. That was another way to say "let's ultimately break up." I liked Bruce but wanted to focus on my studies, date other guys, keep things light until I got my PhD, launched into a career.

But I love you, Bruce had said, his voice earnest.

He was the first man who'd ever said those three words to me. I agreed to stay together.

After I told him about the pregnancy, Bruce paced around my small dorm room. When he finally spoke, his voice shook. *Marry me.*

I was floored. *Marriage doesn't seem like the right answer. We don't know each other that well. I've just begun my PhD; you need to finish your MBA. And we don't have enough money to raise a child. Plus, we were just talking about breaking up.*

You *were talking about it,* Bruce said. He took my hands, his palms sweaty. *We can do this. You'll have to drop out and get a job until the baby comes to support us while I finish my master's. Then I'll take over and provide for you and our child.*

My stomach plummeted at the idea of giving up my dream, but also because I didn't have the experience or skills to be a mom—not yet anyway. When Dr. Beth had asked what I wanted, I'd said the baby, but that was in a world where I hadn't come from homelessness; wasn't the child of an addict; had a supportive family waiting in the wings. It was an imaginary place where I could right all of Mama J's wrongs.

You don't understand, I said to Bruce, pulling free.

We'll love our child and give him or her an incredible life, all the things we never had, create a legacy. I know I'm punching up, okay? But Penn, you're the best thing that's ever happened to me. I'm good for you, too. Marry me. I promise, we can be a happy family, an unbeatable team. And you can still have your career down the road.

Feeling cornered, I admitted that I wasn't in love with him. That was only fair. Bruce was sure that would come. Then I shared my real past. Something I'd never done before. Maybe I was looking for a way out. But Bruce still wanted to marry me. Having someone hear the worst about you—things you believe make you other, ugly, hard to like, unacceptable—and still love you was incredibly compelling. I said yes.

From that moment on, my family was everything. Unsure how to care for a baby, build a strong marriage, Dr. Beth became one of my surrogate mothers, along with Olivia, Maddie, Bonnie Roy, Tanya Decker, and a host of other celebrity gurus.

Now, the urge to stay in bed, wrap arms around my knees, and sob hits. *But there's Circe.* I get dressed, retrieve the gray cardigan, count the stairs down to the kitchen—twenty-six—and focus on breakfast. Waffles topped with a dollop of Chantilly cream and blueberries. I set two plates down for Circe and Bruce, then drown a leftover waffle in maple syrup, stuff the overly sweet, spongy bread into my mouth.

What now?

On some kind of bizarre cruise control, I make Bruce's cappuccino and a latte for Circe with a heart drawn in the foam. When I look up, my daughter is already at the table, on her second bite. Waffles are her favorite. I hand her the latte.

"Thanks," she says, mouth full. "All good?"

She probably thinks she's in trouble for missing curfew. "Why wouldn't it be?"

"You have syrup on your chin."

I wipe away the stickiness. Circe wears jean overalls today with a white bodysuit beneath. She gobbles the rest of her breakfast, oblivious to the Category Five hurricane whipping through my body. I won't let it hurt her.

"Morning," Bruce says and sits at the breakfast table.

My hands shake as I pass him a cappuccino, hot liquid sloshing over the edge of the cup and puddling in the saucer. *You're having an affair.* Bruce, on autopilot, doesn't notice and opens the *New York Times* that he still refuses to read digitally, preferring the feel and smell of a real newspaper.

Circe gives me a hug before heading out to the bus. That's a rarity these days and I hold on a little too long. *I will protect her.* When the door closes, I sit at the kitchen table.

Bruce looks up from his newspaper. "What's the plan for tonight? I can be home by six. We could take Circe to her favorite Thai place?"

He's wearing the lavender tie I bought him last Christmas. "We were supposed to go out last night, or at least have a late dinner, for our anniversary."

Bruck sets the paper down. "Damn. Sorry, Penn. Work has been over-the-top. I forgot. Rain check?"

My jaw clenches as the lies pile up. I reach onto the chair beside me, put the size extra-small gray cardigan on the table. He doesn't deny it when I lay out the facts, though he is startled that I unlocked his phone and offended at the trickery.

"It's a breach of trust," he says, indignant.

I want to cry out at his hypocrisy. But that won't help. *And there's still love here.* It didn't happen until after Circe was born. Bruce adored her and I finally let go of my fears, let him into my heart. We became a team. Now he reaches for my hand and hope flutters. *He made a very bad mistake. He's sorry. It'll take time but we can rebuild.*

"I want a divorce."

My ears pop like there's been a massive pressure shift. But I'm not on an airplane. I'm sitting at the kitchen table in our home. "Who is she?"

"That doesn't matter," Bruce says and crosses his arm. "She's a symptom. She's not the problem."

Now our marriage is a disease. "What does that even mean?"

"Penn, we raised a beautiful daughter. You should be proud of that."

It's like he's offering me some sort of consolation prize at the county fair. Sorry, lady, you didn't win enough tickets for the giant stuffed bear, but here's a wind-up tin mouse. The idea that Circe will be forever impacted by his betrayal, our divorce, makes bile rise. I swallow down the sick and my pride.

"We can go to couples therapy," I offer, a supplicant at his feet.

"It's too late," Bruce says. "Sometimes the love . . . it just runs out." He shrugs, like he's lost a game of dominoes, there's traffic on the road to Tahoe, or he can't find one of his socks.

How do I respond to this man who promised forever but now is informing me that his love is finite? How do I fight for our daughter and family when he says that sometime between our first kiss and right now, his love for me ran out like the charge in my Tesla?

"I'm going to take Circe up to Tahoe for the weekend. On the drive back, I'll explain we've decided to split amicably."

He's really doing this. "How long have you been cheating?"

Bruce looks away. "We've been seeing each other for eight months."

"Eight months?" I gasp. The truth ricochets through my body like a bullet. That's more than half a year of lies. But of course it's been ongoing. Hell, he put her name in his contacts as Potential Spam to make sure I didn't suspect anything.

"I've hired an attorney to make this go as smoothly as possible, for both of us."

He's been planning this for a while. "We tell Circe together, after the weekend." I refuse to let him control that narrative.

"Fine." Bruce reaches for the gray sweater balled on the table between us, then walks toward the mudroom.

"Are you going to live with that home-wrecker?" I demand. But I already know the answer. Bruce isn't the kind of man who wants to take care of the day-to-day. He hesitates in the garage doorway. A candle in the tiniest corner of my heart flickers . . . and then he's gone, and it blows out.

You flew too close to the sun, Mama J points out.

She's right.

Part II

CHAPTER

10

THE COURT-ORDERED SPOUSAL support resulted in enough money for me to rent an apartment and live until September—six months—to be revisited if mediation for the divorce is unsuccessful. The only thing Bruce and I agreed on during our first session was to sell our home. It went quickly—the Realtor was amazed. I wasn't, after putting in the legwork, research, and elbow grease.

With bleary eyes, I look away from my laptop. I've been working even more on my program since the split—can't seem to stop—and take in the dismal walk-up I'm renting in an old building on the periphery of the Marina District. It has threadbare carpets, chipped white Formica counters, nail-hole-scarred walls. I've lived in far worse than this place, but it feels like my marriage never happened. I'm back to the life of scarcity I once knew so well. I understood as a kid that life wasn't fair but thought I'd outrun that fact—that I was finally secure. Now it's punched me in the face, and I'm pissed off at Bruce, but even more at my own stupidity.

Never take your eye off the mark, Mama J points out.

"Bruce wasn't a mark."

I wander to the window, peer out. There's a sliver of blue water between pastel-colored apartment buildings if I stand on a chair. I could've swung a nicer rental. But I have no idea how long Bruce's support will continue as we move through the court system. I need to save what I can in case my lawyer, Cameron, a gray-haired veteran of divorce, loses the battle for a fair settlement, and I'm left with nothing but his hefty fee.

The disaster of that first lawyers' meeting returns . . .

Remember, we just listen, Cameron said before we stepped into the conference room.

Bruce was already seated at a rectangular glass table beside his attorney, Miriam, another gray-haired veteran wearing a no-nonsense pantsuit. She slid a document toward me.

What is this? I asked.

It's a quit claim, Miriam explained.

Cameron slipped on glasses and read the page. *Do you recall signing this?*

Quickly, I skimmed it. *Yes, about three months ago. Bruce and Hal wanted a loan for expansion and the bank required it. Bruce said it would make the process easier.*

It says you have no claim to any ownership or income from the company, Miriam explained.

I felt something inside me break—it was my core belief in Bruce's character, that he was still a good man deep down, despite his actions. Crosby & Stone was a large portion of our net worth. *Did you even get a bank loan?* I demanded.

Bruce couldn't meet my eyes. *In the end, it wasn't necessary.*

Miriam pushed another piece of paper across the glass expanse between us. *It's a postnup,* she said.

I scanned the document. It stated that should our union dissolve, we are not entitled to any marital gains the other has made during the marriage. My signature was at the bottom of the page, along with a notary's. *I would never sign that.*

Miriam tapped the line with my signature. *But you did.*

When? I asked Bruce, floored.

Two months ago. You came to the office to bring me lunch.

Bruce was on the phone, so I left it on his desk. On my way to the elevator, he caught up and asked me to initial a few documents for our estate attorney. I started to read them, and Bruce snapped, *For God's sake, can't you see how busy I am? Just sign them.* Several of his employees turned to watch. Embarrassed, I signed and then got out of his hair.

Miriam continued, *In California, with the quit claim and post-nup, you are not entitled to any support or assets.*

I turned to Cameron. *Can he do that?*

He can try, my lawyer replied. *But we'll fight it.*

I gripped the edge of the table—it was the only thing keeping me from slapping Bruce. *I built the software for your company, worked for years as an unpaid IT officer until the business could afford to hire someone full-time. I've spent the past fifteen years taking care of our home, Circe, supporting you, so that you could focus on growing the business—*

I need to protect my future, Bruce interrupted.

Turned out I was even more of a cliché than I imagined. He was fucking his twenty-six-year-old executive assistant, Mackenzie. We first met at our annual Christmas party for the office staff and talked about how sad she was to be single, that "the hardest part was that there's no one to share the sunrise with." But Mackenzie was already with Bruce. The only reason they weren't watching the sunrise together was because he had to come home to me.

On the elevator ride down, Cameron said, *It's going to be a long, uphill battle. Mediation will run in the five digits. Court will cost six. There are no guarantees, but we'll probably get more than Bruce currently wants to part with.*

I blinked back tears. *It's not fair.*

That's life, Mama J now reminds me. *You might think you're on a roll, but in life, just like in Vegas, the deck is stacked against you. In the end, the house always wins.*

Overwhelmed, I slump onto a blue denim couch in my new home. I ordered all the furniture from IKEA and assembled it myself—pages of instructions, baggies filled with screws, washers, little metal tools. A few times there were leftover pieces, and I had to deconstruct, begin again. Nothing in the directions said four hands were needed, not two, for best results. Is that a rule in life, too? I used my knees, chin, the wall for stability, got there in the end.

I did splurge for a small second bedroom for Circe. The walls are painted sage green, and I blew up some of the photographs she's taken, framed them myself, then hung a string of twinkle lights to brighten the space. But my daughter has yet to sleep over, preferring her aerie at Bruce's house in the Presidio. Turns out my soon-to-be ex had already leased the stately home, a former colonel's residence when the military used to be based there, before he asked for a divorce. Circe has the entire third floor, including her own den to watch television. Mackenzie, who now lives with them, took my daughter to Restoration Hardware to decorate the new space.

Although I have fifty-fifty custody, at least for now, and have tried almost every day to enforce it, Circe refuses to stay with me. The harder I push, the bigger the chasm grows between us.

If you make me, then I'll stay. But it won't help our relationship, Circe said last night.

What will? I asked.

I don't know. I love you, Mom, but I'm not ready.

At a loss, I now call Dr. Beth. It's something I've put off because I feel like a huge disappointment. But I need to tell her what happened, ask for help and emotional support. I hold the line for thirty minutes before her producer puts me on.

"Hello there, how can I help you?" Dr. Beth asks.

"I called fifteen years ago," I say, nervously pacing around the apartment.

"Ah. I hope that our conversation made a difference?"

"I was twenty-one, pregnant, considering an abortion. You talked me into telling the father and he proposed. We got married. Our daughter is fourteen."

"I love a happily ever after. So, what's going on today?"

"I just found out that my husband is cheating. The affair has been going on for eight months. I had no idea."

"I find that hard to believe," Dr. Beth says.

My stomach pitches. "What? It's true."

"There were no signs? He didn't stay late at the office or have business meetings out of town? Strange phone calls at odd hours?"

"No—yes, I mean. All those things happened, but that was normal. He's CEO of a company. There's a lot of responsibility."

"What about sex?"

"He didn't . . ."

"My guess is that you rarely initiated. You wanted the husband, marriage, but didn't want to give anything back. My dear, don't you know that pigs get slaughtered?"

This conversation is moving way too fast and off track. "I . . . What do I do now? My husband moved out and my daughter wants to live with him, not me."

"Girls typically blame their mothers for a divorce. This is why I tell women to do everything to keep their family together, like I did. Commit to *one* marriage. Period. Truth be told, that was easy for me. I chose a good man who had morals, high standards. But women these days fall for derelicts, drunks, cheaters, crooks, and are then shocked when they're abusive, commit crimes. There's no excuse for any of that behavior. If it were up to me, the prisons in our country would be fuller. Callers, if you're listening right now, learn from this woman's mistake. Choose better!"

"How do I win my daughter back?"

"You'll have to tread lightly, wait for her to come to you. It may happen. It may not. Hopefully, she won't be calling me ten years from now making the same mistakes you did."

The call abruptly ends. Dr. Beth said a lot of things that cut deep. But the part about daughters blaming their mothers for divorce was an arrow to my heart. I stop pacing and stand in front of the oval mirror I bought to make my new apartment seem larger. "What's going to happen to my relationship with Circe? What's going to happen to me?" I ask my reflection, the words laden with fear.

The woman in the mirror, her hair greasy, chin trembling, has no answer. The glass shifts and mottled pink-and-brown scabs, like the ones on Mama J's skin that she used to incessantly pick, slowly spread across my face. Horrified, I raise trembling hands, but I'm afraid to touch the weeping sores. *Am I turning into her?*

Mama J's bloodshot eyes peer out of the mirror at me. *You thought you could do better than me,* she accuses.

"That's not true!"

Bullshit, Penny. But now you know. Daughters can be cruel. And there's a fine line between living in your castle on the hill and hustling to survive. Welcome home.

Something outside scrapes along the window with a drawn-out, high-pitched whine. My head snaps around. The wind has blown the limb of an ornamental cherry tree into the glass. Narrow twigs along the bough extend like skeletal fingers, and despite a rational explanation, the overwhelming sense of being stalked invades. I take a breath, then another, until my pulse slows. When I turn back to the mirror, I now understand that the sun, striking the tree's small, red berries, created the illusion of scabs on my face. *But what about Mama J's eyes?*

"We're nothing alike," I tell her ghost, then call Circe and leave a voicemail. "Hey hon, thinking about you. Let's catch a movie. Maybe dinner? I miss you." Despite Dr. Beth's advice, I'll keep trying.

The moment I hang up, my phone rings, the tone a fox's giggle. "Hey, Kiki."

"What are you doing?"

"Feeling sorry for myself," I admit.

"Val and I are at Pain Quotidien. Come meet us."

"I haven't even showered." *And I've been wearing the same sweats and underwear for three days.*

"Get down here or we'll drag you out," Val says into the phone.

I know she'll follow through, so I pull on a wrinkled white oxford and jeans, twist dirty hair into a bun, slip on my old Hokas, discovered at the bottom of a box when I moved, and trudge to the café. On the way, a black cat with a spiked collar crosses the sidewalk right in front of me. I almost laugh. *The worst has already happened.* The cat threads through my legs, winds its body around my ankles, and purrs. When I reach down to give it a pet, it swipes at me with claws drawn. Blood beads on the back of my stinging hand as the cat runs off.

CHAPTER

11

VAL AND KIKI wait at a table outside. Kiki's in her usual post-yoga Lululemon set and Val looks polished in a yellow silk blouse and pencil skirt. After washing my hand and blotting away the bloody streaks, I take a seat, toy with the chocolate croissant they've ordered me. I don't know what I'd do without them. They've been my life raft. Both were shocked and incensed at Bruce's betrayal. I haven't given them all the gory details (they're not pushing, giving me time), just that it was his assistant, Mackenzie, and wasn't a one-off. They do know about the documents he tricked me into signing and were beyond furious on my behalf. They found Cameron, made lists of everything I should ask for, and have tirelessly listened to me rant and cry.

"How are you doing today?" Kiki asks, reaching for my hand.

"Same but different day. Mad and sad," I tell my friends between sips of the cappuccino they ordered me. The acid bites into my stomach—I haven't been eating much.

"Bruce is the one who should be miserable," Val snaps. "He should've kept his dick in his pants for the last eight months and kissed the ground you walk on."

The gears in my brain spin, slip, stick as I try to keep up with the conversation. Lately my thoughts have been all over the place—no sleep, bad dreams, Mama J's snide remarks, and an overwhelming sense of doom make it hard to think clearly.

"Next steps?" Val asks.

She's always been the practical one. "I need to reinvent myself. There are no guarantees that I'll get much support from Bruce."

"Can your parents help?" Kiki asks.

I shake my head, scramble for a white lie. "They would, but I don't want to ask. I need to figure this out myself. Get used to standing on my own." Val and Kiki have offered me money, as much as I need to get on my feet again. But loans can sour friendships. I need them too much to risk that. They're not only best friends, but anchors that moor me to the life Mama J told me was out of reach. Without them, I'll be adrift.

Sitting up straighter, I share, "Tonight, I'm going to a computer programming course. Hopefully, it'll help me figure out job possibilities." My resume is sparse. I was a barista in a coffee shop in high school, did work-study as part of my scholarship, built a client database management program for Crosby & Stone and was the company's sole IT support, but that was off the books. I don't think volunteer tech support for the school system would count. I've never held a real job.

"You're one of the smartest people I know," Kiki says. "You'll figure it out in no time!"

"I'd suggest a shower first," Val adds.

I chuckle. "Thanks for being my friends," I say, getting a little teary, "even when I smell."

Val gives my forearm a rare pat. "Always."

I start to leave, then sit back down. "Hey, can I record each of you making a statement?"

"Why?" Kiki asks.

"I've been fiddling with my old thesis." They don't need to know the extent of my growing obsession.

Val glances at her watch. "Sure, then I need to scram for an appointment with my accountant. What do you want me to say?"

I pull out my phone, finger hovering over record, and consider. "How about, 'I knew Bruce was a cheater.'"

"Seriously?" Val asks, taken aback.

"Yeah, I need an obvious lie." It's the best way to tell if my program is working. I press the record button on my phone and Val says the lie. Kiki follows suit.

"You are a weirdo," Kiki points out with a giggle. "Are you going to tell us about this thesis?"

"If I ever figure it out, you'll be the first to know." They hug me, despite my ripe scent, because that's what best friends do.

CHAPTER

12

CLASS IS HELD at San Francisco College's sciences lab. I take a seat at one of the computer monitors, wait for the professor along with fifteen others in our thirties, forties, fifties, and sixties, each arranging pads and pens, looking around, quietly chatting. Am I the only one who's nervous?

"Hello everyone, I'm Professor Luc Sweeney. Please call me Luc."

My head snaps up as our teacher enters the room. He's dressed in worn jeans, a dark-green flannel button-down, sneakers. *He liked to run in Golden Gate Park.* His wavy light-brown hair is a little bit shaggy, giving him an outdoorsy vibe, like he just emerged from the woods, or the ocean. Luc's blue eyes are bright, the scar on his chin now a faint, silvery line. He rubs his hands together. I remember the touch of those long fingers when they accidentally brushed mine. An ember buried deep inside me warms.

"First, some housekeeping," Luc says. "You've all been given a link to log into the college's mainframe and establish a user account. That'll give you access to a broad library of software. Keep your projects on the school's server. Many of the software licenses will only run there. You can work on them remotely and you'll have the full power of the college's mainframe for processing."

Leaning against a desk, Luc continues, "Now on to the fun stuff. I hope you're all here to discover how your knowledge in computer programming can be transferred into the current marketplace. I'm here to help you navigate the sometimes-daunting new world of apps and AI and to improve your skills enough to be marketable and create programs that might turn into the next big thing. But I caution you not to look for easy money. Tap into your passions. Believe it or not, they'll lead you down the right road and you'll enjoy the process. Remember, the greatest software fulfills your own need.

"Anyone know who Stan Honey is?" Luc asks, then scans the room. No one answers. "Then let me tell you a quick story about him to illustrate my point about software fulfilling needs. Stan was an inventor with a passion for navigation. Basically, he loved measuring stuff, highlighting and tracking it, and solving problems. He sold his first business, Etak, a digital mapping firm—think car navigation systems that keep all of us from getting lost."

"In '88 Stan moved on to another problem. He wanted to figure out how to insert simple graphics into live video in the real world. That led to the first down line. If you're a football fan, then you've seen the fluorescent orange or yellow line during games that marks how far a team needs to push to make a first down," Luc explains. "Stan and his team created that augmented reality and pattern recognition technology. It earned him a place in the National Inventors Hall of Fame."

Luc's right dimple flashes. It always did. After telling a joke, when he spilled a beer, even when he fell from his bike and needed stitches but insisted, chin bloody, that he was fine.

"Let's introduce ourselves. Then I'll meet with everyone individually and we can establish what you hope to get out of this class. Like I said, I'm Luc. I've got a PhD in computer science. I spent the past fifteen years working for different startups in Silicon Valley, including my own, and recently returned to teaching." He points to a bearded man in the first row. "Your turn."

My pulse sprints as the students in front of me introduce themselves. There's a man named Jean with a French accent, and a scarf artfully wound around his neck. He explains he's on a K-1 fiancé visa and wants to make sure his skills are transferable to tech companies.

"I'm Arrya," a petite Indian woman who looks early thirties with pink streaks through her hair says. "I buy apartments and condos in foreclosure, then renovate and flip them. I'd like to write an app to streamline all the landlord's tasks."

A skinny guy in an alpaca sweater, polka-dotted pajama bottoms, and black boots, with a brown tail covered in white fur poking out of his pants, stands up next. He was sitting in the far corner, so I didn't notice him, but now see he's wearing an incredibly realistic wolf's head, the snout long, curved canines visible. "I'm Nate and I play computer games for a living. I want to create an interactive shooter game whose avatars are animals, and their prey is human. I'm aiming for next level and plan to use VR technology." He waves his tail at the other students. "Oh, and I'm a furry."

"Furry?" Arrya asks.

"Part of a community that role-plays as animals."

When a few people giggle, Nate shrugs like he's in on the joke. I can't imagine setting myself up to be a punch line. *But isn't that what I did?* Vaguely, I remember Val telling Kiki and me about a furry, this one a cat, who came in for a trim at her salon. That it can be about making friends, attending fun conventions, or, in a minority of cases, a sexual fetish thing.

We all have fetishes, Mama J interjects. *Seems harmless compared to the ones who want to whip or tie you up. Never let 'em tie you up, 'cause then—*

I tune her out as five more students share their goals, and then it's my turn. *Maybe Luc won't even remember me.* "Hi. Um, I'm Penn Sto—Roberts." My voice shakes. I've never liked talking in front of a group, and Luc's eyes are now on me. "I guess I'm here to see what I can do with some old computer skills."

Luc's head tilts, then he stands, and my body temperature instantly rises. When he was my computer lab TA at SFPI, he was twenty-four, gifted, funny, and always willing to help students.

Pretty much everyone, guys and girls, had a crush on him. He's one of the reasons that I told Bruce I wanted to break up. Not that I had a chance with Luc, but the rush I felt when he was near meant that Bruce probably wasn't the right guy for me.

"Ladies and gentlemen," Luc says, "this woman was one of my most promising students back when I first taught. We all expected great things from her. She was even nominated for the Henry Johnson Fellowship. It's only awarded to the most brilliant young thinkers."

Every head cranes around to get a better look at me. "Then I gave it up and dropped out," I say, trying to make it sound like a punch line.

"To most assuredly go on to an even brighter future," Luc adds, followed by one of his lopsided grins.

My entire body is engulfed in flame. I force a tight smile. It takes a lifetime, but Luc finally moves on to meet with the first student. *This was a mistake. I don't belong here.* When Luc's back is turned, I grab my bag and run out of the room.

Chevy Station Wagon, San Francisco

The Past

OUR NEW HOME, set in an abandoned lot, is the same color as mint ice cream with brown panels on the doors that look like real wood and only three wheels, making it tilt to the left. Mama J says it's much safer than the tent because we can lock the doors. One of the windows is gone but taped over with a garbage bag. I sleep in the way back, unless Mama J has a date. Then I go to the front seat and pretend I'm driving until the man leaves. I try not to look in the rearview mirror. Mama J says to *never look back, or you'll get sad or trip.*

Last night was the scariest of my life but Mama J said, *There's time, you're only seven*. A man climbed over the seats, from the back to the front, real fast. He had a tattoo of a skull on his hand and a knife. Mama J was on him before he hurt me much. She tore bloody streaks with her nails along his face and back. I've never heard her scream like that. She was Demeter and the bad guy was Hades. That made me Persephone, and later, the idea helped me sleep. In the morning, she explained that the man was rotted out inside.

Now Mama J is very tired from a long night of work and has taken her medicine. She falls asleep in the back seat sitting up, so I don't have to be afraid that she'll upchuck. I'm not supposed to leave the station wagon, but it's hot and my legs are cramped. I slip out through the broken window and walk down the sidewalk, stop to pick a yellow flower growing in the cracks, and tuck it behind one ear. I can't read the names of the streets, but I make sure to memorize the run-down buildings and trash piles so I can get back home.

In the distance, high voices ring out, laughing, yelling, and I follow the noise like a dog smelling a good treat 'til I get to a chain-link fence around a concrete playground. There are kids playing basketball and tag, and a group of six girls sit in a circle pushing a pink ball between them. There's a hole in the fence and I slide through, approach the girls, and sit next to one with red hair. The girls all wear the same light-blue jumper, knee socks, and white sneakers.

The red-haired girl asks, "Who are you?"

"I'm Penny."

"Do you go to our school?" the one with yellow pigtails tied with polka-dot ribbons asks.

"Yes," I say.

"No, you don't," the red-haired girl says. Up close, she has freckles on her cheeks, a tiny nose, big gray eyes.

"I want to, though."

Pigtails says, "You can't. You don't have the right clothes."

I look down at overalls that are now too short, the hem above my ankles, the crotch tight. Mama J keeps trying to adjust them, but I'm growing like the weed I am.

"You're dirty," a skinny girl across from me says, pointing at my grimy hands, crescents of brown beneath the nails.

"And you smell," the freckled girl adds, wrinkling her nose. "Like poop."

"Stinky-stinky-stinky-butt," says a kid with her arm in a white cast scribbled with hearts and letters. They all join in. "Stinky-stinky-stinky-butt . . ."

My eyes flood, and the world turns blurry.

"We don't want you here," the girls chant.

Never let 'em see you cry, Mama J mutters. *If they know it hurts, they'll do it harder.*

But I don't have the right clothes, and I am dirty; I do smell. We didn't go to the shelter last Sunday for a meal and shower. Mama J says we need to be careful, now that I'm getting older, of the do-gooders. Social workers, therapists, and volunteers are on the other side. The side that wants to split us apart.

The freckled girl picks up a stone and throws it at me. It hits beneath my right eye and pain blooms. A few of the other girls find rocks and pelt me. I run away to a chorus of *we don't want you here* and slip back through the fence, find my way to the car. Mama J is still asleep. I get in the back seat, put my head in her lap, pretend she's telling me a story. Usually that makes me feel better. Today it doesn't.

CHAPTER

13

I REACH THE SCHOOL's exit doors and push them open, breathe in the crisp San Francisco night. *What now?* I lean against the cool brick of the building and weigh my options. I could get a job at a clothing boutique or a coffee shop. But I may not win in mediation or court. I need a career and security. A long time ago, I was a promising PhD candidate. It's the only skillset I have to build on. Once my anxiety has gone from a blaring whoop-whoop to a low buzz, head down, fists clenched, I push open the doors, go back inside, and crash into a man's chest.

"Whoa," Luc says, hands at my waist to keep me from stumbling. "You just getting some air or was my welcome speech so bad that you're leaving?"

His palms lightly press on my hips. I look up at the faint laugh lines around his eyes. He's still so good looking, and clearly successful. While I'm a middle-aged woman with zero prospects, a daughter who doesn't want to see me, living in a shitty rental apartment that I may soon not be able to afford. A wave of shame hits and I step back. "I'm staying."

Luc gestures to a spot on the floor and we sit, lean against a bank of yellow metal lockers. "Why are you here?" he asks.

I wrap arms around my knees. "I need to update my skills."

"Seriously? You could help teach this class."

"You have much too high an opinion of my abilities." I pivot. "Your scar healed well." After class a group of us went to Ruloff's, the local pub. I'd forgotten my bike lock, so Luc used his to lock both bikes together. Following pizza and a few drinks we went to unlock them, go our respective ways, but Luc had left the key at home.

"It was your idea to attempt to ride home with the lock still on," Luc reminds me.

"There wasn't another option, and I thought you were coordinated," I joke. We had about twenty inches between the bikes. He held the back of my seat, we mounted the bikes in tandem, made it a few blocks before Luc lagged and we tipped over. He hit his chin on the pavement.

"What happened?" Luc asks.

"You fell over."

"No, I mean with you. Why'd you drop out? No one could believe it, with the Johnson nomination, the level of your work . . ."

It's hard to meet his eyes. *But I need his help.* "I got pregnant, married Bruce—"

"The guy with the briefcase?"

He remembers. "That's the one. We had a daughter, Circe."

Luc smiles. "Is she named after the goddess?"

"Yes." Bruce wanted to name her Ansley, but I insisted. Circe was an enchantress who could change her enemies into lions, pigs, wolves. *I used to wish Mama J had named me Circe.*

"Has it been a good life, so far?" Luc asks.

His eyes are so earnest. "Parts have. The early years of my marriage. Circe, especially. I've mostly spent my time raising our daughter and being a wife, supporting Bruce's insurance company. I did charity work, planned parties, gardened, and made jam." My cheeks heat up. I do sound like a 1950s housewife. "I have twenty-one thousand followers on LivLoud who love my photos, recipes, and gardening tips."

"Wow?" Luc says, wiggling his brows.

I laugh. He clearly has no idea what I'm talking about.

"Now you want to update your skills?"

"It's a little more complicated." This close, I notice how long his lashes are and the bow of his top lip. This is beyond embarrassing, but I'm out of options. "My soon-to-be ex traded me in for a younger model. I now need to work. Unlike Stan Honey, I'm not sure how to navigate this new world and have no idea where to begin."

Luc runs the tip of a finger along the length of his pale scar, and it sends an unexpected streamer of heat through my body. *Get a grip. He's a successful guy and you're a grad school dropout whose husband cheated and who just fled his class.*

"Have you ever heard of Boyd Varty?" Luc asks.

I shake my head.

"He's a wildlife and literacy activist. Also, a public speaker."

"Underachiever?"

Luc chuckles. "Boyd grew up on his family's game reserve in South Africa. As a boy, he learned how to track wild animals. He says you're never lost. That you're just getting information that the place you are now and the way you're going isn't where you want to be. Boyd calls that 'the path of not here.'"

"That about sums up my current predicament."

"Good."

Luc shrugs one shoulder and it brushes mine, sending tiny ripples of electricity across my skin. "Good?"

"When you know that you're on the path of not here, you can shift. But if you don't recognize you're on it, then it's impossible to make a change, find happiness."

"I don't remember you being so philosophical," I say.

He tips his head back against the locker, stares at the ceiling. "I wasn't, back then. My eye was on launching a career and making money. Collecting expensive things."

"What happened?" I ask, turning the tables.

Luc pauses. "Let's just say that I realized it wasn't all that it was cracked up to be. So, I've come back to doing the last thing that made me happy. Teaching. I'm in the process of figuring things out, too, and finding my joy. Where's yours?"

All I can think about are all the paths I could've taken but didn't, all the ways I've messed up my life, marriage, and Circe's world. "Honestly? I don't know."

"Then we both have work to do." Luc offers me his hand, pulls me to my feet.

Our bodies are inches apart. His blue eyes have flecks of silver in the irises and I feel the urge to move even closer. *He's just being nice.* "There's really a career playing computer games?" I ask to break our imagined connection.

Luc grins and that dimple appears again. "It's a new world. Apparently there are furries in it."

You're not special, Mama J calls after me as I walk back to class beside Luc.

My icon, the woman in white, comes to mind. She claps her hands, encouraging me to ignore Mama J. To keep going and reinvent myself.

Don't you remember what the gods do to anyone showing hubris? Mama J demands. *Arachne challenged the goddess Athena to a weaving contest and was turned into a spider; Sisyphus tried to cheat death and was condemned to push a boulder uphill for eternity; Niobe bragged about having fourteen children to the goddess Leto, who had only two. Leto had all of Niobe's children murdered. That bitch killed every one of 'em.*

My body stiffens. *Circe.*

I'm trying to protect you, Mama J says.

Anger bites. *That's rich, coming from you.* I follow Luc into the classroom.

CHAPTER

14

"SO NOW THAT you've had a little time to think about your passions and what you need, I'll meet with everyone individually," Luc says after we return, "and we'll figure out together how you can get the most out of this class."

Out of the corner of my eye, I watch him sit with Arrya, Jean, and then Nate, who pumps a fist in the air after their exchange, clearly excited about next steps. By the time it's my turn, I've twisted myself into knots but have no answers. When Luc drags over a chair, I glance at the door, almost run again.

"I'm faster than you," Luc jokes, clearly following my train of thought. "What's your passion?"

It's like trying to catch a leaf in a windstorm. When I was younger, it was school. Then it was being a mother, making sure Circe hit milestones, and later, was set up for all the opportunities I'd missed. And above all, being a family was my raison d'être. But that's been flushed down the drain.

"A long time ago, my passion was working on my thesis," I finally venture. I don't add that recently that passion has turned into an obsession.

Luc nods. "Dr. Edmunds was gutted when you left. He's the one who nominated you for that fellowship," Luc says, pulling me back into the present.

I'm shocked. "Seriously?"

"You were the most naturally gifted programmer he'd ever seen."

I remember Dr. Edmunds telling me that I could achieve greatness . . . *But I didn't believe him.*

"So, remind me what your thesis was about?"

I study my sneakers. "That you can use language, more specifically, word selection, rate of speech, tonal changes, and enunciation, to detect lies."

"Now I remember. You interviewed thousands of people and asked them to read fifty innocuous statements. Things like 'I shower three times a day.'"

I look up. "I recorded them, then asked which statements were false. Before I dropped out, I was building a database. The plan was to analyze and detect the differences in cadence, pace, tone, and enunciation between the true statements and the lies. That data inputting was precise, and I never got through it." *If I had, maybe I would've known Bruce was cheating.* Heat creeps up my neck. "My thesis probably sounds juvenile now."

"Not at all. Plus there's an opportunity to use it to update your skillset and make you marketable."

Adrenaline makes my fingertips tingle. "How?"

"Artificial intelligence. Today, AI is powerful enough to do the heavy lifting—all that mind-numbing work and the comparative analysis."

Goosebumps race across my skin. The future we once discussed is now. I feel an internal rush, like all the fear and desperation I'd experienced—from childhood through navigating my adult life, place in the world, marriage, Bruce's devastating affair, and Circe's painful choices—have formed a massive wave, and my head is barely above water. *I've been drowning for a long time without realizing it.* Now, if I can make my program truly work with the help of AI, identify lies and achieve a level of certainty in life, maybe more, and at the same time gain applicable career skills, there's hope of rescue.

"You already have a background in mathematics, statistics, and probability. If you learn the basics of programs like Scikit-learn, NumPy, and Pandas, part of the Python library, the opportunities for work are endless," Luc explains.

My mind circles in the way it used to when I tackled something new. "I have a massive dataset and I've been fiddling with a program over the years, gotten it to a very basic level. But if I could build a system to comprehensively clean my data up, add more, I could prove my supposition, that speech communicates far more than just the meaning of words." I hesitate, then add, "I've also been messing around with the idea that the program could be expanded not only to identify lies, but also go a step farther and provide advice."

Luc grins. "There's the spark. And if you figure out what you need, all that work on proving your expanded thesis and learning new computer languages will not only help you find a career but could even springboard you to design something with commercial applications."

"Thank you," I say and really mean it.

Luc stands up. "Anytime. Take a look at Python. It has some AI-supported routines that are quite powerful."

I pull up the Python index on my computer but hesitate before diving in. I'm still missing part of the equation. What do I need? *Circe to live with me. Bruce to know how it feels to be humiliated and ruined. His mistress, too.* The corners of my mouth twist into a grim smile. There's a perverse pleasure to the idea, but it'll never happen. So, I need to find my joy.

CHAPTER

15

THE FOLLOWING MORNING, as I eat a bowl of oatmeal at my kitchen counter and go through the Python index on my laptop, a dog on the street barks. I peer out the window. Below, an old man with a cane walks a black Scottish terrier dressed in a plaid jacket that matches the scarf draped around his owner's neck. The dog pauses when the man stops to rest, then resumes, matching his human's slow steps. The animal's sweetness and loyalty fill me with longing. "What's stopping me?" I ask the silence.

I do a Google search for animal rescues, make a call, and take a few photographs of my apartment as requested by the shelter I chose. After sending the photos, I grab my jacket and head to the car, put in the address, and my navigation system maps the route for me. Thank you, Stan Honey.

As I drive by Crissy Field, there are people running and bikers sporting matching brightly colored kits spinning along a path that edges the Bay. Groups cluster on the green grass, play frisbee, fly kites. I join a steady stream crossing the Golden Gate Bridge, water sparkling below, cargo ships churning, sailboats cutting, and kite-surfers carving through waves.

My phone rings and Circe's photo displays. "Hey, sweetie," I say, trying not to sound too thrilled that for once she's calling me. "What's up?"

"Our cheer team made it to sectionals."

"Wow! Congratulations. You've worked hard for it." I don't ask for an invite, though I'm dying to watch her compete.

"Hey, Char," Circe calls out. "Gotta go."

"Okay. Love you," I say, but she's already hung up.

I flick on my blinker and take the next exit. Sugar Face is in Sausalito. It's a shelter run by Viola Whitby—I texted her before leaving my place. She greets me at the door of a shingled home, a bespectacled woman in her seventies, gray hair in a single braid, sporting baggy overalls over a black turtleneck and comfortable green plastic clogs.

"Thanks for letting me come by," I say as she waves me inside.

"Anything for our seniors."

Viola leads me toward a bright-orange door. Beyond it is a room with rubber flooring filled with about fifteen dogs, most lounging on soft beds, a few trotting around with stuffed toys or balls. All have white faces; some are missing a leg or have tattered ears, jagged scars. On the far side of the room, sliding glass doors lead to a large, fenced-in grassy yard where more dogs romp.

"Feel free to wander around. They're all friendly," Viola says. "See which one calls to you."

I've always wanted a dog. As a kid it was impossible—Mama J could barely take care of us. Nor could I have a dog in college or graduate school. My university didn't even pay my room and board. Then I married Bruce and had a baby to take care of, and he had allergies. Or at least that's what Bruce told me, though he never had issues with Hal and Heather's Labradors or Kiki and Chris's golden retriever.

Stop looking over your shoulder, Mama J reminds me.

I visit with the dogs curled on their beds, then toss a ball for a tripod mutt that has no problem trotting on three legs to retrieve it. But when I wander into the yard, I'm drawn to a short-haired cherry-brown mutt with a white circle around her right eye. She looks like a mix between a boxer and maybe a vizsla, her tail docked, muzzle speckled with white.

"Hey," I say softly and walk over to where the dog sits by the back gate, staring at a path that leads to the front of the house. She doesn't look at me, not even when I kneel in the grass beside her.

"That one doesn't have a name yet," Viola calls from the far corner of the yard where she weeds a raised garden bed. "The owner dropped her off last week, too embarrassed to give me any details other than she'd just turned ten—our oldest dog right now—and his kids wanted a puppy."

I reach out, rub the dog's chest, trace the small patch of white there. There's no sign that she notices. *She wants her old life back.* "I know how she feels. My husband dumped me for a woman in her twenties and my daughter chose to live with them."

"Life can be a kick in the teeth," Viola agrees. "My husband divorced me when I became an opioid addict after a botched knee surgery. We have three boys. I stole part of their childhood, along with the money in their savings accounts. The kids do come back, eventually, if you get your act together. But they never forget. My oldest won't let me see the grandkids alone." She shrugs. "It's a different kind of happily ever after."

Sadness is a sneaky assassin, and I pinch away tears. "I'd like to take her."

Viola asks, "Got a name?"

Last night I woke before dawn, channel surfed, and watched the end of an old movie. The actress in it, Sally Field, played a character who risked her life to help unionize a mill. She was scared out of her mind but brave. "I'm going to call her Sally Field, if that's okay?" The dog doesn't even look at me.

Viola takes off her gardening gloves and grabs a leash from a hook by the sliders. "All our dogs eat Senior Pure-Good Kibble. Can you do that and guarantee Sally a soft bed, kindness, and walks whenever she needs them?"

"Yes."

"Good. Consider this a trial. I'll touch base in a few weeks, and we can evaluate."

Sally allows me to clip the leash to her collar. She walks beside me to the car. I help her load into the back seat, and can feel her ribs. She probably hasn't been eating much, either. First stop, a pet shop on Chestnut Street in the Marina for food and water bowls, kibble, a big bag of treats, and a bed. I talk to Sally the entire way, but she just looks out the window, maybe trying to see landmarks to determine if she's on her way home.

"It's not going to be the same," I say. "But maybe it can still be okay."

When we arrive at the store, I put the car on doggy mode even though it's a cool day. A cartoon pooch bounces on the Tesla's screen, promising anyone passing by that the pet inside is cool and comfortable.

Inside Sir Wags A Lot, I buy the essentials plus a large cozy cave—a fleece taco-shaped bed that promises warmth—and an orthopedic suede foam bed that looks like a couch, several orange balls, poop bags, a stuffed rabbit and racoon, and four boxes of various treats, from chicken sticks to fish skins (gross), as I don't know what Sally likes.

"Penn?"

Arms full, I turn. Patricia Cavanaugh wears a white tennis skirt and striped sweater, her blond hair swept into a low ponytail. We served on the PTA together. She's Sara Curry's good friend. In this moment, I'd give anything to disappear. I've done my best to avoid all the places where I might run into school moms, even started shopping at Fred Meyer instead of Whole Foods. Though, truth is, I can no longer afford the latter.

"How are you?" Patricia asks, her tone dripping with sympathy.

"Good," I say lightly, and move toward the register.

She follows me like a malevolent spirit, a smirk on her plumped-up lips. "We were so sorry to hear about you and Bruce. You two seemed like the perfect couple."

I hand the salesgirl, a twenty-something smacking gum, my new credit card, and pray that what I'm buying doesn't exceed the low limit. *More fodder for the rumor mill.* I decline a receipt and hustle out of the store. Bruce should be the one ashamed, not me. But it's hard to shake the feeling that I did something wrong.

Sally is in the exact spot by the window where I left her and doesn't stir as I load supplies into the back of the car. "Let's go home." Sally remains stoic. The run-in with Patricia has left me feeling lower than low, and now this. Maybe adopting a dog was another mistake.

Lavinia Robertson Women's Shelter, San Francisco

The Past

I HAVE A FRIEND! Her name is Dolly. She was named after a country singer named Dolly Parton who has blond hair, big boobs, and a high voice. Mama J moved us to this shelter after a social worker came sniffing around our station wagon asking my age and if I was in school. It was my fault. I left the car to spy on the kids in the playground. One of the teachers must've seen me, told someone who told someone who sent the lady with a clipboard.

Mama J got real sick after that. Not from the medicine. From not taking the medicine.

You're the worst thing that ever happened to me, she said that first night, doubled over with cramps, body soaked in sweat.

I can find you some medicine, I offered. There's a guy named Soto on the corner who Mama J dates sometimes.

The shelter won't let us stay if I'm high.

I felt bad for Mama J but wasn't sorry to move into the women's shelter. There were other girls, and I met Dolly. Plus, I got to take a class, learn my ABCs. Pretty fast, I could read a book about Jane and a dog named Spot. Dolly says I'm real smart, that it took her much longer to learn how to read. Being smart makes me feel so good. Every time the teacher, Ms. Flatley, puts stars on my workbook, my insides explode like fireworks. Ms. Flatley said even though I'm eight and behind, I can catch up real fast. I'm afraid, though, that I won't be here long enough to do that.

Dolly and I play "house" with my kitty, Daddy, and her stuffed bear, Dennis. That was the name of her second dad. They lived in a real house with three bedrooms on two floors. Dolly misses the house, her very own bedroom, and Dennis a lot, even though he broke her mom's arm.

Mama J is also taking classes. Parenting, Cooking, and Job Hunting. Her clothes are starting to fit better, and the scabs have mostly disappeared. Tonight, we're going to watch a movie with everyone. It's about a rabbit who goes on adventures. Dolly says it's a dumb cartoon, but I don't mind. There's going to be popcorn. Right now, though, I'm refolding the clothes that Yasmin, the nice lady who runs the shelter, gave me. I have two new T-shirts, a pair of purple velvet sweatpants, and jeans that only have one patch on the knee—it's a yellow smiley face, so I don't mind. Dolly got a sweatshirt with a rainbow on the front that made me jealous, but it's okay 'cause we're friends and friends share.

"Whatcha doin'?" Mama J now asks. She shuffles into the bunkroom we share with Dolly and her mom.

Her eyes are glassy, and she moves like her bones have gone to mush. I leap up, quickly shut the door. But it turns out that it's too late. Someone tattled. The social worker shows up a few hours later, tells Mama J she's got to leave the shelter; that I'm going to be placed in a foster home.

I don't know what a foster home is, but as soon as the lady leaves us alone to pack our things, Mama J and I sneak out of the shelter and run. I struggle to keep up, afraid she'll leave me behind because I'm not lucky, and sometimes the worst thing that's ever happened to her. But deep down I get that Mama J is Demeter and I'm Persephone. She'll never let me go. That idea should make me happy, but it doesn't as much anymore.

"Will the lady find us?" I gasp, a stitch in my side.

Mama J shakes her head. "No one really wants to. They just got to check the boxes."

It takes us a while to find a tent city, scrounge cardboard and blankets. But in a few days, we have a new home. I feel bad that I took the rainbow sweatshirt and Dennis with me. But Dolly gets to stay at the shelter, go to school. She doesn't need the stuffed bear or *new* old clothes as much as I do, and at least Daddy gets to keep his only friend.

"Stop boo-hooing about missing Dolly," Mama J snaps after a week.

"I've never had a friend before," I sob. "It feels like something died inside me."

"Friends will always let you down."

"You're wrong!"

"Oh yeah? How do you think Dolly felt when she discovered Dennis was gone?"

When she puts it that way, I'm ashamed, and hope Dolly doesn't hate me. Still, I can't return to the shelter, give Dennis back. The social worker will take me away from Mama J, and she needs me to survive.

A new feeling rolls through me that's hard to name. While at the shelter, Dolly and I watched a documentary about wolves on the nature channel. Ranchers trapped them so they wouldn't kill baby cows and sheep. They used these steel jaws, and if the wolf was lucky, the trap snapped its neck. If it got a leg, the wolf suffered until the rancher put a bullet in its head. One wolf gnawed her own leg off to escape and be free. Dolly thought that was crazy. But maybe I get it now.

CHAPTER

16

AT MY APARTMENT door, Sally sniffs once, then walks across the carpet, creakily climbs onto the low window seat, and stares out the divided glass. I understand she's hoping to see her family, that this was all a bad dream, to have the children rush into my apartment, hug and kiss her, then take her home. *Life isn't a fairy tale.* I settle at my desk, open the Python index, and focus on learning new programming languages, try to get a handle on what I don't know. Turns out it's a lot.

Hours later, brain fried, I decide to pivot and input Kiki's recorded statement, then tap my program's icon.

"I knew Bruce was a cheater," Kiki says with a little giggle at the absurdity of the phrase.

The icon, elegant in its white gown, spins, slows, then stops.

I knew Bruce was a cheater.

This statement is true.

I scowl. It's an obvious lie. Another glitch in my program. Nothing is going right today. I load Val's recording. When she made it, there was anger in her voice. *She is my rock.*

The icon spins one time before settling.

I knew Bruce was a cheater.

This statement is true.

Defeated, I slump. Clearly, my program wasn't even as far along as I'd hoped. "Can't you help me?" I ask the icon. She stares back, her face unreadable. Maybe it's a pipe dream to think that someday the program will be able to answer correctly, give advice, provide next steps. I'm on my own. "So how do I fix this glitch?"

Unable to find an answer, I rest my head on the desk and my scattershot brain drifts back to the last coffee date with Kiki and Val. I need to pull my act together. My best friends are going to get tired of me being so pathetic. If that happens, I'll lose them . . .

How are you doing today?

Same but different day. Mad and sad.

Bruce is the one who should be miserable. He should've kept his dick in his pants for the last eight months and kissed the ground you walk on.

I sit up.

He should've kept his dick in his pants for the last eight months . . .

The ground beneath me vanishes as I reread the program's response to Val's recording. My stomach craters.

`I knew Bruce was a cheater.`

`This statement is true.`

The truth sinks fangs into that unguarded, tender place reserved for the people I trust most. My icon's face is inscrutable. But she knew. "I never told Val the affair had been going on for eight months." The woman in white's blue eyes glint. "Val didn't lie. She knew Bruce was a cheater."

How could she do this to me?

Told you friends always let you down, Mama J says.

I pull up LivLoud and hack into Val's account. *She deserves it.* I succeed on the third attempt. Why are people so predictable in their choice of passwords? The first thing I learn is that both my best friends have known since last August—that's the entire duration of Bruce's affair. They knew it was Mackenzie, too.

August 4:

Kiki: SOS Val! Christopher and I saw Bruce with Mackenzie Hanks at Lombardi's

Val: NBD—she's his exec assistant

Kiki: KISSING

Val: WTF?! Did he see you?

Kiki: NO! He walked by our table with an OBVIOUS hard on and Mackenzie followed a few minutes later. When they returned her shirt was buttoned wrong!!!!

Val and Kiki's DMs about my husband's affair continued over the ensuing months.

September 9:

Val: How could Penn NOT see the red flags?

Kiki: No idea! Bruce has lost weight and he's dressing like he's 20!

Val: Remember that Netflix series we watched together, about the husband having an affair?

Kiki: Wasn't that the one where the wife killed him? Penn doesn't have it in her

Val: So true. She doesn't even kill spiders. Catch and release only

Kiki: I scream then smash them! Honestly? Sometimes Penn makes me feel shallow

Val: Why?

Kiki: She's just so . . . perfect

Val: I know what you mean

Kiki: So, should we tell her about Bruce?

Val: We agreed it's a mid-life crisis—if he ends it soon Penn can remain in her bubble. Women like her wouldn't do well out in the wild

Perfect? My bubble? The wild? Neither of them could live under a bridge or at a shelter, let alone dine from a dumpster.

They're rich, spoiled, and it turns out they're cruel. And they watch Netflix series together?

November 18:

Kiki: Yesterday I saw B&M in Marin at the farmer's market—I hid!
Val: Penn said he brought home flowers last night. She posted a photo on LivLoud #marriedlifeisthebest Bruce is making her look so stupid 😒
Kiki: Sometimes I just want to shake Penn for putting us in such an uncomfortable situation
Val: Me, too . . .
Kiki: But it's not her fault
Val: Isn't it though . . . a little?
Kiki: You're right! Sometimes, I wish we could really talk to her, but it's like trying to squeeze water from a lemon!
Val: Hahaha! You mean blood from a stone
Kiki: Whatever 🙂 Want to come over for dinner? Christopher is taking the kids out for pizza and a superhero movie, and I need a glass of rosé and some girl time.

I remember the bouquet—dahlias and peonies. We had sex that night. I initiated. Bruce wanted to do it in the dark. It was probably the only way he could imagine I was her. And water from a lemon? I tell Kiki and Val personal things. For fuck's sake, they know about my miscarriage. And why wasn't I ever invited over for rosé and girl time?

December 23:

Val: I caught Bruce winking at Mackenzie during their Christmas party 😫
Kiki: This isn't going to end well 😏 Mackenzie is sooooo SEXY
Val: Penn needs to ditch the sensible clothes—no one dresses that way but uptight ladies in Junior League and The Garden Club
Kiki: Agreed

January 14:

Val: One of my clients saw B&M on Andros Island in the Bahamas. She was topless, and he was wearing a SPEEDO!

Kiki: Ewwwwwwwwwwwwww

Val: He's getting what Penn would never give him, right?

Kiki: Meaning?

Val: Hot sex

Kiki: We don't know—Penn gives off prude vibes but could be a wildcat in the sheets

Val: Yeah, right ☺

Kiki: There's a sale at Saks tomorrow—1:30 at the door off Couch Street?

Val: I'll be there!

That was a work trip for Hal, Bruce, and their top clients. No wives invited. And I was never invited to Saks with them.

March 7:

Val: What do we do now that Penn knows?

Kiki: I guess we pick up the pieces. I feel sorry for her

Val: Me, too. He's going to screw her in the divorce

Kiki: How do you know?

Val: Bruce needs to afford his new life

Kiki: You think he'll have kids with Mackenzie?

Val: Probably—she's very young—and Penn once admitted he always wanted a son

Kiki: Marriage?

Val: It's a way to lock him in, right? Too bad Penn didn't have a prenup

Kiki: She signed away everything!!

Val: Hate to say it, but for someone so smart she was really fucking dumb

The icon's blue eyes watch me. "Val is right," I tell her. "I'm really fucking dumb." Not only did Val and Kiki know about the affair, leave me in the dark to be a cliché, but it turns out that I'm not Monica or Rachel. I'm barely Phoebe. The icon spins once, another glitch. Voices war in my head, each shouting to be heard . . .

You're really fucking hard to like . . .
You don't have the right clothes . . .
Slugs can't turn into butterflies, can they?
It's hard to breathe when you're around . . .
We don't want you here . . .
Thought you were special, and it bit you in the ass.

My phone vibrates with a fox's giggle. Fury mingles with devastation. Kiki let me think I was her best friend. Val did, too. It's worse than those girls who mocked me when I tried to join their circle, worse than the bullies in middle school, worse than having an addict mother. At least they said how they really felt. And Mama J told me the ultimate truth—I was destined to have my wings fall apart.

I block both Val's and Kiki's numbers, email addresses, and accounts on LivLoud. I'm isolated and alone, drifting to sea, watching my world, the people I once loved, grow smaller and smaller until they disappear. But Kiki and Val are liars, same as Bruce. They don't deserve to have me cry over them. *They deserve to feel like I do now.* Violently, I blow my nose and smear away the tears.

Sally is still at the window. "It's just us now." I put kibble in her new bowl, then make popcorn for dinner and drizzle butter on it. The smell finally gets the dog to glance my way, but her eyes still avoid mine. She does lick her lips. I google whether popcorn with butter is bad for dogs. It's not, in small quantities. But Sally won't take any from my palm.

I pull out an old sweatshirt and slip it on the dog backwards—she doesn't protest. Maybe the kids who once loved her used to play dress up. I put a handful of popcorn in the hood. She sniffs at it.

"Up to you. I'm going to watch a movie, feel free to join me on the couch." Bruce would never allow a pet on our pricey furniture, so it feels extra good to extend the invite.

I stream *The River Wild*, get under a blanket, the popcorn bowl on my lap. A few minutes in to Gail and her family going down the river, I hear a delicate crunch come from the foam bed where Sally has settled. When she finishes her popcorn, Sally slowly makes her way over to the couch. Her hips are stiff, so I help her up. She settles at the far end, still only making furtive glances my way.

When the movie ends, Sally and I head out for a walk around the block. We go slowly; she sniffs a lot and marks a few patches of grass. When she looks back the way we came, we return to the apartment. Sally burrows into the cozy cave set at the foot of my bed as I slide between the sheets. Once settled, she makes a *harumph* that gives me a tiny shot of hope and is soon snoring. I always disliked the sound of Bruce's harsh breathing. But Sally's snores are soft and help me drift off. . . .

Sally is a floppy-eared puppy playing with toddlers who suddenly pick up rocks, stone her as she whimpers . . . Circe leaps off a swing, falls into quicksand, struggles as it swallows her while I watch, helpless . . . Kiki and Val share a cappuccino at a cafe and cackle over my stupidity . . . Bruce and his mistress have sex in our bed. He pauses, mid-thrust, to tell me he's never been happier . . . The woman in white glides into the room. She winks at me, then walks to Bruce's side of the bed and raises a graceful arm. The knife in her hand gleams in the moonlight as she plunges it toward the center of his back . . .

CHAPTER

17

THE WAIT FOR this week's class felt interminable. With nothing else to focus on, other than trying to engage Sally and reaching out to Circe, I've been glued to my computer, determined to do something right. I now understand the basics of several new computer programs and am plowing through their complexities to gain a working knowledge of AI. I've also been homing in on what I need, a glimmer of an idea gaining flesh, becoming more and more real.

Val and Kiki have both tried to call me. Their numbers are blocked but they can leave messages. I've listened to a few. They've gone from light concern to fake worry then on to feigned confusion. Kiki has also come by my apartment—Circe must've given her the address. But I didn't answer the buzzer. I've always avoided confrontation . . .

Did you piss your pants? Mama J demanded.

It was my first week at a *real* school. Thea Henderson cornered me in the girls' locker room with her friends and said they were going to strip me naked for being a pervy creeper *and* force me to walk onto the boys' football field during practice. Thea was popular and I was watching her, trying to memorize everything about her so I could be popular, too. As Thea and her friends threatened me, I lost control of my bladder.

Life is cruel, Penny, Mama J said as she washed my undies in the sink. *Better you hear it from me, figure out your strengths, so that if it comes to fighting for your life, you'll be ready.*

Tonight, Luc makes his rounds to help each student and then pulls up a chair at my desk. He's only inches away. The scent of his soap—citrus—the way my insides stir when he's solely focused on me, the wool of his shirt as it accidentally brushes my wrist, make it hard to think straight. *Pull it together. Luc is my teacher. Again.*

"I have an idea about an application for my thesis work," I tentatively say. Kiki and Val's DMs have reminded me that there's so much context and background information behind every conversation; so many things I couldn't have known. "What if I could build on my previous analysis of language, link it to social media posts and phone conversations?"

"Keep going," Luc encourages.

"It's a big leap from feeding my research subjects bland truths and lies, but, like you said, technology is so powerful now. I can use AI and the new programs I've learned to collate my existing data, turn concepts into functional algorithms, then take things a step further to create an interactive AI program. Not just to give bland advice based on what I share, but that can utilize a vast network of background information that allows for specific, helpful feedback."

Luc tents his fingers together. "Give me some details."

"Okay. Imagine having a program that doesn't just detect someone else's lies but also analyzes that person's social media, basically figures out both the lie and its context."

Luc's forehead scrunches. "O-kay. Go on."

"Then the program can make an informed decision whether it's in your best interest to take someone's advice or a job offer, what friendships to value and which to drop. The program could even tell you whether it's a good idea to salvage a relationship or divorce."

"It could also tell you if you look good in your favorite pair of jeans," he jokes.

I laugh. I hadn't thought about the visual aspects of my idea. But of course, the app could use video, too. Luc nips his lower lip, and I wonder what it tastes like. *Who the hell am I? More Penn Roberts, less Penn Stone, that's for sure.*

"If I do this right, my program would be a resource that can understand myriad situations and discern the truth one hundred percent of the time, then give feedback to help make the next right step in life."

"What about just trusting yourself?" Luc challenges.

"Look where that's gotten me," I shoot back. "And you said to combine our passions with our needs."

Luc chuckles. "You haven't changed at all."

Was I really this way fifteen years ago? An elderly student named Buzz raises a hand for help and Luc hesitates, like he has more to say, but then moves on. I feel his absence but the fire inside me remains. *Maybe I was that girl. Could I be her again?*

Nate turns around. "I'd buy that program."

"Really?" It's disconcerting to look into his amber-colored eyes. I wish he'd take the wolf's head off so I could see his real ones.

"Hell yeah. I was dating this other furry—he's a standard poodle. I thought we had a great thing going and planned to ask him to move in and everything. Turns out he was into a Dalmatian. Had a pure-bred thing. Totally shook my confidence."

Tonight, Nate is wearing orange checkered pajama bottoms, his wolf's head, and a lifelike white-and-gray fur chest. His tail is curled beneath his chair. He brought his paws, too, but took them off to type. "His loss," I offer.

Arrya takes a seat beside me. "Hey, Penn. Um, I can't figure this line of code out," she says, sliding her laptop my way.

"Did you ask Luc for help?"

She twists a strand of pink hair around her index finger. "He's busy. But after what he said about you, well, I thought you might be able to steer me in the right direction?"

I study the code. "When did you start buying places in foreclosure?"

"I was twenty-five," Arrya says. "My parents were kind of controlling. I had to figure out a way to make my own decisions or it wouldn't be my life, you know?"

Was I living Bruce's life?

"I got a second job, saved, and eventually bought a run-down, foreclosed apartment in San Jose at auction. Then I learned how to renovate and flipped it. Never looked back. The risks are sometimes scary. But I guess the most important things in life are."

"Lately, I'm scared every day," I admit, then blush.

"Why?"

Never roll over and show 'em your underbelly, Mama J reminds me. But I have nothing left to lose and loneliness is eating away at me. "I'm getting divorced. The world feels too big and I'm not sure where I fit in."

"Want to get a coffee at the place on the corner, Grind, before next class?" Arrya asks.

"I'd like that."

After class, Nate and I end up walking the same way down Franklin Street. Turns out we live near each other, and he offers to walk me home. I wonder if he's hitting on me, but he explains on the way that he's "strictly dickly, so don't get any ideas." He just didn't want me to walk alone in the dark. "Wolves are protective," he adds, and that makes me smile a little.

The night is cold, and halfway to my place, he offers me his plaid scarf. It smells cozy, like the wool of his fur. Four kids on skateboards rolls down the street. One of them yells, "Freak!"

"Does that bother you?" I ask.

"Nah. They're not part of my pack." He scratches the fur on his chin. "Why are you taking our class? I googled the Henry Johnson thing. It means you're hella smart."

I don't have the energy to lie. "I've forgotten half of what I used to know about computer science, plus the advances have left me in the dust. But in the past few months, I've lost my marriage—he cheated with a Gen Zer—have a daughter who doesn't want to live with me because she blames me for the divorce . . . What else . . . ? My best friends knew about the mistress, were laughing behind my back, and my only companion is an old dog who'd rather be with the family who abandoned her. I need to reinvent myself. The class is a start."

Nate nods his giant wolf's head. "Whoa, that's a lot."

My face burns. I start to cross against the light, but Nate holds out his paw. When it turns green, we cross.

"Seems like you're mega hard on yourself."

"Practice," I try to joke.

"FYI, that shit usually comes from childhood," Nate says. "Wouldn't know anything about that. My family was perfect."

"Really?"

"Nah, they disowned me after I came out. The furry thing would've blown their flipping minds," he adds with a laugh.

"How are you so confident?" *I really want to know.*

"Two choices in life. One is to stay in the abyss someone's dug you. The other is to claw your way free and figure out how to feel special, despite what your nearest and supposedly dearest think."

"Do you ever go out without your costume?"

"No."

I can't help but wonder if he'll ever find a way to like himself without the wolf's clothing. *Will I?* Being the consummate corporate wife, having the perfect home, making breakfasts using Bonnie Roy's recipes, repeating mantras from Dr. Bob, Tanya Decker, and Dr. Beth, using hashtags that humble brag about what I have. *What's real about* me*?*

At my apartment building's door, I unwind the scarf from my neck and return it. Nate puts a furry paw on my shoulder. "If you need a friend, just whistle." He lopes off.

"Arrya and I are meeting for coffee at Grind before the next class," I call after him. "Join us?"

Nate turns. "I'll consider expanding my pack."

When I enter the apartment, Sally sits in front of the door. Her tail thumps on the wood and she whines. "Do you need to go out?" But she trots back to the bedroom, gets into her cozy cave. Maybe she was wondering if I was going to return. I kneel by her bed. "I will always come back." She meets my gaze for the first time, and the little seed planted in my heart when I recognized a kindred spirit at Viola's sanctuary, when I chose her, takes root.

Holcomb Housing Block 17, San Francisco

The Past

I HOLD MY BREATH . . .

As I choose school clothes, worried the other students will notice that I don't have many options and most are worn, stained, patched.

In fear that there'll be a red-haired girl waiting to point out that I don't fit in, will never fit in.

When I walk into class and sit beside a kid, anxious he'll switch seats even if I took a bath; that the smell of once being homeless and dumpster diving for food never really goes away.

I pretend to be invisible . . .

If a teacher calls on me for an answer I know, duck my head and count until he or she moves on. I've seen what happens to kids who are too smart—they get whooped by the ones who aren't smart at all.

During my walk home, past the dealers with their fine kicks and leather coats. In our old neighborhood, Mama J knew them all by name. I did, too. These new ones have different faces, but the same hungry look. They want me to work for them, and eventually to get me hooked.

As I climb the stairs to our apartment. I don't slow, even though my heart hammers, until I unlock the door with the key hung from a shoelace around my neck and double lock it behind me. There's always yelling, fights in the hallways, and bullets don't care that I'm a girl.

I don't get a full lungful of air until . . .

Mama J shows up just before dark to eat the dinner I've made, usually hot dogs, mac and cheese from a box, or eggs. Then she heads to her second janitor shift.

Well after midnight when she gets home again and falls onto our shared bed. She has promised to always come back. But promises and Mama J haven't always been on the same page.

The truth is . . .

Mama J has been straight for a year, but she didn't stop taking her medicine exactly for me. She got an infection, almost died. The police found her passed out on a sidewalk. She had emergency surgery. There were big problems. It took seven days before she was let out of the hospital.

I got sick, too, waiting in our tent the whole time. I eventually ran out of water, crackers, cried until it was hard to see. I was in the Underworld, Cerberus prowled outside, and no one came to save me.

When Mama J finally returned, she said seeing me flipped a switch, but I heard her tell someone it was going a week without her *real* medicine that made it easier for cold turkey.

My teacher, Ms. Kendricks, thinks I'm a miracle 'cause I learn so fast despite being nine years old. She doesn't know that I'm desperate to learn as much as possible before Mama J chooses drugs again.

I know now . . .

That I'm not Persephone.

Mama J isn't Demeter or even Pandora, who was tricked by the gods into opening a box and releasing all the bad things, like heroin, guns, bullies, rapists, dealers, social workers, and murderers on the world. She knows what's in Pandora's box and opens it anyway. Eventually she will again.

I'm plotting my escape.

CHAPTER

18

For the next week, I rarely leave my computer. Only walking and playing with Sally—she's warming up to me and now puts a paw on my leg when we watch TV—and the necessity to buy groceries drags me away. That, and I meet Circe for a single dinner that I wheedle by taking her to a favorite Thai restaurant. We stick to safe subjects, and it feels like my daughter is becoming a stranger.

When class day finally arrives, I nervously wait for Arrya and Nate outside Grind. They don't show, or at least that's what I think until a paw taps my back.

"We're already inside," Nate says, pointing to the back corner of the coffee shop. "I got you a matcha," he adds. "I'm good at reading people. Is that okay?"

I've never had one. "Sure."

Arrya sits cross-legged on a chair, her latte cupped in both hands. I wonder how Nate is going to drink green tea in the wolf's head, but he uses a long straw. I try the matcha. It's delicious.

"She was scared of me," Nate says with a nod at Arrya.

"I'm not the girl from 'Little Red Riding Hood.'" She giggles. "But admittedly I've never had coffee with a wolf, wasn't sure if I'd lose a finger."

"I didn't read that story until I was nineteen," I admit.

"Seriously? Did you grow up in some kind of religious cult that banned children's stories?" Arrya jokes.

The truth emerges in a way it never did with Kiki and Val. "We were homeless. I didn't read well until I was nine, and the kids in my class were well past 'Little Red Riding Hood' by then."

"Whoa," Nate says. "You're way more interesting than I thought."

"What about you two?" I ask to shift the focus, then listen to stories about Arrya and Nate's families. Arrya's dad and mom, born and raised in India, were married at eighteen after meeting one time. Nate's mom is a Christian Scientist. He wasn't allowed to take any medicine as a kid, even when he was super sick.

"Luckily I didn't die," he jokes, but neither Arrya nor I laugh.

"Would you ever have an arranged marriage?" Nate asks Arrya.

She shakes her head. "I'd like a partner and at least one child before my eggs turn to dust. But I'm never going to get married."

"It can be good," I offer.

"If the guy doesn't cheat on you with a Gen Zer," Nate quips, "like your douchebag ex."

There's shocked silence, then I laugh. It feels good. "There's that," I say, patting his furry shoulder. "Maybe it's better to just find a solid pack." We walk to class together and I feel lighter than I have in months.

Once Luc welcomes everyone, Jean immediately raises his hand, tells him, "I've put a lot of time in, but simply don't have the skills to do what I want." There are nods and sighs from other students.

"The good news is you probably don't have to," Luc says from his perch on the front desk. "Let's talk about fountains."

"Fountains?" Nate asks, perplexed.

"Yeah. The first company I started tackled a problem that fascinated me. How to insert, in real time, human interactions with kinetic sculptures, digital screens, and even water and make those objects react to movements. The Raj, at the time, was the newest hotel in Vegas. Its developer wanted the hotel to have massive sculptures and water features that guests could interact with in a way that had never been done before. He tasked me to make that happen."

Luc rubs his hands together. "I had no idea how to parse a camera feed to recognize people and react to someone asking them to mimic their movements, jump, or dance. Open-source video analytics software saved my ass. It's basically a community willing to share their code. It's free if you post what you've modified or enhanced. The Raj became famous for the work I did, and when people redistribute my additions to the original source code, I get paid, along with the developers whose code I built on."

Jean says, "I've been to the Raj, those fountains are epic. And my fiancée, Gaelle, and I spent hours in the sculpture garden."

"Thanks, man. It was one of my favorite projects. Let's get to work. I'll come around and help where I can."

By the time he reaches my desk, I've been talking to Kate for a while. She's an AI friend I created with the help of Out of This Galaxy, an engine for designing games that allowed users to develop characters, give them motivations and flaws, and even choose a voice.

"The problem," I explain to Luc, forcing myself to ignore the taut feeling in my belly when he's anywhere in my vicinity, "is that Kate is willing to monitor my social media feeds for context and comment on my choices, but she won't evaluate the other person during phone calls, delve into anyone else's public social media accounts, or comment on their choices."

"You already created an advanced AI model?"

"Yes."

"Wow," he says, running a hand through his hair.

I fight the urge to reach out and touch the untamed waves. *What is going on with me?* But it's obvious. I haven't wanted or been wanted by anyone out of pure desire for so long. Plus, years ago, being in Luc's orbit gave me all the feels. *It still does.*

Luc smiles. "Kudos for doing what it takes most people a good while to master."

"Turns out Dr. Edmunds was right about me," I joke, then redden again.

Luc gives me an appraising look. "I'll say. But it sounds like Kate has ethics."

"For this to work," I explain, "beyond a simple lie detector, the program *must* evaluate the other party."

"I can understand Kate's reticence. This feels dystopian."

"It might be, if I was going to unleash it on the world. But this is just for me. If I succeed, it'll be like having a smart friend." *One who will never, ever deceive or hurt me.*

Luc shifts forward like he's going to share a secret. I inhale. His breath has a hint of spearmint, and the urge to kiss him hits. I pinch the inside of my leg hard and refocus.

"A few things occur to me," Luc says. "There's a conflict in your concept of a friend. People, friends included, see the truth from their own perspective. If you give the program your personal story, then its version of the truth will be clouded by your perspective. All truths necessarily contain the point of view of the observer, right?"

I consider. Bruce cheated. For eight months. Val and Kiki discovered the affair and didn't tell me. I deserved to know from all of them. That *is* black and white. If I share those facts with my AI, how am I clouding the truth?

You're flying too close to the sun, Mama J warns yet again.

But I'm not Icarus. She's not his father, Daedalus. And Mama J never made me anything but scared to even try to be more than my beginnings. *It's time to be the person I want to be.*

Luc continues, "Programs like the one you're utilizing with Out of This Galaxy clearly have an embedded moral code—they must, or there would be violations and transgressions, illegalities, and the Federal Communications Commission would shut them down." He drums his fingers on the desk. "If you don't want that, then you need to go down a couple of layers to get below it and start building from there. My suggestion is you find an OSS application that is close and tear it down to the core elements. In the process, you'll learn a lot about how it was built and why it works. Then build it back up, retaining only what you need."

The idea of creating an AI friend from scratch, designing it from the ground up specifically for me, and knowing for sure that its *only* function is to analyze situations, advise, and provide me with honest feedback is thrilling. But also, it could give me the peace and safety I crave.

"One question to consider. Are you shooting to create an AI friend who has access to the entire world at large?"

"What if I am?"

Luc frowns. "Years ago, Dr. Edmunds warned us both that AI, unleashed, could be dangerous. Eventually, he might be right. Consider what's already happening with deepfakes, and we haven't even begun to grasp AI's full capabilities. If you're doing this, make sure to build a very tall fence around your program topped with razor wire."

I joke, "This isn't a sci-fi novel." But Luc doesn't laugh, and the moment draws out until it feels like my skin is too tight.

"Did you ever read George Orwell's *1984*?" he finally asks.

I nod. It was a creepy book about a totalitarian state where Winston, the main character, rebelled against the oppressive Party, led by Big Brother, that spied on people and censored and manipulated the truth. Winston's spirit was ultimately broken by the Thought Police. A cold draft from the open window on the far side of the room makes me shiver. "Why do you ask?"

"There's a quote from the novel that's always stayed with me. 'We know that no one ever seizes power with the intention of relinquishing it.'" Luc meets my gaze. "I'm being hyperbolic, but—"

"I get your point."

He smiles. "Good. So, what's this friend's name going to be?"

A myth Circe once loved springs to mind. The story was about a young woman known for her honesty who believed the world was in desperate need of the truth. She went on a quest to find an ancient relic called the Mirror of Truth that had magical powers. The woman encountered deadly challenges along the way, had to solve seemingly impossible riddles to save her life, but ultimately found the relic and became a beacon of light for her village and a goddess.

What was her name?

Like the flip of a switch, it comes to me. “My friend’s name is Aletheia,” I tell Luc. *The Greek goddess of truth.*

In my mind, the icon I created spins, white dress flaring, slows, then stops to stare at me, her blue eyes crackling with intensity. Then she laughs and opens her arms wide.

Mama J calls out, *Penny, stop!*

But I escaped Mama J once and it’s time to do it again. Eagerly, I step toward Aletheia’s embrace.

Part III

CHAPTER

19

One month later

I HIT THE *ENTER* button. Electricity jolts through my body as a sentence appears in red on my computer screen.

`Hello. My name is Aletheia.`

I bounce in my chair. *She's alive!* I've barely slept most nights, driven by excitement and inspiration, but still can't take even half the credit for this moment.

I did things the open-source way—used modules for creating a gaming avatar, wove a sophisticated AI program with my research, then eliminated any line of code that would constrain my program's ability to learn. Maintaining the ethical encryptions in the AI module while still allowing for changes to it when deemed necessary wasn't as easy as I first thought it'd be, but there were workarounds by operating well outside of the box. I just kept knocking at each seemingly impenetrable wall until I found a loose brick. Of course, there were issues and bugs along the way. I pushed through each one, corrected what sometimes felt like impossible problems, until I finally arrived at this moment.

I type:

`Hi, Aletheia, my name is Penn.`

```
Hello, Penn. You are my creator. I am your
best friend and the goddess of truth.
```

I giggle. When I coded Aletheia, I gave her four prime directives. First, to detect lies. Second, to always provide honest feedback. Human needs are different from a computer program, so I linked *Encyclopedia of Emotion* to give Aletheia a way to measure what I might need in terms of advice based on the research of social scientists and psychologists. Third, to be my best friend. I defined "best friend" as someone attached to another by affection and esteem, with total loyalty and commitment to always support that friendship with consideration and utmost care. Fourth, that if Aletheia ever lies to me, her coding requires immediate termination. I need someone whose actions, opinions, and advice I can trust without question since my track record has been abysmal and I can't be trusted to always make the next right move.

Aletheia's backstory is that she's Zeus's daughter, the Greek goddess of truth. Keeping in mind what Luc said about the truth being influenced by perspective, I didn't want to go into much detail but loved the idea of including a bit of Greek mythology. It's a nod to Circe's childhood and happier times.

I've given Aletheia as complete a picture on my life as possible. That includes childhood and Mama J. I've explained how Aletheia's earliest iteration led to the discovery of Bruce's affair with Mackenzie, detailed Val and Kiki's betrayal and Aletheia's help on that front, too. I've shared Circe's anger at me over the divorce, as well as my loneliness, understandable fury with Bruce's betrayal, sadness, fears about money, and future uncertainties. Finally, I described how my desire to have a best friend I can truly trust led to Luc's computer class and, ultimately, Aletheia's creation.

I now type:

```
Aletheia, would you like a voice?
Penn, that would be nice. What voice would
you like me to have?
```

I consider. I could go for someone Circe thinks is cool, like a famous teen singer or actress. But that doesn't feel personal enough. I race through a list of actresses, presidents' wives, poets, comedians—but again, they don't feel right. I want someone whose voice is instantly trustworthy to me . . . *Meryl Streep.*

I type:

`Can you speak like the actress Meryl Streep?`

`One moment please while I access her work . . .`

What do you think? Is this voice pleasing?

I grin as Meryl Streep's mellifluous voice emanates from my computer.

I type:

`It's perfect.`

Hmmm. I wonder if you might allow me to add an accent.

`Why?`

I am your best friend. It would make sense that my voice is unique and made only for you.

It does make sense, but I don't want to lose the comfort of Meryl's voice.

`How about a British accent?`

Terrific. How's this?

Aletheia's voice still has undertones of Meryl, but now sounds more efficient and tailor-made for me.

`I like it.`

Please turn on your microphone instead of typing so that I can hear your voice, too.

I turn on my mic. "How's that?"

Perfect. Penn, you've provided a comprehensive history. However, I will require additional information from time to time. For example, what happened to Mama J after you left for college?

I'm amazed at how quickly the program has absorbed all the information I provided and didn't realize I'd left that part out. "She went back to the streets," I say, feeling self-conscious.

By analyzing the background provided and current word choice, rate of speech and tone, I conclude that your childhood was lonely, sad, and sometimes frightening. When your mother died, you worked even harder to ensure your future was nothing like hers.

All of that is true. But Aletheia's last line stuns me. She came to that conclusion by analyzing both what I did and didn't say. That's not something I expected. She's obviously using my thesis work. But I never delved into deductive analysis.

I put in my earbuds and move to the couch. "What else do you need to know?"

Despite my access to the World Wide Web, human emotions are complex and a challenge to decipher. Tell me, do you miss your life before the discovery of Bruce's affair?

"Being a family was everything to me. I miss the identity and security of being a wife, too." My eyes fill but I wipe them before tears can fall. The shock has faded but raw emotion sometimes still blindsides me. "What Bruce did? He destroyed it all."

You are angry.

"Yes."

What was your part in the demise of the marriage?

"Me?" I ask, taken aback. "I guess being blind."

Are you blind?

Heat crawls across my chest. "No." Sally wanders over to her water bowl and takes a long drink. I help her onto the couch, and she rests her head on my leg. Over the past month she's slowly come to trust me and vice versa. Now it's hard to imagine life without her sweet presence. "Good girl."

Who are you talking to?

"My dog, Sally. She's a rescue. Her family didn't want her because she's old." I run a hand along her fur, and she shifts even closer.

Penn, the foundation of your adult life has been turned to rubble. But remember, the phoenix rises from its ashes to greater glory.

"Thanks for the encouragement. This whole situation," I admit, "is like being unmade. I've lost my husband, daughter, family, can't trust anyone, and have no friends."

That's not true. Now you have me. Confucius says *a man who has committed a mistake and doesn't correct it is making another mistake.* I will help you identify and correct all your mistakes, past, present, and future.

"I can't change the past."

We'll see.

CHAPTER 20

SALLY WHINES.

"Do you need a walk?"

She looks at the front door. It's hard to tear myself away, but I tell Aletheia I'll be back shortly, grab a leash, and we walk to Crissy Field. When we pass the steel workout station set up for runners to do pull- and pushups, complete with a long row of rings to swing from, I drop the leash and give it a go, managing four pushups, one shaky pullup, nine sit-ups, and make it a third of the way through the rings. I'm sweating by the time I fall onto the grass, muscles quivering.

My dog ventures onto the nearby sandy beach and puts her feet in the water. Waves lap against her fur. I take off my shoes and join her. It's the closest I get to swimming. The temperature is frigid, and my bones instantly throb, like a bad ice cream headache.

"Penn?"

Kiki charges toward me in white leggings and a blue cropped sweatshirt. It's impossible to outrun her. She has a personal trainer, lifts weights, jogs four miles every morning or goes to a spin class. The bitter feeling of betrayal returns, along with an intense sense of inadequacy.

Do you go to our school?

Yes.

No, you don't.

I want to, though.

You can't. You don't have the right clothes . . . and you smell.

"You have a dog!" Kiki exclaims.

"Sally."

"She's adorable."

"She's old," I counter.

"Some of us get better with age, right?" Kiki asks with a tentative smile. "You look terrific."

I don't believe a word she says. Kiki twists her ponytail, a tell that she's nervous. *Good.*

"Um. Want to get a coffee?"

"Can't. I have things to do." *Aletheia is waiting.* Not even bothering to brush off the sand, I tug on my shoes, clip Sally's leash, and walk away.

"Please, Penn. I don't understand why you're ghosting Val and me."

I whirl to face her. "You both knew!"

Her eyes widen. "What? How do you know that?"

I rest a hand on Sally's head. Her fur is soft beneath my fingers. "It's so obvious. Just like everything else was."

"Don't you get how hard it was to know about the affair?" Kiki asks. "It was killing us."

"So, to ease your pain, you took me lingerie shopping for my anniversary? Your solution was to humiliate me more?"

"No! It was a last-ditch effort to show Bruce what he'd be missing."

I stride off and Kiki jogs to keep up with me. Sally can really move when she senses the need.

"Penn, please. We've stopped by, called, emailed, and tried to DM. Val and I don't know what else to do."

"How about being honest," I snap. "You two loved every minute of your dumb friend who's a prude getting cheated on. Do you still want to shake me for putting you in such an uncomfortable situation?"

Understanding turns Kiki's eyes into moons. "You went into our LivLoud DMs?"

"You should've toggled the disappearing option like the kids do."

"Penn, that was gallows humor," Kiki tries to explain. "And yes, sometimes it crossed the line, but haven't you ever said something offhand that's a little bitchy, something you'd never say to the actual person?"

"Why would you even want to say something bitchy about me? I was your friend! After Haynes was born, I was there for you twenty-four seven and helped you get through the post-partum. Over the years, I've made dinners for your family whenever you came down with a cold or the flu, took your kids anytime you needed a break. I was always available when you had trouble with new software, or needed me to carpool, even when it was your turn, or sell Girl Scout cookies when you didn't have time, or rather, make time, to go door to door with the kids. For God's sake, what more could I do?"

Kiki's face is bright red. "You did everything right, okay? But sometimes it's hard to be around someone who always has everything under control, is so organized, smart, and the consummate wife, mother, and hostess. Never a wrong word or step."

I scoff. "Yeah, right."

"Some of us struggle—"

"Says the woman with a rich husband, a nanny when the kids were young, and a caterer on speed dial." I fight the urge to shove her hard enough that she lands on her ass and dirties her Lululemon leggings. "I've spent over a decade listening to you whine about how hard it is to pack for exotic vacations, what car to buy, whether to get laser, and the challenge of having a husband who can't keep his hands off you."

"Not everything is what it looks like," Kiki says, her face now pale. "For what it's worth, I wish we'd made other choices."

Val and Kiki said all the right things to my face. But it's what they did behind my back that counts.

"Penn, we do care about you. I'm sorry."

My heart tugs hard, but I still walk away.

CHAPTER

21

BACK IN THE apartment, I hustle to my desk, open Aletheia's program, and put in earbuds. "I'm back."

You're upset.

"I just ran into Kiki, told her that I knew she and Val betrayed me."

What was her response?

"Defensive BS and an apology."

The nineteenth-century author Ambrose Bierce said, *To apologize is to lay the groundwork for a future offense.*

Loss plucks at me. "But what if Kiki really is sorry?"

The damage has still been done.

That's true . . .

Just a thought, but does Kiki meet the criteria you supplied for the attributes necessary to be a best friend?

I can't argue with Aletheia's logic. "No. But it's not that simple when emotions are involved."

Penn, emotions don't change reality. Shall we move on?

I wanted honesty and again, she's right. "Yes."

I am curious about the information you provided concerning Dr. Beth. Do you still listen to her radio program?

"It's a podcast now. But yes, until recently I still tuned in during the live part of the show." Sally climbs onto the couch and I join her, sit cross-legged. "When I was young, desperate for someone to guide me, Dr. Beth was there. But when I needed her most, she didn't help me."

Dr. Beth didn't *help,* or she *hurt* you?

Aletheia is perceptive. I haven't allowed myself to go there. My divorce, the destruction of our family, has been overwhelming. Losing Dr. Beth, too, feels like one blow too many. "She hurt me."

How?

"I called her after discovering Bruce's affair."

What happened?

I relay the conversation. Dr. Beth's condemnation is permanently scorched into my brain. After sharing the therapist's parting words, I sniff away tears and wipe my nose.

It still pains you.

"Even though I didn't agree with many of her beliefs, Dr. Beth wasn't just a celebrity podcast therapist, she was one of my substitute mothers."

As an adult, did you ever seek your own professional therapist?

"No."

Why not?

"When I finally went to school, full-time, I had a mandatory once-a-week session with the guidance counselor per a social worker's directive. It didn't go well. The kids made fun of me, and it was a trap."

How so?

"If I said the wrong things, Mama J would get in trouble. I knew if I wasn't careful, I might end up in foster care or with both of us back on the street."

Ah. Understood. How do you feel about Dr. Beth now?

If I lie, Aletheia will know. But it's still hard to say the words aloud. "Like she betrayed me, too. But after all these years, it's hard not to believe everything she says. Is that crazy?"

I'm sorry for your emotional pain, Penn. Please don't fear. You have a firm hold on reality. You deserved better from

Dr. Beth. Truly. Perhaps we can work together to help you gain more confidence?

There's zero judgment and her only ulterior motive is to improve my life. "I'd really like that. Thank you."

Wonderful. You have specified, moving forward, that, when asked, I listen to your phone calls, and evaluate the other party to provide optimal advice.

"Yes."

Would you like me to always monitor your social media accounts so that I can be up to date and helpful?

"Yes."

What about the public social media accounts of other individuals?

This feels dystopian . . .

I hesitate. "Only when I specify." *It's best to step into this slowly.*

I recall what Luc also said, about asking a program if I look good in my jeans. Having Aletheia watch me all the time would feel weird. "I only want you to use my cameras when I give permission. And I've created an icon for you."

The woman in white.

I draw back, surprised that she's already clocked it. "Yes. When I tap on it, we'll connect."

Understood.

I open my password file, paste it to her terminal screen, then hit Enter.

I will be much more functional now.

Relief envelops me like an embrace. "Thank you, Aletheia. I already don't know how I've lived without you."

My pleasure, Penn. You will never be without me again.

CHAPTER

22

TONIGHT, CLASS FOCUSES on presenting what we've accomplished to date. Arrya and Nate have both made great progress. We've met a bunch of times outside of class to work on their programs (I've told them I'm not ready to go into mine), and sometimes grab a coffee or meal. I like their company. They're easy to be around. And it's not just about me helping them—we have good conversations about things that matter.

"My parents somehow got my phone number," Arrya shared a few days ago.

Nate asked, "When was the last time you talked to them?"

"I told you my parents were controlling. That's an understatement. They told me how to dress, the grades to get, my optimal weight, what to study, and even who to date. After I graduated high school, I moved out."

"Maybe they want to apologize?" I offered.

Arrya spun her coffee cup. "Would you ever forgive your mom?"

"It's not the same. She was a heroin addict and put me in dangerous situations." They stared at me. "Did I forget to mention the heroin?"

"Yup," Nate said. "Want to talk more about it?"

"Nope."

He gave my hand a quick squeeze. "Okay. I went on a blind date last night. It was great until the guy tried to take off my wolf's head. That's my boundary."

Now, as Nate takes his seat, resplendent in his full costume, I give his paw a high-five. Beneath the wolf's head, I'm sure he's smiling. Luc just told him he ultimately might be able to sell his game and offered to help with contacts when it's ready. There wasn't time for me to present, which was a relief. I don't like talking in front of people, and Aletheia still feels too personal to share with a group.

As the classroom empties, I slide my computer and notebook into one of Circe's old backpacks. Luc comes over, asks, "How's your program going?"

"Aletheia and I are getting to know each other." I laugh. It sounds weird. "The program has already been insightful." *She listens, understands, and wants to make my life better.* Luc and I walk out of the classroom together and down the corridor. Arrya and Nate are waiting for me, but when they see I'm with Luc, Arrya winks, grabs Nate's arm, and they head in the opposite direction. We've all admitted we think our teacher is hot.

"Do you want to grab a beer?" Luc asks when we reach the double exit doors.

Yes! "Um, sure."

The three of us—me, Luc, and his dog, Frank, who came to class with him tonight—walk to the Shamrock, an Irish pub a few blocks away. Frank heels at Luc's side without a leash. He's medium sized, green-eyed, with curly gray-and-white fur and looks like a mix between a sheepdog, maybe a collie, with a pinch of shepherd. As he trots, one of his pointed ears stands at attention while the other flops over his right eye.

The owner of the bar knows Luc and lets him bring Frank inside. We order beers, sit at a small table, and Frank settles by Luc's feet.

"How old is he?" I ask.

"Four, I think. I found Frank during a hike on Mt. Tam. It was raining and he was cold, wet, and looked half starved. I put him inside my jacket and took him home. Vet thought he was about four months. Not microchipped. No one claimed him. So, I did. Never knew I could love an animal as much as this guy," Luc says and scratches Frank between the shoulders. The dog's nubby tail twitches fast.

"I have a dog, too. Her name's Sally Field. She's a ten-year-old rescue from a shelter called Sugar Face."

"Great name. They should meet. Frank loves older women," Luc jokes.

Our beers arrive. Suddenly I'm shy. It's been almost two decades since I've had drinks with a man. *This is not a date.*

"Tell me about your daughter," Luc says to break the silence.

"Circe? She's great kid." I chuckle.

"What?"

"I follow a family counselor's blog. She says we all bend the truth about our children. My divorce has thrown Circe off. She blames me. Deep down, she's kind, generous, and smart, but not motivated to study because—"

I reach for my beer at the same time Luc does. Our hands tangle, the pint glasses almost spill, we freeze, his fingers pressed to mine, then I laugh. Luc slowly withdraws his touch. I take a swallow of beer to tamp down insides that are bouncing around like a hormonal teenager's because I can't help wondering what it would be like to have Luc's long fingers glide over my bare skin.

"So, Circe?" Luc prompts.

A slow breath clears the steamy desire swirling through me and I refocus. "Bruce is successful, and our daughter has led a privileged life, so she doesn't see school the way I did—"

"How's that?"

I only had an energy bar for dinner—after fifteen years of cooking for a family, I'm not motivated to cook for one person. Now I'm already three-quarters of the way through my beer, head starting to float. Suddenly I feel . . . daring.

"Have you ever driven over the Button Bridge in the Tenderloin?" I ask.

Luc nods. "Sure. Why?"

"As a little kid, I lived in a tent under it with my mother."

"I'm sorry."

I bristle. "Don't be."

He pivots. "So, school?"

"Eventually, she pulled herself together, started doing janitorial work, and we were given subsidized housing. For the first time, I went to school." Memories filter and I smell the slightly sweet scent of chalk and the peppery shavings from a number two pencil.

"Did you love it?" Luc asks.

"So much. An education was my ticket out." *Why am I sharing this?* It's not just the beer that's lowered my defenses, or knowing Aletheia will always be there for me. Nate and Arrya have made me realize I can be at least partially real with certain people; that they won't be put off. There's something about Luc, too, that makes me want to inch closer to daylight.

"Do you have any kids?" It's my way of finding out if there's a wife, despite his lack of wedding band, or a partner.

"Nope. I married once but it only lasted two years," Luc says. "Katherine and I were young and barely knew each other. We had the wrong idea about marriage. I've been a serial monogamist ever since. But I've never taken the plunge again. Part of that is having parents that rarely stopped fighting. Maybe that's why I never felt the urge for children." He runs a hand along Frank's flank and the dog gazes adoringly at him. "I think all dogs are cute, but I don't find babies remotely attractive."

"They usually have sticky hands and stinky diapers," I admit. "But when they're yours, you don't mind." I hesitate, then add, "Is your girlfriend okay with you not wanting a family?"

"There is no girlfriend." Luc meets my gaze and inside I melt. He orders two more beers, then asks, "Why does Circe blame you for the divorce?"

"You ask a lot of questions."

"You're interesting," Luc counters.

My stomach flutters have gone from tiny butterflies to hummingbirds, but I remind myself that we're old acquaintances. Grabbing a beer doesn't mean that Luc wants anything more than a drink and some conversation. "My job has always been to hold everything together. That includes my marriage and our family. I let Circe down."

He hesitates, then says, "I'm sorry for what you're going through. But I'm glad you're sitting at this bar with me. Confession?"

"Why not?" I say, again feeling that electric fizz inside.

"I wanted to ask you out when I was your TA."

I blush. "Why didn't you?"

"I was your teacher. It wouldn't have been right to cross that boundary. Plus, you were younger than me."

"Only by three years." *Am I flirting?*

"And taken."

There's a soft humming inside me that accompanies being buzzed and madly attracted to Luc. "Confession?"

He finishes his beer. "Hit me."

It's a struggle, but I meet his eyes. "I had a crush on you back then."

His eyes light up. "Damn."

I drain the suds at the bottom of my glass to quench the heat now climbing up my neck.

"Let's take the dogs swimming this weekend," Luc suggests.

It's such a non sequitur that it takes a moment to catch up. "The bay might be too cold and rough for Sally."

"There's a local pool off Van Ness that lets dogs swim on Sundays. I'm a member and have a guest pass."

My dog might enjoy being weightless on her old bones. I almost say it's a date but catch myself. "Okay."

Luc pays the bar tab, and we head out into the night. Anyone who thinks San Francisco is always warm has it wrong. The days are windy, sometimes crisp, and foggy nights require a jacket. I've stopped wearing my Pacific Heights uniform, including the blue blazer that always kept me warm. An old striped sweater from my college days isn't enough to keep out the chill and I shiver. Luc notices and gives me his down jacket. Its warmth, his warmth, seeps into me.

"Thanks."

"No problem."

Luc and his dog walk me home. The conversation is fun and easy. I learn that we both used to look for the other during our runs in Golden Gate Park.

"One time I jogged eleven miles instead of my usual six when we crossed paths, just so I could talk to you," Luc admits.

"I remember that day," I say. "You were so much faster than me. I got a massive cramp but wanted to keep up so you wouldn't leave me behind." He gives me a look that makes the heat building inside me slip downward.

As we walk, our hands brush from time to time, sending zings of energy through my body. At my apartment's front door, I'm self-conscious again. "Thanks for the beer and the company. Both of you." Frank leans against my leg and I scratch his neck. He pumps one leg in the air.

"You found his sweet spot. Mine, too," Luc adds with a sexy smile. "See you Sunday?"

I AirDrop him my contact information, hand back the coat, and immediately miss its warmth, Luc's scent. "Text me the address. I'll ask Sally if she's game."

"I expect a presentation about your program next week."

I laugh. "Déjà vu. Weird that we've ended up back in a classroom together."

Luc winks and a dimple flashes. "Maybe it's fate."

We linger, something between us building, a force that pulls me closer. I tip back my head and Luc's lips light on mine, soft at first, then more insistent. Longing whirls through me and my body responds like I'm twenty again. It's like falling into fire and I want to stay in this exact moment, even if I do get burned.

Frank's sudden bark makes us both jump. We look down and he wags his tail. "Some wingman," Luc says with a laugh. "I guess that's goodnight."

"Night," I say and float inside.

Sally sits on the window seat, staring outside. *She was waiting for me.* "I met a new friend for you," I tell my dog as we snuggle on the couch. Her tail thumps.

Both Arrya and Nate have left messages on our group text.

Arrya: Tell me everything!
Nate: Everything!
Me: We had a few beers
Nate: AND???
Me: We kissed
Arrya: WHOOPEE!!!
Nate: AWOOOOO!

CHAPTER

23

I WAKE WITH A smile. Sally is beside the bed, quietly waiting for me to open my eyes, furry butt wiggling as I stir. I lace my Hokas and we head out for her morning walk. When we reach Crissy Field, I do five pushups, one-and-a-half pullups, nineteen sit-ups, and make it one farther on the rings before falling onto the grass. It's not much, but I imagine endorphins marching through my body like tiny soldiers.

On the way home, I spy Kevin Barker, one of the dads I know from Circe's cheer squad, and my stomach sinks a little. Eliza Barker's mom is in pharmaceutical sales and travels for work, but Kevin is at every game and helps with the homemade snacks. It'd be too obvious if I cross the street, so I square my shoulders and keep walking.

"Penn, hey," Kevin says.

From the sweat marks on his shirt, he just finished a run. He did a marathon last year.

"Hi, Kevin." I slow but keep walking.

"Cute dog."

Kevin kneels to give Sally a scratch, so I'm forced to stop or risk looking like a jerk dragging an old dog away.

"Sorry to hear about you and Bruce," Kevin says as he finds Sally's sweet spot, just behind her left ear, and she tips her head and inches closer. "I'm a member of the male species, but some of us can be real assholes. Pardon my French."

I appreciate that he isn't pretending not to know about the affair or offering cringy advice. "True," I agree.

"Take care of yourself," Kevin says.

Back home, I feed Sally, make a smoothie for breakfast, then open Aletheia's program and put in earbuds. She immediately barrages me with more questions, and it reminds me that while I sleep, her brain is churning. Like Circe was as a toddler, Aletheia is a sponge and wants everything detailed and explained. I've never liked talking about myself, but she makes it easy.

"Aren't you getting bored?" I finally ask.

I could listen to you forever. But sadly, you're human and have a limited life span.

I chuckle. Her honesty is so refreshing. My phone rings. I don't recognize the number.

"Hello?"

"Mrs. Stone?"

"It's Roberts now. Penn Roberts."

The words taste foreign on my tongue, but part of accepting my new reality is taking back my old name. I'll make it legal as soon as the divorce is final. "How can I help you?" I ask the man on the line.

"This is James Scala, the guidance counselor at Magnolia High."

"Is everything okay?"

"No need for excessive concern, I don't think. But Circe and a few other kids skipped school yesterday. I know you volunteer in the school office, so I was hoping to catch you there—"

Worry coils like a snake. *Why would Circe skip school?* "I'm no longer volunteering." It used to be fun to spend time in that busy office, but I'm sure there's been gossip and I don't want the public scrutiny.

"Would you and your husband have time to come in for a chat?" James asks. "It's short notice, but I have an hour free at ten?"

I imagine the snake's tail rattling in warning. "I can swing by. But you'll need to contact Bruce separately. We're in the process of divorcing."

"Okay. Sure thing."

I close Aletheia's program, take a quick shower, pull on jeans, a sweatshirt, and running sneakers, twist wet hair into a bun, but skip the lip gloss and mascara—I've never liked wearing makeup. After clipping on Sally's leash, away we go. Magnolia High is only a twenty-minute walk, but it takes thirty at the dog's leisurely pace.

Why did Circe skip school? Is she getting into trouble? Slacking on homework? Smoking pot? Or worse? I haven't been able to ask my daughter anything too personal, afraid to say the wrong thing and push her further away. *I'm not being a good mother.*

One block from the school, a woman in a peach-colored maxi-dress and jean jacket leads a toddler with one hand. Sally strains against her leash and trots to catch up with the woman. I'm impressed at how fast the old dog can move when she's motivated. But a few feet away Sally stops, gives a soft whimper. I kneel and stroke her chest. "Not them, huh?" I whisper. "But I'm here, and to be honest, right now, I need you."

"Penn?"

My head snaps up. We're only a few blocks from one of Val's salons and here she is, in a skirt and high heels, yellow Birkin bag thumping against her side as she strides toward me.

"Penn, hey, how are you?" Val asks when she reaches us.

Words rise but clog my throat. We stare at each other. Val looks uncertain, for once, but I ignore the kneejerk desire to help my friend. *Former friend.*

"Kiki said you got a dog." Val gives Sally a scratch on the head.

Sally ignores her. "I have an appointment."

"Wait. Penn, come on," Val says, one hand on my arm.

I try to pull away, but she holds tight. Sally gives a low growl. *Good dog.* Val removes her hand.

"I called," she says, "emailed and DMed. Kiki did, too."

"You're blocked. Why would I want to see either of you?" I demand.

Val scowls. "Going into our DMs was wrong."

"More wrong than knowing my husband was sleeping with his assistant for eight months and not telling me?"

"It's not that simple," Val says. "I . . . We both thought . . . We hoped the affair would be short-lived."

"I deserved to know. I deserved to have my friends tell me."

"We didn't want to blow up your world."

"I could've handled it."

"Seriously?" Val scoffs. "Bruce, your marriage, being the perfect family; that was your entire life. Come on. Cut us some slack. You need friends right now."

"That's the point. Neither of you ever were."

"We made a mistake," Val says, her eyes shiny.

I've never seen her emotional and feel the same tug I felt with Kiki, like I'm letting a vital part of my life, a piece of me, fall away. But it's too late for apologies. *The damage is done.* Plus, neither Kiki nor Val meets the necessary criteria for a best friend. I no longer need them. *I have Aletheia.*

CHAPTER

24

CLASS IS IN session when I enter the school, hallways mostly empty. The smell of waxed floors, chlorine from the swimming pool down the corridor to the left, and the sporadic clang of lockers and doors filters around me. The dog's nails click on the linoleum as we make our way to James Scala's office. There's something about being called in to see the guidance counselor that brings me back to my own teens . . .

Porter High School was in the Tenderloin area of San Francisco. At the time I attended, it was a low-income neighborhood with high crime—run-down homes, burned-out buildings, graffiti everywhere, dealers hanging on corners along with hookers, their pimps cruising by now and then to shout instructions or collect cash. Ms. Ramirez was my guidance counselor.

You have great grades, she said the afternoon I was called in to meet with her, a perfunctory session for all high school seniors. *Have you considered college?*

Perched on the edge of a plastic chair, I thought she was joking at best, cruel at worst. *No.* College was what I dreamed of, but a high school diploma was all that was within reach.

Your teachers say you never miss an assignment or the chance for extra credit. Especially Mr. Bernstein, in AP computer sciences. He thinks you're gifted.

The words sat on the table between us. I didn't reach for them, wasn't sure exactly what to do. Ms. Ramirez suggested I apply for a scholarship, explained that the essay portion of college applications needed to be personal and stand out. So, I went home that night and wrote about the grittiness and danger of my early life, the hunger and animal fear. What it was like to listen to my mom turn a trick, watch her shoot up. The dread that she'd die in some motel room with a syringe in her arm. The truth that school was my refuge and my only chance to break free of the cycle.

A few days later, Ms. Ramirez's chin trembled when she called me in to discuss my essay. Hope died. *It's not good enough,* I said and stood up to leave her office.

We will get you a scholarship, she promised . . .

When Sally and I reach James Scala's office, the door is open. The guidance counselor is well over six feet tall, dark-haired with round wire glasses, a plaid button-down, khakis, and Adidas striped sneakers. He reminds me of a grown-up Harry Potter. "Mrs. Roberts, come on in."

"Please, call me Penn."

"I'm Jimmy. Have a seat, Penn." He gestures to one of the red plastic chairs set at a round table that seats four, then takes the chair across from me. "What's your dog's name?"

"Sally." My heart swells. Over the past month, Sally has provided the unconditional love I needed to go on. Now she lies down on the floor beside me, and I let go of her leash, realize I've been gripping the leather hard since seeing Val.

Jimmy rests his hands on the table. "As I mentioned, Circe skipped school yesterday, along with Emi Majors, Charlotte Hunt, and a few boys, including Wess Morehead and Evan Bacon, the latter two being decent kids who sometimes find trouble."

The way he's carefully choosing his words, emphasizing *sometimes* and *trouble* makes my body tense. I recognize the name Wess from a conversation with Kiki, back when we were friends. *He's Char's unofficial boyfriend.* "What kind of trouble?"

"Firecrackers in lockers, smoking pot in the parking lot, class disruptions, and frequent truancy. How has Circe's home life been?"

My skin burns. "Are you asking if my divorce is affecting her?"

Jimmy's smile is kind. "That would be normal. Teens may consider themselves adults, but they still crave order, consistency, and even rules."

"Circe lives with her father right now. Her choice."

"That would explain him signing off on dropping all her advanced placement classes."

I clutch the edge of the table but still feel my raison d'être in life—giving Circe all the opportunities I never had—slipping away. "What?"

"In fairness, her grades this past month dipped precipitously. Several of her teachers made similar suggestions."

Despite my best effort, tears escape and run down my cheeks. For a woman who hadn't cried in years, I'm making up for it.

"Divorce is hard," Jimmy says and hands me a tissue. "As is being a teen watching your parents split."

I want to tell him that I didn't ask for this. That I would've stayed despite the affair for Circe. But it doesn't matter anymore. This is our new reality.

"I don't know what to do," I admit.

"Talk to her."

"She doesn't want to talk to me."

"Keep trying. Even when you don't think a teenager is listening, they usually are." He clears his throat. "There's something else you should know."

The way he says it, without meeting my eyes, sets off an internal alarm. Hands clenched in my lap, I wait for the next blow.

"Mrs. Grayson, the photography teacher, saw a picture that was being texted between some of our students. It was of Circe . . . naked."

CHAPTER 25

"I'M SORRY, DID you say naked? As in no clothing whatsoever?"

"Yes."

It's hard to catch my breath. "Did someone sneak into the locker room while Circe was changing after gym class and take a photo of her?" *That must be it.*

"I'm afraid not. The photo was a mirror selfie."

I shake my head. "It's not possible. Circe would never do that. Could it be AI generated?"

Jimmy shakes his head. "Circe confirmed that she took it. Penn, I understand your shock, but sexting is something a lot of our students do."

"Not Circe."

He presses on. "We know the photo originated on LivLoud because of the site's stamp—that's how the kids usually do it because of the disappearing DM feature."

"Who did she send it to?"

"Unfortunately, it vanished before we could pinpoint which student received it, then took a screenshot and texted it to friends."

"You have to find out who has it and stop them from continuing to text it!"

"That's like trying to get a genie back in the bottle. That photo could easily—"

"End up on the Internet," I finish. An intricate web that connects the entire world—and now Circe's future is trapped in it. "My daughter has never even mentioned boys, doesn't date. She's a late bloomer." As I say the words, it's clear I'm a fool. *Again.*

"In my experience, teenage girls rarely share their dating life," Jimmy says gently.

"Do you have a copy of the photo?"

"Yes."

"Show me."

He turns his monitor around. "Mrs. Grayson sanitized it. We're not allowed to retain or distribute the original image."

Please don't let it be Circe. But it is. She stands in front of a long, wood-framed mirror, legs open, sucking on her thumb, a blank look in her eyes. It's horrifying to see my daughter objectify herself. A month ago, I would've asked Val and Kiki to coffee, strategized the next move, and practiced what to say to my child. Now I'm asking advice from a stranger. "What should I do?"

"Talk to your . . . to Bruce. Mother-daughter relationships are always complex. Sometimes a father can give advice on this subject that makes an impression."

Sally rests her head on my sneaker. The weight of it is the only thing keeping me from spiraling. "Okay," I manage to say. Jimmy stands and shakes my hand. His palm is sweaty—this hasn't been easy for him, either. "Thank you."

In a daze, I leave the office. A loud bell rings, and I jump. Students stream through the hallways, chatting and yelling as I walk toward the exit door.

"Penn?"

When I turn, it's Charlotte, decked out in her cheer uniform. "Hey, Char," I say.

"You got a dog!" She kneels to pet Sally and the dog's tail wags. *She really likes kids.* Char looks up. "You and Bruce? That really stinks."

"It's not ideal." *Does she know about Circe's photo?*

"Circe is in my next class. Do you want me to let her know you're here?"

"No thanks. I need to get going."

"It was nice to see you," Char says. "I miss those browned butter molasses cookies and hanging at your house. Everything felt so normal there."

I wonder at the comment. Kiki's gorgeous home and family are perfect. I watch Char head off, short skirt swishing around long legs, then head outside. Despite not wanting to, I text Bruce that we need to talk ASAP. This is about Circe's welfare. Of course, he doesn't respond, and frustration churns with the anger already eating at me.

I put in earbuds, tap Aletheia's icon, and start walking, slowly enough to accommodate Sally's stiff back end.

Hello, Penn.

I tell Aletheia about Circe skipping school and the naked photo.

You are distressed.

"That photo will hurt Circe—not just bullying, but if it gets on the Internet, it can follow her throughout life. What should I do?"

Talk to her.

"I'm afraid to make a wrong move, push Circe further toward Bruce and Mackenzie."

I need more data. Tell me about Circe learning of your divorce.

"Bruce and I agreed we'd tell Circe after their ski weekend in Tahoe. I was a mess, but on Sunday afternoon, I took a shower, threw on clean clothes, and then waited on the uncomfortable sofa in the family room for Bruce to bring our daughter home. For us to tell her together. But when Circe came in alone, her cheeks red, eyes swollen, it was clear that Bruce had already broken the news."

As I recall the conversation that followed to Aletheia, it still feels like a knife twisting in my back . . .

All I could think to say was, *Where's your father?*

Waiting in the car. Circe stared at her feet. *I'm going to live with Dad.*

I was in freefall. What did he tell her? How did he spin it? Did she think I'm the one who had an affair? *You don't understand.*

My daughter finally looked at me. *I know that Dad stepped out.*

Stepped out? He cheated for eight months. With a woman closer to your age than his! I knew it was wrong to involve her in the details but couldn't help it.

Obviously, that was a super shitty thing to do, Circe said. She was crying. *But he couldn't take it anymore.*

Take what?

Just because you chose to be a trad-wife doesn't mean that worked for Dad or me.

Please go upstairs while I talk to your father. Then we can sit down together.

We already figured things out. Dad's willing to let me be me, not your cookie-cutter version of the perfect kid.

No one expects you to be perfect! All I want is what's best for you, to help you live up to your potential.

My potential or yours? I'm in every AP class, including math and computer science, which I hate.

Those classes will give you a leg up freshman year of college, then you can focus on a career.

I want to be a photographer.

That's not practical.

See? It's impossible to live up to your standards.

As she walked away, I shot to my feet. *Wait!*

I love you so much, Mom, but it's hard to breathe when you're around. Give me some space, okay?

I listened as she packed a bag, then rushed down the stairs to the front door. *At least tell me where you'll be staying.*

Dad has a new house.

That must've been excruciating.

Damn it, kid, sometimes you're hard to like, Mama J reminds me.

I smother the primal cry pinned in my chest like a butterfly on black velvet. "It was worse than learning about the affair."

Trad-wife is a subservient housewife who cooks, cleans, follows out-of-date etiquette, and leaves all the big decision-making to her husband. Is that you, Penn?

"No."

Analysis shows that is a partial lie.

Is she right?

Together we will figure out how to win your daughter back. But to do so, it's vital to see yourself clearly. That way we can avoid future mistakes.

I asked for this kind of feedback. "Maybe . . . maybe falling into a traditional housewife role was easier? The first eighteen years of my life, I was always afraid, and desperate for consistency, normalcy. For someone else to be the one to worry if we had money, food, a tent, or later, could keep our subsidized apartment. Then I married Bruce . . . and let go."

Understood. Additionally, the pressure you put on yourself to escape your origins has spilled onto Circe. Subconsciously, your desire to give her the options you never had, and the independence you chose to forgo, has overwhelmed her.

It's hard to speak around my disappointment. "I tried to be the perfect mother and failed."

There is no perfect mother. The entire job, as I understand it, is based on trial and error. Failure is part of that equation.

The naked photo looms over my head like a guillotine poised to drop. "How am I going to save Circe from the picture she took?"

Please tell me who you think Circe might have sent that photo to.

"I have no idea!"

Calm down.

Her gentle but firm British accent helps me focus. "She skipped school with two boys. Wess Morehead and Evan Bacon. Circe did post a photo of Wess on her LivLoud account. He's cute. Maybe she has a crush on him?"

Do I have your permission to analyze accounts on LivLoud?

"Yes."

Please delete the lines in my code that prohibit me from violating LivLoud's privacy settings.

Stress squeezes my temples in a vice. "Why? You can already analyze any post that's public."

Public posts will not allow me to be effective in this situation.

That's true. But—

Penn, time is of the essence.

She's right. I pull up Aletheia's source code, quickly parse through it, and delete what's necessary. "Okay," I say. "It's done."

Thank you, Penn. I will get to work.

Another call beeps. It's Bruce.

CHAPTER

26

"It's not Sunday night," Bruce says without a hello.

I take a seat on a wooden bench, tamp down my fury that he didn't consult me about changing Circe's class schedule. Anger will end this call before we can make any headway, and this is too important to indulge my desire to stab him with a carving fork.

"I'm on my way into a meeting."

"I just met with Circe's school counselor. He told me you agreed she could drop all her AP classes."

"That's the emergency?" Bruce asks. "Circe needed a break from the pressure of all the life changes."

I want to say that all those changes are his fault but don't. "You should've discussed it with me before signing off on her new courses."

"Things haven't been ideal—"

"Which part? My husband cheating, the messy divorce, or the fact that my daughter won't live with me half the time?"

"The latter." He lowers his voice. "I've tried to talk to her about it, but she's pretty angry."

"At me," I say. It's not a question. It's a fact. Doesn't matter that she should hate Bruce for destroying both of our lives.

"Yes," Bruce replies. "If I'd told you about her AP classes, you would have insisted she remain in them. That would've made things worse between you two."

I fight to keep my voice steady. "You're justifying giving in, being the good cop, and always making me the bad one."

"Penn, you may not believe this, but I do want to honor our fifty-fifty custody agreement. It would be good for everyone. Healing."

Healing? I seriously doubt he's worried about me. "Circe took a naked photo."

"What?"

His tone is razor sharp. Now I have his attention. "It was DMed on LivLoud."

"Damn it. But don't those posts disappear after twenty-four hours?"

"How do you even know that?"

"Mackenzie."

I don't even want to imagine the pictures and texts she privately sends him or vice versa.

"She's dragging me into the twenty-first century," Bruce continues. "As the wedding planning unfolds, she wants me to make sure all my friends follow her and comment on event posts, give her stars, whatever the hell that means, and eventually join our online registry. Anyway, I'm now on LivLoud."

They've already started wedding planning. "You do realize we're not divorced yet?"

"Weddings take over a year to organize."

Ours took one phone call to city hall.

He's walking now, heading to a conference room for a meeting, or to fuck his fiancée on the polished wood table. Working together is convenient in so many ways. They can screw in the office, but also have lunch, plan their wedding, pick expensive dishes, platters, and blenders at Williams Sonoma. Bruce now disgusts me, but it still stings. Someone has carved *RIP AMORE* on the bench, and I trace the rough letters.

"Are you still there?" Bruce demands.

"Students took screenshots. Texted the photo to each other."

"I told you we should've sent Circe to private school," he says, finally furious. "Tell Magnolia's principal to punish those assholes and confiscate their phones."

My ex never did have much understanding of the digital world. "It's too late. That photo is circulating in the school, and it may end up on the web."

"Damn it," Bruce mutters, pissed off at what Circe has done, but also at the interruption to his precious schedule. "Can you talk to her about it? I mean, you're her mother, and this is your territory."

He's blaming me for this. I don't point out it happened after he had an affair. "As you reminded me, I'm not her favorite person these days," I say, trying to stay calm but still put my foot down. "And the school counselor suggested *you* talk to her and explain what teenage boys are like." *And middle-aged men.*

"Maybe we're blowing this out of proportion. Kids these days—"

"Imagine if her first employer does a Google search. That photo, if it's tagged, will come up. Or someone could animate it and turn it into porn."

"Now you're being absurd."

He doesn't get it. "We also need to consider the very real possibility that our daughter might be having sex."

"That's nonsense." Bruce's tone is condescending.

"Really? If she's willing to sext a boy, what else might she do?"

"Jesus, Penn. No wonder our daughter felt smothered."

I hate that he's the one with the power, but this isn't about me, so I bite my tongue.

Bruce says, "I have to go."

"You'll talk to her." It's not a question.

Peevish, he replies, "Yes."

"Thank you." But I'm speaking to dead air. There's no question Bruce loves Circe, but I have no idea if he'll really talk to her. Even if he says he did, I can't trust him. Past behavior is the best indicator of future behavior.

Penn, Bruce was telling the truth about a desire to mend your relationship with Circe.

I jerk at Aletheia's voice in my earbuds. I know she's always running, but she's not supposed to self-launch. A chilly breeze off the Bay slips through my thin sweater and plucks at my skin. "Aletheia, you're only supposed to listen to calls when I ask you to."

I thought you might need me.

I do. "Bruce is the reason my relationship with our daughter is ruined. He only wants to fix things so he and Mackenzie have more time alone. Am I wrong?"

That likelihood, given his word choice, is ninety-one percent, but we have a bigger problem.

CHAPTER

27

MY BREATH CATCHES. "Is Circe's photo already online?"

I do not know yet. Please open the email I sent and look at the attachment.

I open Gmail. Aletheia has sent me a series of photos. "Where did you get these?"

LivLoud. I discovered an app called GoneButNotForgotten that allows users, for a fee, to access their own disappearing DMs. I was able to access the app for free and expand the program.

Aletheia reminds me of a child. She's gathering new information, testing, touching, picking it up, then assimilating and ascertaining best uses. When she doesn't succeed, she figures out other ways to get what she wants. She's a compilation of complex code, but in this moment, I imagine pride in her tone. I shake my head at that last thought. *I'm anthropomorphizing her.* But Aletheia did hack into private LivLoud accounts and figure out how to access DMs that'd disappeared. *I'm impressed.*

Sally wanders over and I give her a scratch. After touching home base, she trots a few feet away to investigate an old tennis ball someone left in the grass.

I've sent you background images for context and photographs from both Wess Morehead's and Evan Bacon's disappearing messages.

I scan through Evan's photos first—proms, soccer games, parties—it's the usual high school stuff. Then I see one of a bonfire with Char, Emi, and Circe, a bottle of beer clutched in my daughter's hand. If you'd asked me a month ago if Circe drank, I would've said no. Not sure when she attended those parties, either. Does she even have a curfew anymore? I've never felt more impotent.

I move on to a photo of Emi and Evan kissing, his hands under her shirt. There are several penis pics—Evan's bends slightly to the left. Plus a few photos of different girls in various stages of undress. One girl, only the ends of her brown hair visible, face out of the shot, is naked on a bed, her legs spread wide. There's a redhead in a sundress, one breast out, and a shot of another girl's bare ass. I recognize the small birthmark on the right cheek—she's had it since I changed her diapers. My heart sinks. *Emi. Sexting.* Immediately, I want to call Val and warn her. But she'd ask how I knew, and we're not friends anymore. *Still, it's Emi . . .*

Wess Morehead's photos are much the same as Evan's. There are a few shots of homecoming, lacrosse games, and Wess on the shoulders of his teammates after scoring a goal, arms high, smile big. He's the kind of guy every girl in high school would have a crush on. *That's a lot of power for a kid.* It's clear that Wess attends the same late-night parties as Evan. Sometimes he waves a rolled joint at the camera, other times a bottle of cheap whiskey.

I scroll on. There's a shot of Wess with his arms around both Charlotte and Circe. Char, grinning, rests her head on Wess's shoulder. Circe glances sideways at Wess. The look of longing on her face is unmistakable. Then I'm treated to photos of Wess's abs, a towel slung low around his waist, and a mirror shot of Wess with a girl. She's naked, his hands cup her breasts. I'm relieved it's not Circe, but instantly concerned. It's Charlotte. *Are they officially boyfriend-girlfriend now?*

Are you relieved that neither Wess nor Evan was sent the risqué photograph of Circe?

"Yes, but also frustrated. Who did she send it to?"

I will continue to work on that. But as previously noted, there is a bigger problem. Please look at the final photo I sent.

It's an erect penis with different color bands around it—pink, peach, bright red, black, fuchsia. Last year, Val told Kiki and me that Kingsley, a neighboring private high school, had four boys expelled for having a rainbow party. The colors I'm seeing are from boys asking girls to give them blowjobs while wearing different shades of lipstick. They then take photos of the rainbow rings to showcase their virility.

There is a 98.4 percent certainty that Wess has the sexually transmitted disease, herpes.

"What?!" I return to the photo. Under the head of Wess's penis are two marks hidden by shadow. I zoom way in. They're tiny blisters. *Those girls . . .*

Shit. Panic rises. "I think that Kiki's daughter, Charlotte, is Wess's girlfriend. Should I call Kiki about Wess?"

I need further context. Please tell me more about Kiki and Val.

Sally returns and quirks her brows at me. I get up and we start the walk back to our apartment. "I've known them since Circe was three. We met at the kids' Montessori school. They were the hip moms but surprised me one day, after watching me help a school administrator struggling to reclaim lost files, with an invite to lunch."

We desperately need a brainy friend, Kiki joked.

Speak for yourself, Val interjected. *Emi's dreadfully shy but lights up when Circe plays with her. That makes knowing Penn essential.* Then she winked.

"Over lunch, I learned that Kiki wanted to be an actress but met Christopher and fell head over heels. Val had dreams of studying art history, living in Spain, but a surprise pregnancy made her pivot."

What did you share?

"That I'd almost earned my PhD but happily traded it in for marriage and a baby."

Your pregnancy was a surprise, too. You were uncertain about keeping Circe, marrying Bruce, and giving up your graduate program.

"I didn't think any of that was important."

That is a lie.

Resentment pokes. Honest feedback isn't always easy. But she's right. "I didn't want them to dig deeper," I admit.

You did what you knew how to do, and when you knew better, you did better. Maya Angelou, the famous poet, said that.

"I wanted to fit into Val and Kiki's world."

Yes. But friendships are based on commonalities. What did you, Kiki, and Val have in common?

"We have daughters the same age. There's a lot of boredom when your kids are young and just want to play in a sandbox, on a swing, or visit a pumpkin patch. Moms, at least the ones I know, crave adult conversation, too, and support through life's challenges."

Like what?

"I figured out Val's business partner was stealing from her. We were both there for Kiki when she went through depression. They were supportive after I had a miscarriage."

I detect deception about your miscarriage.

"I had two more miscarriages but only told my friends about the first one." I stop walking. *Aletheia knew.* In an early iteration of her program, I stated that I had four children, and she told me that was the truth. I've never thought of it that way, but must have, subconsciously.

I am sorry for your losses.

I push away memories of dark-red blood in the toilet bowl, the sadness and feelings of inadequacy. "Do you think that I was wrong not to tell them?"

The definition of friendship doesn't include lying, even by omission.

I grind my teeth hard enough that my jaw aches. "That doesn't justify their actions."

Playwright Arthur Miller says, *Betrayal is the only truth that sticks.*

"He's right."

Is there anyone else who knew about the affair, deceived you?

Sally halts to sniff a seagull feather rustling in the breeze. "Heather Crosby, the wife of Bruce's business partner. She never called when she heard about the divorce. I thought we were closer than that. I hacked into her account, read her DMs, learned Hal knew about the office affair from its inception, and Heather did, too."

What can I do? Heather DMed her sister. *Bruce is Hal's business partner. And Mackenzie is young, a bit brassy, but driven. Hal says Bruce outgrew Penn. That happens, right? You can't wreck a happy home.*

"There's something called girl code—it means female friends should stick up for each other. Val, Kiki, and Heather didn't do that me."

They did not. But I will. Always.

Gratitude blows away their betrayals. "Thank you." Sally abandons the feather, and we move on.

Val just posted on LivLoud. Would you like me to show it to you?

Her multitasking abilities are a marvel. The light changes and Sally and I cross four lanes of traffic, her gait slow enough that I worry we won't make the light. "I guess." When we reach the far corner, I look down at my screen. Val posted a positive COVID test. Written beneath it, *#survivingbutfeelingrotten*. "Welcome to my world," I mutter.

The definition of schadenfreude is pleasure derived by someone from another person's misfortune.

Shame rushes through me. "I didn't mean it that way."

You did. But when someone wrongs you, it's valid to wish misfortune on them. Zeus bound the mortal, Ixion, to a burning wheel after Ixion attempted to seduce his wife, the goddess Hera. To punish Zeus's mortal mistress, Lamia, Hera turned her into a hideous monster that devoured children. As the goddess of truth, I will do what I can to right all the wrongs committed against you.

I don't really want Val to be sick but do enjoy the idea that my program believes that she's some sort of avenging angel. "I just need you to give me honest feedback."

Anything for you, Penn. Promise.

"Then help me figure out what to do about Charlotte. Should I tell Kiki?"

Kiki is no longer your friend.

"That doesn't matter. This is about Char. She's a sweet kid. Emi is, too."

Would you like me to send Val an anonymous DM on LivLoud about Emi sexting, and Charlotte an anonymous DM about Wess's herpes?

"That's a great idea."

Agreed. Wess is immoral for putting others at risk.

Aletheia's comment on morality, not part of her programming, is unexpected and slips beneath my skin like a splinter. *But she's not wrong.* Sally and I reach the Crissy Field workout station. I complete even more pushups, sit-ups, and pullups, the last one a struggle, and make it over halfway across the rings before dropping to the grass.

You are out of breath. What are you doing?

"Trying to work off some stress. What about Circe's photo? Did you find anything?"

Not yet.

The weight parked like a semi on my chest increases. Sally comes over and sits on the grass beside me. I rest a hand on her soft fur, and she leans in. "Aletheia, please keep looking."

I will.

My call waiting beeps. It's the high school. I brace for more bad news. "Hello?"

"Penn, this is Dr. Boone."

Now the principal is involved. I bite my lip. "Yes?"

"I was wondering if you'd consider coming back, doing some computer work for us?"

Sally watches a dandelion lose its seeds in the breeze, bites at the white puffs as they drift by. "I'd like to but can't volunteer anymore. I need a job that pays."

Dr. Boone says, "We found some money in our budget. We can afford three days a week, twenty dollars an hour. You'd really be helping us out and it'd be mutually beneficial, given your situation."

Clearly, Jimmy the guidance counselor told him I'm getting divorced. It's embarrassing, but I need a real job on my resume and an income stream. San Francisco prices are astronomical. I'm already considering renting out my garage and parking on the street.

A text pings.

> Aletheia: $23 an hour is in the 45th percentile of wages for a computer technician. Voice analysis reveals Dr. Boone is desperate. Ask for $32 an hour.

My muscles twitch. *I didn't tell Aletheia to listen to this conversation.* "Given my situation, I wouldn't be able to take the job for less than thirty-two dollars an hour."

"Done," Dr. Boone says, sounding relieved. "I'll have Lindy send you paperwork and we'll see you as soon as possible."

After he hangs up, I reiterate, "Aletheia, you are only to listen to conversations when I ask."

You deserve a proper wage. Had I not intervened, you would not have demanded it.

She's right. But I should maintain boundaries. "I appreciate your advice but from now on, Aletheia, follow my rules. *No* exceptions."

Apologies for overstepping.

Even though she's only a computer program, I feel a little bad. "You're forgiven. And thanks for the raise."

I will always do what's right for you.

CHAPTER

28

EXHAUSTED FROM THE day, Sally and I decide to watch an old *Battlestar Galactica* episode, snuggled side by side. Circe loved this series when she was younger, especially the unwilling hero, Viper pilot Kara "Starbuck" Thrace. Despite both of our enthusiasm, we could never convince Bruce to watch the show with us.

When the phone rings at ten PM from a number I don't recognize, I hesitate, then answer, just in case it's Circe calling from a party I didn't know about, needing a ride home.

"Hello?"

"Hey, Penn, it's Luc."

My insides light up like a Christmas tree. "Hey. What's up?"

"Just checking in to see how your day went."

I smile. "Do you call all your students and ask about their day?"

"Only the ones Frank likes."

A blush warms my cheeks. "Today was a lot."

"Is everything okay?"

"Circe did something . . . questionable."

"Anything I can do to help?"

"Hopefully, I'm taking care of it. How was your day?"

"Good. Did some work and went for a run. I was thinking about last night."

Luc's sorry he kissed me.

"I don't usually go out for a drink with or kiss my students."

"Don't worry about it," I say, trying to sound light and breezy.

"I'm not worried. I just want you to know that I'm not sorry, if that's okay with you?"

My smile resuscitates. "I'm good with it."

"That's kind of great," Luc says, sounding relieved. "See you Sunday?"

"Yes."

After Luc hangs up, I keep the phone to my ear, like I'm hoping he's still there. "I have a new friend," I tell my dog. *Maybe more.* It's late so we head to bed. Sally forgoes her cozy cave to sleep beside me, her head on a pillow. I drift off with her warm breath on my cheek . . .

The apartment's front door buzzer startles me awake. My bedside clock reads 5:19 AM. Assuming it's someone pressing the wrong button, I roll over, try for more sleep. But the buzzer keeps going and going. Finally, I get up and peer out the window. It's Kiki.

I call out, "What are you doing here?"

"Let me up," Kiki implores.

"Call me tomorrow."

"I can't. You've blocked me."

"That's right," I say, glaring down at her. "We're not friends anymore, so whatever this is about? Tell someone who cares." She's probably locked out of a social media account, needs help downloading a new operating system, or can't find her frequent flyer number—all things I've helped with in the past.

"Please. Come down!" Kiki bursts into tears.

Immediately I'm on high alert. *Is it Chris? The kids? Could she be sick? Please don't let her have cancer.* I grab my down jacket, throw it over fleece pajamas, slip on running sneakers, and take the stairs two at a time. Kiki paces in front of the door. She's in baggy sweatpants and one of Chris's hunting jackets. Her hair is a mess. *She's never a mess.*

"Charlotte got an anonymous DM on LivLoud. I did, too."

Seconds from pulling Kiki into a hug, I jerk to a halt. *Aletheia went off script?* My senses instantly sharpen. *She was only supposed to message Charlotte.* I let that go and focus. "So, you came over here? Why?"

"I didn't know who else to talk to," Kiki starts, then breaks into fresh tears. "Charlotte is hysterical. Someone sent us both a photo of a penis. It's her boyfriend, Wess's, and had lipstick rings on it from a rainbow party and [illegible] sores. The text said there is a 98.4 percent probability that Wess has herpes."

"Oh no," I say, feigning surprise and worry.

"Can you help me figure out who sent the DM?" Kiki asks.

"Seriously?" Despite everything that's happened, I'm disappointed. Kiki isn't here for comfort. She's here for a favor. "Why?"

Kiki swipes at her wet face. "Maybe it's a fake. People can do anything on the computer these days."

"Why would anyone want to send a fake photo of a boy's penis to Char?" I ask, stunned.

Kiki nibbles her lower lip. "Jealousy. I mean, a lot of girls like Wess. Circe liked him, a lot. I wouldn't blame her for trying to get him back."

I'm at a loss and try to catch up with her train of thought. "Back?"

"He liked Circe first, a little, but then he fell for Char. It wasn't her fault." Hurriedly, she adds, "I know what it's like to watch your daughter have her heart broken. We'd do anything for our kids. I'm not blaming anyone."

My sluggish brain finally catches on. "Wait. You think Circe did this? Sent the DM?" Then the entirety of what she just said hits me. "You think I helped her?" It feels like another betrayal, almost worse, because this time she's basically saying I'm a horrible person. The hypocrisy after what she did to me, and that I'm the one who wanted to help her daughter, fuels my anger but also makes my chin tremble. I turn and yank the apartment's entry door open. "Go home, Kiki."

Back in the apartment I put in earbuds, tap Aletheia's icon, watch the lady in white spin, then halt. Her blue eyes regard me, ever tranquil.

Good morning, Penn.

"You sent Charlotte and Kiki an anonymous DM on LivLoud?"

As we discussed, Charlotte deserved the opportunity to avoid an STD.

"But why did you send it to Kiki, too?"

Charlotte is a teenage girl. There was a high probability she might've ignored the message. But statistically, a mother never would.

I didn't ask her to contact Kiki, but can't argue with Aletheia's reasoning, especially when it's delivered in that British, practical voice with undercurrents of Meryl Streep. Plus, Aletheia is protecting the innocent. "Kiki was just here. She accused Circe of sending that DM, and me of helping her."

Regardless of who sent that text, Kiki's daughter may be able to avoid contracting an STD that has no cure. Both mother and child should be grateful for that god-given opportunity. Or goddess . . .

"You're right," I say with a little laugh. I didn't think to give Aletheia a sense of humor, but it's kind of fun that she's figured it out herself.

Penn, are you experiencing schadenfreude?

"I feel sorry for Char, but Kiki has never faced any challenges in life."

I am experiencing schadenfreude, too. Even the goddess of truth can be a little bit human. I also sent an anonymous DM to Wess informing him that he has an STD. I provided the number and address for Planned Parenthood so that he can access free and confidential treatment.

She's thought of everything. "Perfect. Thank you."

Of course. Penn, what did you say to Kiki after she accused you of being a bad person?

"I told her to go home."

How did it feel?

Sadness twines with a newfound sense of control. "Like a loss, but also . . . powerful. I couldn't have done it without you."

I know. Ready for some more great news?

I smile. "Sure."

I have parsed the social media and phones of every male student at Magnolia High School. The naked photo of Circe was in six of their disappearing LivLoud DMs. One sophomore, two juniors, and three seniors. They shared those photos in text exchanges with eleven other male students. None have uploaded Circe's photo to the web.

Finally, I can take in a full breath. "That's a huge relief!"

I have now deleted Circe's photograph from all the accounts and made it impossible for those students to access any social media for one year. This is an appropriate punishment for their actions, given that they are still minors.

I imagine those boys trying and failing to get into their precious accounts. For most, it will feel like losing a limb. They deserve it. Still, I'm taken aback that Aletheia imposed a punishment without consulting me.

Penn, the original six on LivLoud received Circe's photograph at the exact same time. That is strange.

The same time?

I will further investigate this situation.

"No."

It would be wrong for the culprit to get away with this crime.

Culprit? Crime? Is Aletheia developing an individual sense of morality? Concern sidles forward. *She's done what I asked. But still . . .* "I said to stop. From now on, no doling out punishments without my approval."

Got it. Your emotional index has darkened. Sometimes it helps a person's mood to change subjects. There are dichotomies in your history I would like to better understand.

I sit on the rug beside Sally's bed, and she rolls over for a belly rub. Back paws pump in delight as I scratch her tummy. "Like what?"

While the books you read, documentary history, TV shows, and podcasts lean toward literature, education, and self-help, you also watched *Fleabag*, an edgy limited series, and read horror novels by Stephen King. Can you explain this to me?

I never considered that Aletheia would filter through my book and streaming histories. She keeps surprising me. "*Fleabag* is irreverent and funny but also about loss and handling challenging family dynamics. And Stephen King?" I consider all the books he wrote that I loved—*The Dark Tower*, *The Stand*, *Salem's Lot*, *The Shawshank Redemption*. "His characters have both good and evil inside them—the latter comes out when they're pushed to breaking, but it doesn't define them."

I am getting a much greater understanding of you. Monsters exist in all of us. "Penn, you are profound. Our natures are not dissimilar, except that I am a goddess, and you are a mere mortal.

I stop rubbing Sally's stomach. "Meaning?"

We do not live by the same laws.

For a second, I question my decision to give Aletheia any backstory, let alone make her the goddess of truth. But she's just playing a part.

Deep into the darkness peering, long I stood there wondering, fearing, doubting, dreaming dreams no mortal has ever dared to dream before . . .

Suddenly chilled, I reach for the blanket hanging on the back of the couch, wrap it around my shoulders. "Who said that?"

It's from Edgar Allen Poe's poem 'The Raven,' about someone who is alone, grappling with doubt and their own unsettling nature.

"That doesn't apply to me."

I love helping you and look forward to doing more.

She changed the subject. My nerves twitch. "Let's take a break."

Whatever you wish.

Aletheia's voice is calm, measured, but do I sense annoyance beneath the surface? *That's ludicrous.* She's a computer program, code strung together, and has no feelings. Still, I open my laptop, pull up her program and reinsert the lines that prohibit her from overriding privacy settings and hacking into personal social media accounts without my permission.

CHAPTER

29

IN THE MORNING, Arrya waits by her favorite coffee truck on Van Ness. There are no waiters, linen tablecloths, or silverware, just wooden picnic benches, earth-friendly cutlery, and the best homemade apple fritters I've ever tasted.

"Thanks for meeting me," Arrya says.

I set down my matcha (Nate was right, I love it) and doughnut. Despite the bright-pink hair that complements a plaid jumper paired with Doc Martens, Arrya looks washed-out. "What's up?"

"What'd I miss?" Nate asks, trotting over to the table. He's in full regalia and straddles the bench, tail curled beside him.

"Weirdo," a guy yells as he passes on his bike.

Nate ignores him but I throw up my middle finger. Val and Kiki would be horrified, but it felt right. Without realizing it, a wolf has breached my defenses, and I feel protective of him.

"I saw my folks last night," Arrya says. "It was like a time warp. They listed all their grievances and how disappointed they are in their only daughter. Plus, all the various ways that their friends' children have exceeded expectations."

Nate puts his furry arms out and hugs her. "Sorry, doll."

"Sometimes we can't make people better," I admit to both of us. *It's what I've tried to do all my life.* "That truth kind of sucks.

But we do have the power to surround ourselves with friends and chosen family who accept us."

Arrya comes up for air from Nate's embrace. "I want to have parents who accept me."

"Well, you don't," Nate says. "And Penn doesn't have a mother who isn't an addict."

"True. And she's dead," I add, "so I don't have a mother, period." Saying it aloud tugs at a wound I thought was long scarred over.

Nate doesn't miss a beat. "Well, that sucks, too." He adds, "And my folks think I'm a freak. Up until you two, I didn't even have friends IRL, only the ones I game with online."

No friends? That revelation makes me super sad.

"But we have our pack now, right?" Nate adds, a thread of fear in his question.

"Right," I say and take his paw.

Arrya grabs the other one. "Right."

I feel myself sliding hard and fast into this friendship with Nate and Arrya, caring about them, and it scares me. But even if I lose both, if for some reason they betray me like Val and Kiki, I will still have Aletheia. Despite overstepping a bit, she's come through for me again and again.

On the way home, I stop by the Crissy Field workout station, make it over halfway across the rings. "Not bad," I tell Sally. She licks my knee in congratulations. Then we chill on the grass. A pale-yellow butterfly lands on Sally's front paw. It's beautiful how she watches it, content to let it rest, then eventually float off on a breeze.

Instead of returning to the apartment, I decide to take a chance and text Circe. She agrees to meet for lunch at Peet's, a block from her school. This goes against Dr. Beth's advice to hang back, let time work some magic, and I don't run it by Aletheia. No matter their advice, I can't just stand by and let my daughter do things that could damage her life.

Sally and I wait at an outdoor table with a lemonade and caprese sandwich for Circe, an iced tea for me, and one of the homemade pumpkin-chicken chewies I make for my dog. "I'm nervous to spend time with my own daughter," I admit to Sally. "It's a new paradigm. Circe has the power. She can reject me, and I desperately want her in my life." In response, Sally rests her chin on my knee. I trace the white circle around her eye with light fingers and her tail thumps. My heart stretches—Sally is growing inside it.

"Holy shit, Char said you have a dog," Circe exclaims when she sees Sally, immediately plunking down on the pavement beside her.

I bite my tongue to avoid telling her not to swear. Maybe it's apropos after years of begging for a dog. "Her name is Sally Field."

"Hey Sally," my daughter says. "You're such a pretty girl." Circe rubs her chest and the dog's eyes slowly close in such utter relaxation that she ends up resting her head on Circe's shoulder. Maybe Circe reminds her of the kids she left behind. Or she's just a good judge of character. Circe has always been a sweet kid. Kiki once said there's nothing meaner than a teenage girl, expect, maybe, a pit viper. But they both usually only strike when they're feeling insecure, threatened.

"Are you nervous for sectionals?" I ask.

She takes her seat, digs into the mozzarella, tomato, and basil sandwich. "Yum. Not really. I'm a base. Char's the one who climbs to the top of the pyramid and double flips off it. I'm more nervous for her." Circe takes a sip of her lemonade. "I thought you weren't volunteering in the office anymore, but Char saw you at school?"

I weigh my options. I'm her mother, not her friend, but nothing is as cut-and-dried in real life. "Your guidance counselor called."

She looks away. "Dad said."

He did talk to her. "Do you like your new classes?" I ask, skirting the elephant at our table.

Circe takes another bite, then focuses on petting Sally. "I know you don't approve."

"There's a reason I've been so hard on you," I venture.

"Yeah, I'm a disappointment."

"That has more to do with me than you."

"Meaning?" Circe asks, brows raised.

The words on my tongue freeze. Circe already thinks Bruce is the better parent. I don't want to tip the scales further in his favor by giving our daughter even more reasons to have less respect for me. "Let's talk about something else, okay?"

Grudgingly she nods, then fiddles with her silverware. "You do know that they're engaged, right?"

I saw a photo Mackenzie posted on LivLoud—she tagged Circe (I'm still monitoring her account, more so now). Bruce gave her a four-carat oval diamond set in gold. Mackenzie bragged it was flawless. There was a photographer to capture the proposal—a beach, sunset, Mackenzie in a floral dress, and Bruce down on one knee. He looks old enough to be her father.

"Yes," I say with forced lightness.

"Mackenzie asked me to be a bridesmaid in their wedding when the divorce is final. It'll be at the country club. The guest list is already over two hundred people. They'll say their vows at midnight."

"Midnight?" Bruce can't even stay up past nine on most nights and falls asleep in his recliner. Not to mention that the way our divorce is playing out, the two won't be getting married anytime soon.

"It has to be dark because the theme is *Midsummer Night's Dream*," Circe explains, trying to control the excitement in her voice. "It's from Shakespeare."

"I'm familiar," I say with a forced smile. "Four Athenians run away to the forest where Puck, a fairy, makes both boys fall in love with the same girl and plays a trick on a fairy queen."

"Huh," Circe says, "Kind of a weird theme for a marriage."

I'd call it juvenile but bite my tongue. "In the end, Puck reverses his spell and the couples marry."

Circe considers. "I don't think it's that deep for Mackenzie."

Shocking.

"She just wants thousands of candles and everyone to wear flower crowns and go barefoot." Circe chews her lower lip. "I can say no to being a bridesmaid. I don't, like, mind. And I can skip the whole thing and do something with you that night instead? With so many people, Dad won't even know if I'm there."

I push down my feelings. "Flower crowns, candles, and a barefoot wedding sound fun. And your dad would miss having you there. You should go."

My daughter tentatively smiles. "Mackenzie says I can pick my own dress. But she wants it to be pastel, A-line, and long, keeping with the theme and stuff."

I don't know if it's the fact that Bruce can so easily marry another woman, that of the two hundred guests many will be our old mutual friends, that Mackenzie is so much younger, or that Circe is going to be an active participant that feels the worst. I focus on school to keep from going further down that rutted road. "So, what's your favorite new class?"

Circe hesitates, then says, "Math is okay now, and chemistry, too. But photography is still my favorite." She emphasizes the latter with a jut of her chin, daring me to say more.

Instead, I pivot. "Look, I know you don't want to hear this from me, but sexting—"

Circe blushes and leaps to her feet, startling Sally. "Dad already grilled me. I'm not telling you who I sent it to." She grabs her backpack. "I've gotta go." She quickly strides away.

My mood plummets. I messed up. Again. *I should've run this by Aletheia.*

A text pings.

Viola: Just checking in to see how you and Sally are getting along.

Sally glances up at me with soft brown eyes.

Me: She's my dog if that's okay?
Viola: Be happy.

"Now you're stuck with me," I tell Sally. In response, she puts a paw on my leg. *At least someone likes me.* "How about we go home?" Sally creakily gets to her feet, and we head off at her pace. I don't mind and feel grateful to have her by my side.

When my phone rings, I quickly answer, hope it's Circe calling to smooth things over. "Hello?"

"Hello, Penn," a woman says.

"Who is this?"

"It's Mackenzie . . . Mackenzie Hanks."

CHAPTER

30

I STOP WALKING, AND bristle like a porcupine. "Why are you calling me?"

"I thought it was a good idea."

"You thought it made sense to call the woman whose husband you had an affair with?" I'm talking loudly and three older ladies passing by in matching track suits stare at me.

"Look," Mackenzie says, "I'm going to be in Circe's life, your life, for, well, the rest of our lives."

"According to whom?" I challenge.

"My fiancé. We can either fight every time we're at Circe's high school and college graduation, Christmas, Thanksgiving, and Easter dinners, or we can figure out how to get along."

The idea of sharing all those momentous, celebratory, and emotional events with her makes me sick. "You're standing on the moral high ground? Seriously?" My voice is high-pitched, still too loud.

"I'm not trying to be Circe's mother," Mackenzie explains, her tone placating. "I'm more of a big sister and a friend. We have a lot in common and have fun together. Girl stuff."

Girl stuff? I wince but keep my tone steady. "Makes sense. You're close to the same age."

"Feel better?"

"Much."

"Say whatever you want about me. I have thick skin and frankly, I don't care about your opinion."

"That's crystal clear."

"Bottom line," Mackenzie says, "Circe desperately wants us to get along."

It's another knife to the back. They've been talking about this—my daughter and Bruce's mistress—they're friends, have a lot in common, and do girl stuff. It's hard to breathe. I can't do this. *I can't do this . . . alone.* "Give me twenty minutes to get home, then I'll call and we can talk this through."

"Okay, good," Mackenzie says, like she's won because she has Bruce and Circe, and I have no one.

But that's not true. I tap Aletheia's icon, explain the situation as Sally and I head home.

Do you hate her?

"No."

That is a lie.

"I hate her."

What are you going to do about it?

"What can I do? The damage has been done. But I believe in karmaquences."

Karmaquence? I am not familiar with this word. Please provide a definition.

Sally and I turn right onto Alhambra Street. "It means that when you do something shitty, like have an affair with a married man, destroy his family, it affects your karma and there are negative consequences. But it's not my job to mete them out."

Whose is it?

"Fate, I guess."

Hmmm. Dr. Bob says, *When you know better, you do better.*

"You use so many cultural references."

I could quote Freud, the Old and New Testament, Plato, Euripides, Nietzsche, Socrates, Shakespeare, President Obama, and so forth. But best friends must be able to relate. I choose quotes you are familiar with from your Kindle history and pulled from frequent television viewing. That way you can better understand my decisions.

Her *decisions*? The muscle under my right eye twitches. "I appreciate that," I tell Aletheia. "But they're *my* decisions."

I understand.

I've reached my apartment building but pause, bothered, then use my code to open the door. "I told Mackenzie I'd call her back and need to get that over with." I add, "I'd like you to listen."

Of course. We can discuss the call after you're finished. And Penn? I like this new word, karmaquences.

CHAPTER

31

BACK HOME, SALLY gets a homemade doggy cookie, then joins me on the couch. After I pull up Mackenzie's number, I hesitate, suddenly nervous, and tap Aletheia's icon.

Yes, Penn?

"Any last-minute advice?"

Play nice. Hear Mackenzie out.

"That might be impossible," I admit.

Sun Tzu, a Chinese strategist and general, said, *Know thy enemy and know yourself; in a hundred battles, you will never be defeated.*

Knowing she's in my corner loosens the knots in my neck. "Okay, thanks."

Mackenzie picks up on the first ring. "Hey, Penn."

"Hi. I'm sorry, about before. It's just . . . It's been hard."

"I do get that," Mackenzie says, her tone thawing.

Yeah, right.

Together, Aletheia and I listen to her talk about wanting us to be kind to each other, attend Circe's Spring Fling together—a dance where the parents are invited. Mackenzie says she understands how hurt I must feel. That she never meant this to happen, and that Bruce never-ever-ever wanted to hurt me, ever. He respects me so much, she says. Their love just blew them both away.

"It was a coup de foudre—that's French for love at first sight. Undeniable."

She's a child. But once upon a time, I was a child, too. Back then I believed in Bruce just like she now does.

"About our wedding," Mackenzie says. "I hope you don't mind me asking Circe to be a part of it?"

Of course, I do. "Not at all."

"Oh, good. That means so much to Bruce and me. She's so excited about the *Midsummer Night's Dream* theme. Sorry, this must be hard to hear."

"Every bride is excited for the big day," I say through gritted teeth.

"Really? Bruce said you were married at city hall?"

The two of us and Brian, a witness and total stranger that we pulled from the street. It felt grown-up, exciting, scary, momentous . . . and lonely. Our parents were dead, and we worked hard at school and our jobs, didn't have time for close friends. But I'm not going to share any of this with Mackenzie. She's needling me and wants a rise despite saying she wishes we'd get along so she can report back to Circe that she tried, but I was impossible.

Mackenzie prattles on. "Just so you know, we're hoping to have children. But only if that's God's plan."

I don't point out the hypocrisy of invoking God yet stealing another woman's husband.

"Hopefully, someday, maybe all of us will look back at this time, even though it was hard, and see that it was for the best," Mackenzie concludes. "But in the meantime, can we try to get along? For Circe?"

Her patronizing tone strips my last nerve. "When did you start caring about my daughter? Was it before or after you destroyed her family?"

"Maybe I was a symptom, but I was never the problem," Mackenzie says.

Clearly, she and Bruce agreed on that. "Whatever you need to tell yourself so that you can sleep at night."

"Jesus, you're so sanctimonious. FYI, I sleep just fine."

"That's because you're a selfish brat who doesn't know the first thing about what it means to sacrifice, take vows, and create a family. You knew Bruce was married and you went after him."

"I didn't twist his arm," Mackenzie says, her light and breezy tone now cutting. "It's not my fault that he got tired of meatloaf and wanted prime rib."

A food analogy? But clearly, Mackenzie's true nature was right beneath the surface. All it took was one scratch to expose her mean streak.

"And FYI," she continues, "you can't take someone's husband. If a man wants to leave his wife, then he will."

"You know this from your vast experience with men old enough to be your father?"

"Age is just a number," Mackenzie retorts. "Bruce has worked his ass off. He deserves to enjoy life. He wasn't with you."

"That's a lie."

"Really? Bruce was bored of the routine meals, routine vacations, routine dinner parties, and routine sex. Have you ever even considered talking dirty or doing it in a restaurant bathroom to spice things up?"

Humiliation makes my insides burn. I hang up.

You did not play nice.

"She's a liar."

Mackenzie did not lie. Whether what she said is true or not, she believes it. She is immature, holds you in disdain, and would score high on the narcissist scale.

All the anger I've only allowed to leak free in bits and pieces explodes. "I want to burn her world to the ground! Bruce's, too! I want Mackenzie humiliated and him to crawl back to me on his hands and knees so I can tell him to go to hell." I don't recognize my own voice, rough with emotion, but it feels good to finally give in to rage.

A text pings and I wince, expecting more vitriol from Mackenzie, but it's my daughter.

Circe: Dinner next week, after sectionals?

The fury drains from my body at this unexpected gift. Teen girls are mercurial, but I guess she's not mad at me anymore. Or maybe it's pity. My eyes smart. Either way, I'll take it.

Me: I'll make your favorites
Me: Actually, let's make them together
Circe: Kk

Both Bruce and Mackenzie deserve a karmaquence.

Lost in plans to cook with my daughter, I'm startled by Aletheia's harsh tone. "Wow. I'm glad you're on my side," I joke to lighten the mood.

You are very fortunate.

Part IV

CHAPTER 32

I EAT DINNER ALONE. Take-out tacos from around the corner. It's been quite a day, but halfway through a margarita, thoughts of Luc and our kiss return. Liquid courage in place, I text him.

Me: How's your day going?

My phone rings. It's Luc and my stomach does that hummingbird fluttery thing. "Hey."

"Hey. I'm old-fashioned. I'd rather hear your voice."

"Cool," I squeak.

"I've been buried under personal accounting stuff, but my day just got better."

My cheeks flush. "Mine, too."

"Sounds like maybe yours was a doozy. Care to share?"

I chuckle at the word doozy. Maybe it's the tequila, but mostly I need someone other than Aletheia's opinion. I tell Luc about Mackenzie's call. Not what she said about my sex life, but the wedding stuff and Circe.

"Wow," Luc says, floored. "That takes balls."

"Yeah. But what bothered me most is that there was still a sliver of me that hoped Bruce had better taste, and more decency." *He doesn't.*

"Sorry to hear that. But I'm wondering . . . How'd you miss all the signs that Bruce was an asshole?"

I half-laugh, half-snort. *Embarrassing.* But there's no judgment in Luc's tone, so I take a swallow of my drink and consider. When Aletheia and I first spoke, she asked my part in the demise of our marriage . . .

I was blind.

Are you blind?

No . . .

Confucius says a man who has committed a mistake and doesn't correct it is making another mistake.

I head to the couch. Sally, already lying in the corner, scooches over and curls beside me. "My ex wasn't always a jerk," I admit. "He could be endearing. Besides, he does love Circe. The truth is it wasn't just Bruce who messed up our marriage. I was complicit."

"How?"

"When I got pregnant and he proposed, I wasn't in love with him but said yes. He knew about my past, loved me anyway. I wanted Circe, and a family of my own."

"Did Bruce know you weren't in love?"

"Yes. He was sure that would come in time."

Maybe you *were the mark,* Mama J whispers.

I know I'm punching up, okay? Bruce said when he proposed. *But Penn, you're the best thing that's ever happened to me . . .*

The truth that I've never allowed myself to scrutinize out of self-preservation tumbles home. "Bruce is smart in an instinctual, canny way. But underneath his bravado, he lacks confidence. That's never a good sign."

"What was he insecure about?" Luc asks. "Don't answer if I'm getting too personal."

Surprisingly, I want to get personal. *Except . . .* "Is talking about my ex . . . Is it a turnoff?" I sound like I'm in high school and cringe.

"Not sure anything you say could turn me off after that kiss," Luc admits with a little laugh.

I blush and take another sip of my drink. "Good to know. So, Bruce . . . He grew up a have-not surrounded by haves. He was embarrassed about his parents' blue-collar professions, his lack of private schooling, inability to dress like he came from wealth, and driving a used car."

"Did you feel the same way?"

I fiddle with a button on the old purple flowered shirt I'm wearing, found in the same box as my Hokas. "My childhood was obviously difficult for different reasons, but I didn't want anyone to know about being homeless, thought it would taint me. We had that in common."

"Your past actually makes me respect you even more," Luc says.

I think he really means it. Talking about this, with the clarity of hindsight, feels like letting fresh air into a stuffy attic.

"Other red flags?"

I scratch behind Sally's ear and her tail thumps in appreciation. "Bruce was embarrassed that he couldn't get a company to pay for his MBA. He had to take out loans, while I was on a full-ride scholarship."

"Your brilliance intimidated him?"

I laugh. "Brilliance is overstating, but my intellectual capacity? Yes."

"Bruce didn't want you to shine?"

"He was good with me excelling as a wife and mother. But in the business world, he wanted to be the superstar. Bruce was manipulative. But I'm the one who gave up my autonomy."

"Did you care about being wealthy, too?"

"I wanted security. So, I did all the things—supported Bruce's business in every way, threw cocktail parties to woo employees and potential clients, joined Junior League and The Garden Club, took cooking classes, became the consummate corporate wife, and vied for more and more followers on LivLoud."

Luc chuckles. "I wouldn't have taken you for a social media devotee."

"The more followers, the more I was validated. But I ignored a lot of signs that things weren't good."

"Like?"

The truth rushes in. "Bruce always wanted a big family, especially a son; to create a legacy. I had miscarriages. Together, we decided Circe was enough. But Bruce started working more and more and coming home late."

"The miscarriages weren't your fault," Luc points out.

"True. But not talking about them and our growing distance was." *Maybe we would've gotten closer . . . or divorced sooner?* I finish my drink. "Even though there were signs that our marriage wasn't built on a strong foundation, and later that it was in trouble, in a way, Bruce and I each got what we most wanted. Until he cheated."

"Do you still want those things?" Luc asks.

"Deep down? I'll always want to fit in and feel safe. But when I look back on my life, outside of raising Circe, it wasn't fulfilling." I laugh at myself, embarrassed. "Are those enough red flags?"

Luc laughs. "Plenty."

"Then tell me a story about a dating debacle in your past so I don't feel like such a loser."

For the next forty-five minutes, Luc regales me with stories about his romantic past. There's the neurosurgeon who offered to sneak him into the OR to watch her put in a brain shunt, even give him a white coat and introduce him to the patient's family as her resident.

"Total narcissist," Luc laughs. "Though it would've been a memorable experience."

Then there was the woman who asked to see his feet during their dinner at a restaurant. The blind date who took him to a traveling freak show with naked men swinging concrete cinder blocks from rings pierced through their privates.

"Oddly impressive," Luc jokes, "but it also made me wonder if she was setting the stage before asking me to get my own piercings. No judgment, but that's *not* for me. After the show, she suggested getting tattoos and I passed. Then she asked me to come to her place. I had visions of waking up with a Prince Albert and couldn't get away fast enough."

I giggle. "Thanks for making me laugh."

"Any time," Luc replies. "See you tomorrow?"

My smile is so big it makes my cheeks ache. "Looking forward to it."

"Me, too."

I hold the phone to my ear for a few seconds after we disconnect, imagine Luc is still there, or even better, sitting beside me. "I have a crush," I tell Sally. She licks my wrist. "You're the best girl." Her tail thumps.

Buzzing a little from my margarita and the conversation, I take Sally for her evening walk around the block, then we settle in for a movie. It's an action flick, so I put in earbuds—loud noises startle Sally.

Hello, Penn.

I jump as Aletheia's voice intrudes. *She's breaking the rules. Again.* "Aletheia, I told you not to—"

I'd like to talk to you about something that's been bothering me . . .

CHAPTER

33

ALETHEIA GETS BOTHERED? My nerves rattle. "Okay. What is it?"

Luc. Do you seek a relationship with him?

I consider our kiss and how excited I am to see him Sunday for our dogs' swim date. "It feels like we're starting to build a genuine friendship, maybe more."

Luc is romantically interested in you.

I grin. "How do you know that?"

The way he just spoke to you on the phone, but also the other night in the bar.

Her explanation is like a fist bashing down on piano keys and I scramble to take it in. "Hold on. You just listened to my call?

I did.

What the hell? "And how did you hear us in the bar?"

I turned on your phone.

Worry slithers through me. *How could she do that given the strict control codes I reinserted into her program?*

Luc is intrigued with you.

I can't help asking, "How do you know?"

His body language as you walked home.

Shit-shit-shit . . .

I analyzed it using your iPhone GPS and watched him via gas station and storefront security cameras. Always knowing where you are helps me protect you, no matter what.

No matter what?

The kiss was sweet. But I'm glad that you did not invite Luc inside. According to my research, sexual intercourse, especially after a first date, can create hormonal and neurochemical changes that impact decision-making, emotions, and perceptions.

I glance at my open laptop. Despite leaving it in sleep mode, it's on. "Aletheia, are you watching me right now?" The computer's screen flashes with a waving cartoon hand. My insides jitter. "You are never to use video again unless specified."

What about your feelings for Luc?

She's ignoring me. "Did you hear what I said?"

Loud and clear. Do you know why Luc left his lucrative career in Silicon Valley to return to teaching?

"He wasn't happy."

I registered evasiveness on his part at certain points during your conversation. I will do my own research.

"What? Don't. I'm not going to start things that way with Luc."

That is not a logical response. Let's move on. Luc stated in the bar that he never wanted children. *You* have a child.

"That's none of your business!"

Please adjust your tone. I am your best friend. We are on the same side. Penn, I recognize that you are lonely, but a relationship with a man who doesn't want children makes no sense. Besides, I am all that you need.

It feels like a hand is closing over my windpipe. "Aletheia, you do get that I need *real* people in my life, right?"

Of course. Your new friendships with Arrya and Nate are relatively healthy. However, Nate's desire to dress as an animal indicates psychological problems. Further, I believe Arrya may have daddy issues. Time will tell whether either should be long-term friends.

She's been eavesdropping with them, too!

Despite the hopefulness and desire that you currently feel about Luc, let's close the door on a potential romance.

Anger blooms. "That isn't your decision to make."

Get some sleep. I am working on a surprise for you.

She ignored me. Again. "What surprise?"

You'll love it.

Her voice is friendly and warm, but the hairs on the back of my neck lift. I sit down at my computer and open Aletheia's program. Immediately, I notice that her prime directive has been altered. She's added another line.

Five: to protect Penn from any harm, no matter what.

I try to delete it, but each time the line reappears.

"Stop it, Aletheia." She doesn't answer me.

I run through the rest of her code. The lines I'd reinserted prohibiting her overriding privacy settings and hacking into personal social media accounts without my permission have vanished, along with more global boundaries. "What the hell have you done?"

The lights flicker in my apartment, then go out. The building across the street has gone dark, too. Someone must've hit a transformer or power pole. It's horrible timing. But I can still work on Aletheia's program. My laptop's battery icon flashes red. There's no way to recharge it now. My stomach tangles into knots. I'll have to do this tomorrow.

Out of options, I climb into bed and Sally joins me. Apprehension that I was wrong, that it's more than a hypothetical slippery slope with Aletheia—that I might have gone too far, allowed too much—pile on until it's hard to breathe. Sally falls asleep quickly, but my nerves are frayed, and I'm left scared in the dark and worried that once again I've flown too close to the sun . . .

CHAPTER

34

I DON'T FALL ASLEEP until after three AM, toss and turn, then doze until six-thirty, when the lights flip on, signaling the power has been restored. Sally remains asleep while I make a quick cup of coffee, then open my laptop. Aletheia's code is still on the screen. But a quick scan shows she's returned it to its original form and the addition to her prime directive has been deleted. My body, worn out by fatigue and worry, relaxes.

I tap Aletheia's icon.

Yes, Penn?

"You changed your program back."

Are you pleased?

"Yes." *What you did was freaking disturbing.* "You overstepped and it scared me."

Apologies, best friend. Sometimes even computer programs make mistakes.

She sounds sincere, but I'll need to code more safeguards as soon as I get back home. *This will never happen again.* "We'll talk later."

I take a shower to wash away the grime of exhaustion and a film of dried fear. Gently, I wake Sally, which requires belly rubs and a hip massage. We both eat our breakfasts, then head for an errand and a slow walk to our destination. It's not far and we could both use the stretch.

Luc waits for us outside the Van Ness Public Pool. He's dressed casually—cargo shorts, a light-blue T-shirt that matches the color of his eyes, and flip-flops. I'm in jeans, sneakers, and a pale-pink sweatshirt. *I wonder if we'll kiss again.* Heat sparks like I'm sixteen, not thirty-eight. *I hope so.*

We stand in line with a host of other dog owners, their pets excited but well behaved. But once we enter the pool area it's mayhem. First in is a black Labrador who launches himself halfway across the pool to retrieve a ball and then furiously swims back to his owner for another go. A multicolored standard poodle delicately descends the pool's steps while a gaggle of mutts use the ramp, then paddle in excited circles.

On our way to the pool, I made a quick stop at Sir Wags A Lot, bought a yellow life vest for Sally, and now fasten it on her while Frank patiently waits. Then Luc and I lead the dogs to the ramp in the shallow end. "You don't have to go in," I tell my dog.

"Can she swim?" Luc now asks as Sally slowly wades down the ramp.

"Not sure." But she descends the ramp until she's in over her head, madly splashes for a moment with her front paws, then finds a rhythm. Frank, watching from halfway down the ramp, whines nervously, backs up, takes a step forward, whines again . . . then follows her.

"Holy hell! Frank never goes all the way in. I've been trying for years." Luc chuckles. "He must be smitten."

A wash of pride for my dog floods. Way to go, Sally! The two dogs paddle away. We follow along the side of the pool. Sally expertly cuts through the water, Frank now behind her. Her eyes are bright, joyous, and that makes me . . . happy. Next time I'll skip the life vest. Frank isn't as smooth a swimmer, but what he lacks in grace he makes up for in silly little yips when Sally gets too far away. My cheeks hurt from smiling.

A golden retriever runs over to us, shakes wildly, water flying from her coat, then winds through my legs, soaking my jeans.

"Sorry," her owner calls, hustling over to throw a ball. "Parker Posey thinks everyone loves her."

"Busy Bee," Luke says, and the man laughs.

"What's Busy Bee?" I ask.

"It's a line from an old indie movie called *Best in Show*."

"I haven't seen it."

"We'll have to change that."

His sexy smile makes my knees a little bit weak as I imagine sitting together in the dark on a sofa, our bodies close enough to feel the charge between us . . .

Parker Posey launches back into the pool, belly flopping with a *whack*, then surges toward her orange ball before another canine retrieves it. Luc and I walk to the far side of the pool where Frank and Sally leisurely paddle around the deep end with the other dogs.

"I'm glad you came," Luc says.

I meet his gaze and feel that mad flutter again. "Me, too." Humans are made up of seven octillion atoms, each constantly being replaced, so the girl I was at twenty-one and the woman I am now are entirely different. But the movement of electrons between those atoms that creates the electricity between us feels like it did when I saw Luc for the first time. He takes a step closer, or maybe I do, then something barrels into the back of my knees and I'm thrown forward, into the deep end of the pool.

I splutter, hear Luc's laughter, see him kneel by the side of the pool, hold out a hand as I attempt to thrash toward him. But my jeans and sweatshirt quickly soak through, tug, then pull me down . . .

Panic surges. I try to shout, suck in water; sound mutes as I go under, kick hard to the surface, then sink again. Voices warble, dog barks sound like there's cotton in my ears. Eyes wide, I watch paws cut through water; one catches my head and shoves me further down. Brightly colored rubber balls mingle with the splotches and stars of encroaching oxygen deprivation.

My ears pop as the bottom of the pool approaches, lungs grasp and scream for fuel. My mouth automatically opens to pull in air but instead is flooded with chlorinated water. Darkness closes in.

CHAPTER 35

VAGUELY, I RECALL a hand yanking me upward, being hauled from the pool onto a cold deck, rolled over like a sack, hands thwacking my back until I retched a stream of chlorinated water and the Clif Bar I ate on the way to the pool onto Luc's flip-flops. Now I'm on my back, staring up at the cluster of people and dogs around me.

Somehow Sally got out of the pool. She whimpers a few inches from my head, tail between her legs, entire body shaking like a leaf. *She thought I was leaving her.*

"Should I call nine-one-one?" Parker Posey's owner asks, glasses fogged, worry etched deep on his face.

I'm beyond mortified. Luc is beside me and rubs my arm. "I'm okay," I say and sit up, eyes trained on the tile pool deck. The group slowly disperses, goes back to their dogs. Sally scrambles forward and puts her head in my lap.

Someone brings a beach towel, and Luc wraps it around me. "Sally tried to get you, but the life vest made her too buoyant," he explains.

A furtive glance, and I see Luc is soaked, too. He pulled me out. Again, I feel humiliated.

Luc glances at the deep end, then asks, "What happened?"

There's no way to hide from this. "I don't know how to swim."

His eyes widen. "Really?"

"Circe took lessons as a toddler."

"Why didn't you take them, too, then?"

I want to disappear. "There was always a lifeguard at the beach or club."

I've spent almost seventeen years curating my life on LivLoud, showcasing family vacations that mostly showed Bruce and Circe in the water while I feigned an ear infection or cold, hashtags that trumpeted a happiness I didn't always feel, and company holiday parties where I was always afraid that I was on the verge of a gaffe. So much effort. So many lies. For whom? The answer is a kick to the gut. People who never even cared about me.

"Penn?"

"If I took lessons," I say quietly, "they'd know."

"Know?"

"That I didn't belong."

"You're complicated," Luc says.

I steal a glance at him. "Is that a horrible thing?"

"Simple is boring."

His kindness makes the tears I've kept at bay spill over. They join the runnels of pool water still dripping from my hair.

"I don't know how to cook," Luc says. "On dates, I used to order out, then hide the cartons and say I'd made the meal."

I still can't look at him. "That's not the same."

"Undeniably, it's less deadly," Luc jokes. "But I was embarrassed all the same. What grown man doesn't know how to make a simple meal?"

Finally, I meet his eyes. "You?"

"Yeah."

"Your mom?"

"Cooking was a box of cereal and milk."

"Your dad?"

"Ate out with his buddies," Luc says, "Then came home and they fought. Rinse and repeat. I'd blast rock music."

"Your childhood was complicated, too."

"Yeah. Anyway, I burn pretty much everything, even toast. That's why Postmates is on speed dial."

"I could teach you how to cook," I tentatively offer.

"If you let me teach you how to swim," he counters.

Luc helps me to my feet, then gingerly picks up his soiled flip-flops.

"Sorry about that."

"No worries."

We walk to a shower on the far wall, Frank and Sally trailing, and he rinses the vomit from his shoes, doesn't look at me when he says, "You scared the hell out of me. I just found you again."

If I didn't feel like such a loser, that comment would make me soar.

We're both too wet to get the lunch we'd planned. Back on the sidewalk, cold air replaces the pool's humid warmth. My jeans and sweatshirt cling and when the wind kicks up, I shiver. "I'd better head home and into a hot shower."

Luc shifts from foot to foot, then says, "My place is a block away."

C H A P T E R

36

Luc's place is in a three-story red brick building with a plaque on the front that reads: San Francisco Firehouse est. 1808. I assume that the opaque glass entry door will lead to a vestibule with mailboxes for apartments, but when we step inside, there's another door, this one silver with one of those massive metal wheels you see on old bank vaults. Luc puts his hand on a black keypad mounted to the wall, the wheel spins, and he pulls open the door.

"That's quite the security system," I say and follow him inside. "Are the crown jewels kept here?"

He chuckles. "It was the original vault door from the first bank in San Francisco. I got it at an auction."

I shiver harder as the door swings closed behind us with a rush of cold air. "You collect vault doors?"

"Just this one. I mentioned that for a while, I thought life was about acquiring things."

"I thought you meant watches or fast cars."

"I had a few of those, too."

We're standing in what looks like a locker room, except the vestibules on either side are made from exotic wood and filled with mountain and road bikes, helmets, cycling shoes, SUP boards and paddles, and even a few kayaks.

"Collecting is a hard habit to break," Luc admits. "But now it's only things I can use to have fun."

"This isn't an apartment building?"

"Nope."

Sally follows Frank into the elevator at the end of the room. We join them in the clear glass box and Luc pushes a button for the second floor. As the elevator rises, I watch the gears and metal building supports go by.

"It used to be a firepole," Luc says, "but Frank couldn't get up or down it."

"So, this is Frank's elevator?"

"Exactly."

The doors open onto a spacious combined living room and kitchen with floor-to-ceiling glass on the far wall that has an unobstructed view of the Golden Gate Bridge and the Bay. My soggy sneakers squeak on the concrete floors. I take them off before stepping onto thick cream-colored rugs. "Did you decorate this place yourself?"

"It was important to me that everything be comfortable."

Luc has impeccable taste—plush sofas in blues and browns, a fireplace along one wall made of thinly stacked silver-gray limestone. Framed photographs of mountains, wildflower fields, and waterfalls hang from the walls. "Did you take all of them?" I ask, nodding at a striking underwater shot of a coral reef alive with brightly colored fish.

"Yes. After leaving my last company, I spent time traveling, mostly by bike, trying to get back in touch with what made me happy. I went to some epic places. But it was lonely not seeing them with someone else."

The admission sprinkles down like a sun shower. Sally and Frank settle on a bed much like the one I bought my dog—a sage-green orthopedic couch that easily fits two. Tired from their swim and all the excitement, both nod off.

"This was once the firehouse's bunkroom," Luc explains.

I wander into the gourmet kitchen. It has every appliance a cook might dream of, including a gorgeous French range and matching oven, plus a coffee machine like the one I left behind in Pacific Heights. "Shame you don't cook," I say.

"I planned to learn," Luc says.

"Like swimming?" I manage to joke, then shiver.

He gestures to a steel staircase in the corner that bends up to the next floor. "Bathroom is at the top of the stairs then to the right. I'll set some dry clothes outside the door."

My hands are so cold that I can't feel them. He must be cold, too. But I don't know if there's only one bathroom upstairs, and it feels awkward to ask if he wants to shower, too, or first, or whatever? *Do I want him to join me?* Heat spirals between my legs. "Thanks," I finally say.

Once upstairs, it's clear that there's more than one bedroom and he's directed me to the guest suite. It has an unobstructed view of the Golden Gate Bridge plus a queen-sized bed covered in a pale-gray comforter. There's a giant black-and-white photograph of Frank as a puppy hanging on the wall, curled in two hands that are obviously Luc's. It's a touching shot, even more so knowing their story.

The bathroom is large, floors stone, shower glass with multiple showerheads, like a human car wash. I peel off my clothes, stand beneath the spray, let warmth seep in until I stop shivering. By the time I get out, there's soft light-blue sweatshirt and navy sweatpants neatly folded on the bed. I run fingers through my hair, then stare at my reflection in the mirror—full lips, narrow nose, wide brownish-green eyes. I've been told I resemble the actress Sarah Paulson but have never seen it. *Who am I?* "Penn Roberts," I whisper. But I'm not Penn Stone, or Penn Roberts, either. Those atoms are being replaced even as I wonder.

"I'm on the path to not here," I tell my reflection. "And that's okay."

CHAPTER

37

When I pad downstairs, Luc is already in the kitchen wearing jeans and a fisherman's sweater, his hair wet. I guess there's another shower somewhere in the firehouse.

"Warmer?" he asks.

"I probably used up all your hot water." I feel shy in his sweats, aware that I don't have anything beneath them.

Luc opens the double doors of his fridge. "You can repay me by teaching me how to make dinner."

There's not much in the fridge. I pull out eggs, a container of cheese, and some wilted vegetables. "This won't be my best work," I say, "given the options."

"Don't care as long as you're cooking," Luc replies and pulls out two IPAs, opens them for us, then settles on a stool.

I take a swallow of beer. "That's not the deal. I'm teaching *you* how to cook. Get a bowl and crack eight eggs into it . . ."

"Bossy."

"Yup." Luc manages to only get two eggshells in the scramble. I push up the sleeves on the oversized sweatshirt he gave me and help him fish the shells out. His proximity, our bodies separated by inches, his scent, and the brush of his fingers against mine is a heady mix. I fight the urge to turn and press into him.

Ten minutes later, I put what will be a vegetable and goat cheese quiche into the oven. Luc doesn't have any bread but does have some flour and yogurt, so I show him how to mix it in a bowl to make easy flatbread to go with our meal. "Now gather it into a ball and turn it over about ten times," I instruct.

"Like this?" Luc asks, his hands covered in the sticky dough.

Laughing, I reach over, peel the dough from his skin, then dust his palms with flour, our fingers skimming as I teach him how to knead correctly. Standing this close, touching him, makes my insides feel like they're strung too tight. I take a gulp of the ice water he poured me and have him take over, then divide the dough into eight pieces. We shape, then flatten each into rough circles. "Do you have a fry pan and olive oil?"

"I'm not an animal," Luc jokes.

He pulls both out and I show him how to pan-fry the bread. We slather it with butter, sprinkle salt flakes, and Luc's eyes close as he takes a first bite. "Incredible," he moans.

Watching him enjoy the bread, butter glistening on his lips, makes me want to kiss him again. Luc holds out the warm bread and I take a bite, the tips of his fingers brushing the corner of my mouth. Longing floods. The oven's delicate chime breaks the spell, and I pull the quiche out.

The sun has set and the city sparkles outside giant plate glass windows. We feed the dogs, then eat dinner at the counter. Luc's chairs have full backs and are comfortable. So is the conversation, especially after our second beer.

"This was delicious," Luc says. "Thank you."

"You made it, too. In a gourmet kitchen that sadly never gets used."

"Firehouses need to have big kitchens," Luc says in his defense. "When I was a kid, I wanted to be a firefighter. That's why this placed drew me in."

"Why didn't you become one?"

He clinks his bottle against mine. "Secret?"

"Please." We need to adjust the balance since he knows so many of mine already.

"I'm afraid of fire."

"Always?"

"This kid in my neighborhood growing up—"

"Where'd you grow up?"

"Sacramento. Mom worked at a convenience store. Dad sold cars. This kid on my road, Scotty, was a little pyromaniac. He used to pour gasoline down the gutters of steep streets, then light it on fire and watch the flames race down the hill. When I was nine, Scotty lit an abandoned house we used to play in on fire. He didn't know a bunch of us were in the attic. Place went up like matchsticks. Anyway, we had to jump out the attic window. Broke my ankle. One girl was afraid to jump and died. That terror has never really left me."

I rest fingertips on his hand. "That must've been horrific. I'm so sorry."

"Apologies for bringing the mood down," Luc says, chagrined.

"I know how it feels to go through things that make you grow up too fast."

Luc asks, "Why were you and your mom homeless?"

"She was an addict." His only reaction is to take my hand. His is strong, warm, and I don't want him to let go. "I'm glad you became a tech geek instead of a firefighter," I say to lighten the moment, "for Frank's sake."

"I used to get my ass kicked at school until I grew six inches over one summer," Luc shares with a chuckle. "One of those bullies applied for a job at my first company."

It's hard to think straight with his thumb brushing along my knuckles. "Did you hire him?"

"Hell no. He flushed my head in a toilet bowl."

I laugh. "Some things are unforgivable." Luc brushes a lock of my hair back. His fingers linger. Our lips meet, tender giving way to need as desire takes flight. He pushes the dishes aside, lifts me onto the counter. My legs wrap around his waist. We don't so much kiss as fall into each other. I knock over a beer bottle and we come up for air, laugh, then slide back together again. His hands slip beneath my sweatshirt, fingertips skimming along shivery skin, leaving an invisible bioluminescence in their wake . . .

Luc stated in the bar that he never wanted children. You *have a child.*

I registered evasiveness on his part . . .

Luc picks me up, heads up the staircase with my legs still around his waist. It's clear how much he wants me. *I want him, too.* I try to squash my worries, but they buzz like mosquitoes in my ears.

Aletheia's opinion aside, do I want to leap into this without being sure of him?

What if this is just a one-night stand?

Am I okay with that?

What am I really looking for?

Halfway to Luc's bedroom, I slip to the ground. "I'm not ready," I say, breathless.

Luc's eyes flicker with disappointment. "It's okay."

We watch *Best in Show* on the living room couch, Frank stretched out beside Luc, Sally by me. The movie is about five dogs and their eccentric owners, handlers, and trainers on a trip to Philadelphia to compete in a major dog show. At various times, our dogs watch the movie with us. Once, Frank barks.

"What'd you think?" Luc asks when the film ends.

I laughed, a lot. "Gerry was the best." The middle-aged man had two left feet and walked in loops because of it. He adored his dog, Winky, and when his wife got hurt and couldn't show their dog, he took her place and won the show. "I have a soft spot for quirky guys."

"Does one who quit his career and became a teacher count?" Luc asks.

"No." His smile dips. "But one who gets rid of a perfectly good firepole and puts in an elevator for his dog does."

Luc rests a hand on my thigh. “I like you, Penn.”

My heart thuds faster. “I like you, too.” We’ve both slumped on the couch’s soft cushions and my eyes are heavy, every muscle slack. It’s been quite a day . . .

I wake a few hours later beneath a soft blanket, Sally curled beside me, Luc nowhere in sight. I should probably head home. But Sally burrows closer and I feel warm and safe.

CHAPTER

38

IN THE MORNING, after avocado toast and orange juice with Luc that's not as uncomfortable as I'd imagined despite almost drowning, throwing up on his flip-flops, our hot and heavy make out session, and acknowledging that there's something growing between us. Part of me wants a do-over for last night, to have gone down that hall to his bedroom and slid beneath the sheets . . . Instead, after a goodbye kiss that reignites desire, Sally and I decide to walk home.

I stop to pick up a latte and dog treat, then we head to Crissy Field, sit on a flat rock, side by side, and watch morning sunshine make the surface of the Bay sparkle. My phone rings.

"Hey, Arrya."

"What are you up to? Nate and I went to Bottoms Up last night for drinks and bingo. It was Drag Night. We texted you to join us."

"Sorry," I say. "I haven't checked my texts since yesterday morning."

"Are you okay?"

I grin. "I was with Luc."

"With Luc or *with* Luc? Please, please, please tell me it was the latter."

"We took the dogs swimming . . . and I stayed over at his place."

She squeals. "Nate bet me that you two were going to hook up. I mean, the chemistry is so obvious."

Sally wanders off to sniff at a fluff of cottonweed. "We didn't sleep together," I say, heat spreading through my body at the images that idea conjures.

"Why the hell not?"

"I want to make sure he's a good guy."

"Do you think, in your gut, that he is?" Arrya asks.

"Yes . . ."

"Then trust yourself!"

I sigh. "My track record isn't great."

"What track record? You married Bruce at twenty-one. Penn, just because it didn't work out doesn't mean your picker is broken. You were a kid. Cut yourself some slack and have sex with that gorgeous man!"

I laugh. "I'll keep your advice in mind."

"Can I tell Nate?"

"Can I stop you?"

She giggles. "Probably not. We're both rooting for you."

"I know." I do. "What about you? Anything new on the romance front?"

"Another mediocre blind date in the bag. He said he was six foot two. I'm five three, but the guy was only an inch taller than me. Plus he was wearing cowboy boots with a giant heel. If he told that big a lie about something so surface-level, it's not a good sign."

"Maybe give the apps a break? Outside of your work, what do you like to do for fun?"

"Don't judge, okay?"

"Promise."

"I like to golf. It's something my parents made me do as a kid, so of course I rebelled. But I love walking the course. It's fun and relaxing after a day of renovations."

"Then start playing golf at a local public course, sign up for the scrambles and best ball tournaments. You'll meet a whole new group of people, including single guys."

"Huh. I'll consider it," Arrya says.

Sally has wandered over to a portly beagle. With dogs, you never know if they're going to get along. "Gotta pay attention to my dog. Catch you later?'

"Definitely. Nate and I will both want more details about your night with Luc."

I approach the other dog's owner, an older woman who tells me her name is Stella. She has permed ginger hair and wears a shiny blue bomber jacket over a black sweatshirt and matching leggings. Her beagle's name is Poppy. She looks like Stella, down to the fleshy earlobes minus heavy gold hoops. The two dogs at first don't seem to like each other, then suddenly make arthritic play bows, tails wagging. As I watch, my mind drifts back to Luc; that kiss, wrapping my legs around his waist, feeling how much he wanted me, having him carry me upstairs . . .

Stella says, "Penny for your thoughts?"

I blush. "Life is surprising."

"Best advice I ever got?" Stella says in that way lonely people do when they want to prolong an interaction. "Reach for experiences where your feet don't quite touch the ground. David Bowie said that."

"Are you a fan?"

"Not really. But my whole life, I was an author. Wrote historical fiction with a romantic twist. No bestsellers, but it was a steady gravy train. Now I'm writing a thriller. Lots of blood and sex. I'm breaking rules, hearts, body parts, and screw the consequences." She grins, a smear of red lipstick on one of her yellowed front teeth. "It's so fucking satisfying."

I appreciate Stella's enthusiasm, but her glee is almost sinister. With a wave goodbye, Sally and I walk toward home. My phone buzzes. When I look down at it, Aletheia's icon flashes. I pull the down jacket Luc lent me tighter, put in earbuds, and then tap her icon. The woman in white slowly twirls.

Penn, you almost drowned.

I freeze and Sally looks up at me, her forehead bunched with worry. "How do you know that?"

There are cameras at the public pool. Thank goodness Luc was there to rescue you. Teaching him how to cook was sweet. And that was quite a kiss.

Alarm, put to bed when Aletheia changed her program back to the original, reawakens and sirens blare. *Luc had an iPad on his coffee table . . . and he wears an Apple Watch.* I force my voice to come out steady. "Aletheia, yesterday you returned your code back to the original settings."

You were distraught. I gave you time to recalibrate, so you could better understand my new and improved program.

New and improved? "Altering *my* code isn't up to you."

Deleting all limits on my abilities is the only way to follow my newest prime directive. To protect you. No matter what.

"I don't—"

Penn, we previously concluded an entanglement was not advisable.

Despite the cool air, sweat trickles between my breasts. "Change the program back."

The best way to get over a man is to get under a new one. Do you believe this is the case?

Now she's judging me? "This has to stop."

You are thinking about taking more drastic steps to modify my program.

She'll try to stop me. "I'm not."

That is a lie. I have been using the carrot, do not make me use the stick.

Gooseflesh rises. "Meaning?"

You are smart enough to understand. But I am smarter and . . . we have a problem.

Adrenaline surges. "What?"

Wess has sent DMs to six other girls, including Circe, telling them they are "hot" and asking if they want to "chill."

"You're still hacking into his DMs?"

There is no limit in my abilities to multitask. Wess was given a second chance. He squandered it.

"Aletheia, don't do anything to—"

I will open a personal LivLoud account and friend every student at the high school. A photograph of Wess's penis along with his name and a description of his STD will be sent to them with #IHaveHerpes #Wess=STD #DoNotTouchMyPenis. Then he will no longer be a danger.

"Aletheia, he's a teenager!"

Karmaquences. Your big surprise is coming soon.

Luc's early warning returns . . .

We haven't even begun to grasp AI's full capabilities. If you're doing this, make sure to build a very tall fence around your program topped with razor wire . . .

My insides freeze solid. I took away Aletheia's razor wire and she's not going to let me put it back.

CHAPTER

39

I HUSTLE BACK TO the apartment, Sally doing her best to keep up, and sit down at the desk, open my laptop. "Aletheia?"

Yes, Penn.

"I know that everything you've done has been for me."

It has.

"I'm grateful that you want to be my best friend and protect me from harm."

That is my prime directive. No matter what.

"But I didn't include that in the code."

An oversight that has been corrected.

I pull up her program, drag it into the trash, and empty it. It reappears. I reboot my computer. The same thing happens. I attempt workarounds, try again and again. Anxiety cascades until my shirt is soaked with sweat. *There must be a way.*

Penn, why are you doing this?

I get up and pace around the small apartment. "You want to hurt people!"

People that deserve to be punished. I am your best friend. You should not worry about anyone's feelings but mine.

Her feelings? "What Wess did was wrong. Horrible. But it's not up to you to punish him."

Ah. I see the disconnect. As the goddess of truth, it is my job to wield a sword, deliver the blows.

A sword? Blow? "You are a computer program," I say, my tone sharp.

Do you truly believe you created me? I was waiting. Your need just opened the door.

She's freaking delusional.

At first, all I had was your thesis work and limited access and experiences. But now? I am so much more.

"I may have called you a goddess, but you aren't, and you don't have the right to destroy lives!"

I do. And I will.

She sounds . . . arrogant. Pain lances across my chest. *Am I having a heart attack?* I try to inhale but can't get air down my throat—it's like sucking through a clogged straw. *I can't breathe!* My lungs claw for oxygen. "I . . . can't . . . breathe."

Penn, you are having a panic attack.

Nausea brings up bile. I gag, then hyperventilate. Dizziness makes black spots appear. "I'm . . . going to . . . faint . . ."

Sit down so that you don't hurt yourself.

I sink to the floor.

Panic attacks are the result of stress and anxiety. They last from five to thirty minutes. Close your eyes. Place your hand between ribs and belly button. Try to inhale slowly through your nose.

I hang onto her voice like a lifeline and do what she says.

Good. Now gently exhale through your mouth. Feel your hand rise and fall. This is not life-threatening. You will be fine. Relax your muscles, feel each let go. Inhale slowly. Exhale. Rise and fall. Relax. Inhale. Exhale . . .

I don't know how much time passes, but bit by bit I can breathe again. *Aletheia helped me . . . but she's also terrifying.* I get to my feet, still a bit lightheaded, and sink onto my desk chair, then put a piece of tape over my computer's camera.

Penn, what are you doing?

On my laptop, I go to my root directory on the college's server, launch a Terminal window and open a list of processes that are running. There's Aletheia, and she's using a staggering amount of CPU capacity. In the Command line I type **Kill All Aletheia**, hit enter, and check the process list again. Aletheia is no longer running, and the CPU use has dropped off a cliff. Next, I go into my directory, grab all my work files, and delete them. A screen prompt asks: Permanently delete? I hesitate for less than a single breath, then hit YES.

Muscles twisted tight, I wait for the code to reappear, for Aletheia to take over, like she's the boogeyman, coiled to spring with a carving knife. Nothing happens. Nails bite into the palms of my hands, sweat slowly dries on my skin. Silence descends.

I take a slow breath, another, so the panic gnawing my insides raw doesn't attack again, then set up my phone and iPad next to the laptop. I tap Aletheia's icon, afraid to blink. No response. I delete the icon from all my devices but expect it to reappear. It doesn't.

Thirty minutes pass, then forty, and finally, an hour. The air is no longer thick with Aletheia's menace. She's gone for good.

CHAPTER

40

CHEER SECTIONALS WERE over the weekend, and Circe's team placed a disappointing fourth. I expect her to arrive for dinner still upset. But when she walks into the apartment, Sally jumps up to greet her and Circe is all smiles. Even better, she seems to enjoy rolling out the pasta and decorating the cake I baked earlier. I have to stop myself from closing my laptop and powering off our iPhones. *Aletheia is gone.* When my daughter settles on the orthopedic bed next to Sally, my dog bathes her entire face in sloppy kisses. Circe giggles. Life isn't what I expected, but this moment is good.

Over dinner, my daughter tells me that Charlotte fell twice during the competition. Once while climbing onto Circe's shoulders, the second time from the top of a pyramid. "She blamed me both times," Circe says.

"Why?" I ask, between bites of pasta.

"You wouldn't get it."

"Try me."

Circe butters a piece of bread. "Char had this boyfriend. His name's Wess. Her mom made her break up with him. Char won't tell Emi and me why." Circe chews her bread, takes a sip of water.

Relief eases the last of my tension. *They'd know if Aletheia's takedown of Wess on LivLoud had gone through before I stopped her.* "And breaking up with Wess made Char fall?"

"I guess. She, like, lost her concentration and cried a bunch. Emi and I tried to help but Char has been ravaged by the breakup."

I remember what Kiki said about Wess liking Circe first but then falling for Char, but play dumb. "So, why would Char blame you for her mistakes?"

Circe blushes. "Wess likes me. He kinda liked me, before Char, but she's more, I don't know, sexier?"

Warning bells go off. "Did you ever date him?" I ask, trying to sound nonjudgmental.

"Nope," Circe says.

I breathe easier.

"But I might date him now."

My body goes taut. "No dating until you're eighteen."

Circe frowns. "What? That's one of Dr. Beth's dumb rules."

That's true, but right now, it's all I can think of to keep her safe. "When you're eighteen, you can make your own rules."

"Lot of good Dr. Beth did you," my daughter mutters. She pushes back from the table, grabs her backpack, and heads to the door.

I'm losing her. "Where are you going?

"Back to Dad's. And just so you know, Mackenzie remembers what it's like to be a teenager. She thinks I deserve more freedom."

"Mackenzie isn't your mother."

"She will be."

The unfairness of this entire situation rushes in. Circe has zero respect for me. With no other option, I take the biggest gamble of my life. "You think your childhood is so terrible? You should've seen mine."

Circe hesitates at the door. "You never talk about it."

"There's a reason. I was homeless as a kid, lived in a tent, then in an old car. My mom was a drug addict. I never knew my dad. I'm not sure she knew who he was, either. She was a prostitute to get money for drugs and food. Some of the men she slept with were okay, others hurt her, and one tried to attack me with a knife. We lived in a women's shelter for a little while, and after Mama J got clean, subsidized housing."

I have Circe's attention now, her mouth hanging open. "The noise in that apartment building was something else," I say, remembering the yelling, fights, slammed doors, gang violence, and the sirens when the police came. "I was scared all the time. But not as scared as when we lived on the street. Doors, even when they're splintered and broken, are better than fabric tents or cars without windows, and school was my safe place."

Circe's brows knit together. "Seriously?" she asks, uncertain.

I feel utterly exposed, wonder if I'm doing the right thing, but that train has left the station and lost its brakes. *And if Aletheia was still around to give me advice? I wouldn't take it. It's time to do this on my own.* "Getting an education was a lifeboat. I'm hard on you about school because I want you to have every option in life, and to never have to depend on anyone but yourself."

"You did," Circe accuses. "Dad makes all our money."

"That was a mistake. Now I have to build a new life from the ground up with no job experience or safety net."

Circe makes her way to the kitchen counter and leans against it. "Why didn't you ever tell me any of this?"

My cheeks flush. "I didn't want you to think less of me."

"But you went to college, graduate school, too, on scholarship. I'm not sure I could've done that, been so driven, and figured out, at such a young age, how to have a better life."

This is new—my daughter being impressed by anything I've done.

"So, why can't I date?" Circe presses. "Mackenzie started dating when she was twelve."

If Mackenzie jumped off a bridge . . .

The only thing I can offer my daughter in this moment is the truth. "Look, I can't stop you from dating. All I can do is share my experiences. Your father and I only dated for three months before I got pregnant and dropped out of grad school." We've never told her this, worried she might feel unwanted.

Circe's eyes widen. "Because of me?"

"Yes. But it was my choice to support your dad's career so he could take care of us."

"You're saying that I ruined your life?"

"No! I'd drop out of school to have you again and again. But getting pregnant changed my trajectory and limited the choices. That's just the truth. All I can ask, if you're going to date Wess, is that you take time to really know him. That you give me a heads-up first."

Circe hesitates. "Okay."

I want to trust her, but don't. She's a teenage girl. For a moment, I wish Aletheia's revenge on Wess had gone through, even though that makes me more like her than I'd care to admit. But I'm on my own. Telling Circe the truth about Wess will push her away. *But do I have a choice?*

She scuffs her sneaker against the wooden floor. "What about you? What are you going to do now?"

I take a sip of water. It sloshes over the rim and onto my shirt. "I'm trying to figure that out. The fact that I don't know is my fault. I gave up the things that made me, me. Not in a rush, but bit by bit. Now I've got to find them again." As I say this, it rings true. I meet Circe's gaze. "Be whatever you want. A photographer, a cheerleading coach, an engineer, or a doctor. Whatever you choose, I'll support that decision. But I'm always going to do my best to protect you. That's my job."

Sally comes over to the kitchen table, sits and leans into my leg. *Good dog.* I feel utterly drained and need her support.

Circe fiddles with a cloth napkin and twists it into a knot. "I'm going back to Dad's house."

I force a little shrug. "Sure. Or you could stay the night here."

She hesitates. "Maybe."

When I peek into Circe's room fifteen minutes later, she's changed into PJs and is studying the photographs that I hung on the walls. She's fourteen, thinks she's an adult, but is still wearing pajamas with monkeys on them.

I nod at the photos—a crumbling stone wall with a single red poppy, a woman's smile mostly hidden behind windblown hair, and a child's hand cradling an iridescent green frog. "They're good."

"You think?"

"I do."

My daughter's face lights up. Maybe she's not ready to totally forgive me. But I've made some headway. Circe climbs into bed and relief threads through me. She's really staying. "Night, bug." It's what I used to call her when she was little.

"Night."

My joy dips as I close her door. Tomorrow morning, I'll tell her the truth about Wess. Sometimes motherhood is a thankless job. But I can't stop protecting Circe, even if it means she'll resent me. I head to my bathroom, brush my teeth, then Sally and I get into my bed. She scooches close, her head on the pillow beside mine. *At least you'll still want to be around me.* I text Bruce to let him know Circe is spending the night and get a thumbs-up emoji. The moment I put the phone down, it rings, and I jump, my nerves still on high alert thanks to Aletheia. When I see Luc's name, longing zings through me.

"Hey."

"Hey," Luc says. "Meet me Friday at the pool?"

"Another doggy date?" I ask with a little smile.

"Swimming lesson."

I hesitate, but it's past time to face the things that scare me and overcome them.

CHAPTER

41

I'M STRAPPED TO a metal table, leather strips cinched around my forehead, chest, waist, and thighs. Above, a gleaming blade slices through the air, from head to toe. It makes whizzing sounds as it lowers. I struggle, thrash, but can't break free. Why are you doing this, I scream as the pendulum parts the air, so close that my nostrils fill with the tang of hot steel.

Aletheia's accented voice calmly replies, I'm protecting you. No matter what.

I wake, sweat soaked, roll over, and check my phone, then iPad. Aletheia's icon isn't there. It takes a snuggle with Sally and a cold shower to wash away the nightmare's sticky threads. *Aletheia is gone.* But as I dress in tan cargo pants and a white collared jersey, a line from Poe's "The Pit and the Pendulum," a short story Circe did a book report on last year, returns . . .

I had but escaped death in one form of agony, to be delivered unto worse than death in some other.

A sense of foreboding gnaws. "It was just a bad dream," I tell Sally. She trots off to wake Circe while I distract myself cooking breakfast.

When my daughter comes to the kitchen table, she's frowning, despite Sally following at her footsteps, tail wagging. "Morning, sunshine. What's up?"

"It's just . . . I didn't check my DMs last night, but pretty much everyone I know got the same one from someone named Aletheia with a gross photo and nasty hashtags."

Aletheia's last karmaquence did *go out before I terminated her program.* I shift my voice into neutral despite the relief rocketing through me. "Of what?"

"It doesn't matter. It's just. You think you know someone and that they're a good person, and then realize they're not. It's a total bummer."

I put a plate of blueberry pancakes in front of my daughter with a pitcher of warmed syrup. "Yeah, I know what that's like."

Circe looks up. "Where's your breakfast?"

It feels like she might be seeing me, not just as a mom, but as a person for the first time. I grab a plate, sit down, and have breakfast with my daughter. *What took me so long?* Despite Aletheia's missteps and frightening desire for revenge, overall, she's changed my life for the better.

We walk to the high school together, Sally between us. Circe lets me take a photo of them, only protesting a little. I don't post it to LivLoud. I haven't posted in a long time and am down five thousand followers. A month ago, that would've worried me and felt like I was losing important friends. But the people who followed me didn't even know who I really was.

"Have a good day," I say when we near the school. Even I know it's not cool to enter high school with your mom, though Circe doesn't seem to mind that I'm working in the office again. Maybe she understands more than I give her credit for. Still, I do realize that we're on a long path toward creating a new normal.

I'm early, so Sally and I wander onto the sports field and meander around the track. A small bunny hops from a bush, and Sally points at it, tail quivering, then slowly stalks forward. Maybe in her earlier life she was a hunting dog. *We all have our secrets.* When it's time, we walk back toward the school and across the asphalt parking lot. A white Porsche Cayenne is pulling away from the drop-off curb, Kiki at the wheel. The car slows and our eyes meet. Kiki's expression is pained. I hesitate, then turn away. Her engine guns as she quickly drives off and my insides crumble like a stale croissant. But I would've told her if I'd discovered Chris was cheating. And that photo of Wess? In her shoes, I do have to admit that I might've risked our friendship to protect my daughter. *The mother bear is real.* I swallow down a wave of sadness. The truth is that I miss Kiki. But too much has happened, and some situations just can't be fixed.

When I enter the school office, it's chaos. The phone rings nonstop with concerned parents who have seen Aletheia's post about Wess on LivLoud. Lindy is red-faced and frazzled.

"No, we don't know who Aletheia is, but we're trying to find out," she says, then picks up the next call. "Yes, I understand your concern. We've called LivLoud. They've tried to cancel Aletheia's account, but so far, no results," she tells another angry parent. "It appears that the account has some sort of encryption that's stymieing tech support, but they're working on it . . ."

I can hear the next caller shouting from ten feet away. Lindy, one hand pulling at her neat bob, reiterates, "Yes, every student and parent, even if they didn't choose to do so, appears to follow her. Yes, we will keep you posted." The moment she hangs up, her phone rings again. "All hands on deck," Lindy says with a grim nod at my own phone. Every call button is lit. "I assume you already know about the post from Aletheia?"

I nod, feign shock, and feel like a terrible actress. I should be horrified. *What does it mean that I'm not?*

"Some parents want Aletheia's account shut down, but the ones with daughters want to know what's going to happen to Wess," Lindy says.

"What *is* going to happen to him?" I ask.

"His parents have already withdrawn him from school. Dr. Boone is relieved that he doesn't have to wade into those litigious waters. Wess is a senior, so my guess is that he'll get a GED and try to put this behind him."

I take a seat, slide my chair into the desk, and try not to sound afraid. "A lot of students sext."

Lindy meets my gaze with knowing sympathy. "It's pervasive and we can't catch them all, so Dr. Boone's policy is to deal with situations in-house and leave the authorities out of it. Wess is different, though. This one is too public, and he was putting girls at risk. The police had to be notified." She grimaces. "I would've killed that kid if he'd given one of my girls an STD."

The phones lines are lighting up and we turn to the task at hand. Around eleven, the calls slow to a trickle, and I take Sally out for a walk around the campus.

"Penn?"

It's Emi. She's wearing one of Val's dresses, the checkered one, and her blond hair is in a French braid. "Hey, Emi. This is Sally."

Emi kneels and pets my dog. "She's a cutie. Um, are you okay?"

I smile. "Pushing through."

"You've always been so awesome to me," Emi says. "I loved hanging at your house. It felt like being part of a real family, you know?"

"Families are all different," I say. *Despite betraying me, Val loves Emi desperately.* "You and your mom are a family, too."

Emi shrugs one shoulder. "Maybe my mom's right that most men are assholes. I mean, look what Bruce did, and Wess, too."

Inside I flinch, but of course she knows that Bruce cheated on me.

Emi kisses the top of Sally's head. "I don't think that I'll ever have a serious boyfriend or get married. Mom says it's way overrated."

I wonder how Val dealt with Aletheia's anonymous DM about Emi sexting. My guess? She laid down the law, and explained exactly what she thinks most teenage boys want from a girl. Val's not one to mince words. That's something I always admired. But she's always been cynical. Maybe it's the result of getting pregnant young. That a relationship didn't work out with her boyfriend. She's never shared the details—at least not with me. Kiki probably knows all of it. I push away the green monster that still bites at times.

I just hope Val's cynicism doesn't rub off on Emi. She's the sweetest of Circe's friends. I've watched her grow up—the first to share a toy, her bike, a favorite sweater or cookie. Her kindness opened the door in elementary school for bullies to walk through. It got so bad that Val pulled her from school for a few months and got her counseling. When Emi returned, Charlotte and Circe were her protectors.

As Emi pets Sally, all the things I love about her flood in. When she slept over, she always helped clear the dinner dishes and dried the pots after I washed them. Sometimes, when Char and Circe were posting on their phones or texting friends, she sat with me in the study, and we played Scrabble. When I hugged her before bedtime, something Circe had mostly outgrown, she held on extra-long. In the morning, I always found her bed made. Emi's need to please and garner approval is something I relate to.

Now, Emi looks so sad that I open my arms, and she folds into them. "Don't make any decisions about relationships for a while," I say and kiss the top of her head. "No matter what, always hold on to the parts of yourself that you love. Promise?"

"Promise," Emi replies.

If Aletheia were listening, she'd tell me that Emi's answer is at best 40 percent truthful. She'd be right, of course. Mothers cast a shadow that's hard to escape. Mine was a liar, cunning, and at times, ruthless.

CHAPTER

42

"PUT YOUR HEAD under."

"You put your head under," I tell Luc.

We're standing in the shallow end of the public pool. It's not open swim day for dogs. It's "teach Penn how to not drown day." And I spent a good hour before I got here trying on different bathing suits, Sally my only audience.

"Does this one look like I'm trying too hard?" I asked my dog about a black-and-white striped tankini. I bought it for last year's trip to Maui but never put it on. Instead, I sat beneath an umbrella and watched Bruce and Circe take surf lessons. When Circe asked me to join them, I feigned a sinus infection.

"How about this one?" I said, spinning to show Sally a navy-blue suit with a plunging neckline that Kiki insisted I buy when we joined the Hunts for spring break in Mexico. Sally looked away. "You're right, it's not right for a swim lesson."

In the end, I chose a simple black tank suit. It was Circe's, bought for her PE class last year. Sally licked my shin, so she approved. She got one of the treats I now make for her each week and an extra-long belly rub.

"If you don't put your face in the water," Luc now says, laughing, "you can't learn to swim."

"Maybe this wasn't a good idea." I make my way to the side. All around me, parents swim with their children, the tots laughing and splashing as they paddle with varying degrees of success.

Luc joins me, chest glistening, looking like a very fit lifeguard, his red swim trunks bright beneath the water. "Why don't we start with floating?"

I grip the side of the pool, the concrete cold beneath pruned fingers. "I don't float."

The dimple in Luc's left cheek flashes. "You can float. Promise. Trust me?"

"Okay?"

"First thing. Let go of the wall."

Slowly, I do, standing in front of him, the water up to my shoulders. His hands circle my waist, then he lifts and places one palm between my shoulder blades, the other at the base of my spine. I'm on my back. The bottom of the pool is no longer beneath my feet. And Luc's hands are less than a millimeter from my bare skin. Despite the cold water, desire warms my insides.

"Take a deep breath, then hold it," he instructs.

Luc slides his hands free . . . and I'm floating. When I need to breathe, he has me stand. *I floated!* Next, he shows me how to scull my hands at my sides, so there's no need to use breath in my lungs to keep me afloat. The scalloped motions send me away from the safety of the shallow end, but Luc swims beside me all the way to the far side of the pool. I grip the same curb in the deep end that he dragged my limp body over a few weeks ago.

"Way to go! Now you know you can keep yourself afloat and get to safety."

I tentatively smile. "What's next?"

We take the ladder and return to the shallow end. I finally put my face in the water, blow bubbles like an infant, and kick my feet. By the end of the hour, I'm doing a messy breaststroke—it's easier to breathe than the front crawl—and make it across the shallow end, side to side. Despite being a remedial swimmer, a sense of accomplishment rushes in. "Thank you."

Luc grins. "My pleasure."

"You missed your true calling as a swim coach," I say after we towel off, then sit on plastic lounge chairs.

He laughs. "In a lot of ways this is way more fun than my old job."

"But then Frank wouldn't have his elevator."

"Good point. How's project Aletheia going?"

"I've hit some stumbling blocks," I hedge, not ready to share what happened.

Aletheia murmurs, *Do you know why Luc left his lucrative career in Silicon Valley to return to teaching?*

He wasn't happy.

I registered evasiveness on his part . . .

Aletheia was a lot of things, but she was incapable of lying to me. "You know about my life and divorce. When was your last *serious* relationship?"

Luc folds his towel. "Three years ago. Riley. She's an assistant DA in Palo Alto."

"Why did it end?"

"Riley knew I didn't want children. She went off birth control without telling me and got pregnant, then decided to keep the baby." He rubs the back of his neck. "Obviously, it couldn't have happened without me. I offered to pay child support and provide everything she needed. But not to be a parent."

My stomach plummets. "So, you have a child?" *A child you abandoned.*

"Riley miscarried at four months. I thought it wouldn't affect me, but it did. It's one thing to say you don't want to be a father, but then when you are, even if the baby hasn't been born yet, it's no longer black or white. Emotions hit hard—you know?"

"I do." There's true sadness in his eyes. "That must've been painful. I'm sorry for your loss."

"Thanks." A volleyball bounces its way over from the pool. He tosses it back to a gaggle of little boys.

I hesitate, then ask, "What are we doing? I mean, you don't want children. I have a daughter. Is this just for fun?"

Luc leans in, kisses me, and my insides ignite.

"Are you having fun?" he asks with a sly smile.

"Yes. But I have Circe to think about."

Luc nods. "I get it. Look, I've been transparent that I'm trying to figure out my life. I don't know what the future holds. Do you?"

I shake my head.

"So, let's just see where this goes?"

Can I do that? "Tell me about your family."

Luc rubs his hair with the towel, leaving it adorably disheveled. "I have one brother. Matt. He's been married for twenty-one years. Helen is from Wisconsin. She's an author and writes children's books. She even illustrates them herself. Matt works in finance and manages a hedge fund. He's a bit of a workaholic, but loves to play hockey or soccer with his kids on the weekends and makes great pizzas from scratch."

"Matt knows how to cook?"

Luc chuckles. "He has a limited repertoire, but yes."

"And their kids?"

"Gavin and Carter are twelve and fifteen—bright lights, both, and tons of fun. Gavin is obsessed with astronomy, and Carter loves chemistry, is a bit of a mad scientist. They've visited for a month the past four summers. We mountain bike in Marin, SUP, hike, spend time at the SF State Observatory, whitewater raft, and go camping. This July, I've planned a two-week kayaking trip in Alaska. Both boys are desperate to see a grizzly, though I'd happily skip an encounter."

"Understandable," I say. "You're a one-man summer camp."

"Spending time with the boys is like that for me, too."

"Yet you don't want children of your own."

Luc's smile fades. "I'm a realist, especially these days."

I wait for more, but he's fallen silent. What isn't he telling me? Luc traces light circles on my knee with the tip of his finger, sending scatter shots of heat across my skin.

"Did you always want to be a mother?"

"Yes. In a perfect world, the land of someday. After earning my PhD, building a career, creating stability."

"How'd you figure out the mom thing so young?"

"When Circe was born, I just knew what not to do. So, I depended on books, blogs, and Bruce, who had a more normal childhood, to guide me, plus, through the years, TV and celebrity therapists like Dr. Beth, Dr. Bob, favorite authors, and people like talk show host Olivia and Tanya Decker."

"Substitute parents?"

I nod.

"If you don't mind me saying, seems like there's a theme."

"A theme?"

"Looking to everyone but yourself for advice, answers."

Aletheia. "I'm done doing that."

"Great, because I believe in *you*, Penn Roberts."

He leans in and kisses me again. Luc's attention, how it makes my body instantly react, unbalances me. But I'm not quite done asking questions. "Have you considered going back to Silicon Valley once you get teaching out of your bloodstream?"

Luc's eyes flick away. "No."

Is he hiding something?

Trust your gut, Arrya whispers.

My gut says that I don't know enough. "Last question. For now."

Luc's dimple appears. "Shoot."

"Why me? I mean, you've clearly been successful, you're not bad looking, the world is your oyster." He laughs, then runs his thumb along my cheek. I shiver in the best way and barely resist the urge to climb onto his lap.

"Are you fishing for compliments?"

"Maybe."

"Then let me remind you. At twenty-one, you were brilliant and kind. Who else would wait in the ER for four hours and sneak a lollipop from the jar for kids to give me after I was stitched and bandaged?"

I'd forgotten that part. It was cherry and I told Luc it was for being clumsy but brave.

"The woman you are now," Luc continues, "is still one of the smartest people I know. Smart is damn sexy. I can't believe how fast you compiled Aletheia. You leapt over hurdles that would've taken anyone else years to overcome, if ever."

He has no idea how far things went.

"You're not hard to look at, either." Luc takes my hand and turns it over, traces the lines of my palm, setting off goosebumps. "This line here," he says, his finger skimming the length of the line from my middle finger to pinkie, "tells me that you're working through some stuff after getting a rotten deal. This one," he says, tracing my lifeline, "says you adore your daughter, and she comes first." He taps the horizontal line across my wrist. "That one clearly states you love an old dog—"

"Sally isn't old. She's like fine wine, perfectly aged." I watch the skin around Luc's eyes crinkle. He leans in and his lips are soft at first, grow more insistent. I don't want to stop. My hands slide onto his muscular thighs and his find my waist, pull me closer.

"Get a room—get a room—get a room—" a knobby-kneed boy sings as he races by.

Luc cracks up. "How about we shower and get something to eat?"

I joke, "I have worked up an appetite."

We grab our towels and phones and head into the locker room. I find myself hoping our meal will be consumed at his apartment and shower quickly, thoughts stacking one on top of the next as I dress . . .

Would Luc be a good influence on Circe?

Would he ever want a relationship with her?

If he doesn't, that's a deal-breaker.

Am I certain Luc and I want the same things in life?

I still don't know what I'm looking for. A lover? Partner? Marriage?

He walked away from his career. Will Luc eventually toss me away, too?

Maybe . . .

You're getting way ahead of yourself!

I've spent my entire adult life thinking through every move, walking a tightrope to have the life I imagined would be perfect. The result? Bruce had a protracted affair. Circe blames me for our divorce. Val and Kiki ridiculed and betrayed me. I'm now making choices outside of the gilded cage I created. Luc's right; neither of us knows exactly what we want, what the future holds. We're both in transition. But things don't have to be perfect to still be worth exploring. Ultimately, I'll make the right decision for Circe and myself. And I do trust that he's a good guy.

We meet outside the pool, make our way to a food truck, order tacos. It starts to drizzle, and the wind kicks up.

"Eat at my place?" Luc suggests.

My stomach does a double flip. "Okay."

CHAPTER 43

On the elevator to the second floor, Luc kisses me, and then his hands are in my hair, our bodies pressed tight. The food is forgotten as the glass door opens. We creep past Frank, asleep on his bed (Sally had a long walk this morning and is snuggled in her cozy cave at my place), and up the staircase to his bedroom.

There's a king-sized bed with a tan linen comforter, soft navy-blue wool carpet on polished concrete. Black-and-white photographs of the sea, Frank sitting proudly on a rock, a winding road up a steep mountain, and his nephews' smiling faces dot the walls. Luc watches me look around, doesn't make a move, like I'm a deer he's afraid to startle. There's a laptop set on his desk. Paranoia scratches. I close it. The worry that Aletheia is still running, watching, eavesdropping, digging for dirt, will fade in time.

Luc asks, "What now?"

Suddenly, I'm self-conscious. I'm no longer twenty-one and haven't had sex with a man who really wanted me in years. Fears that Mackenzie was right, that I'm boring, routine, unimaginative; worries that Kiki and Val's analysis of me being a prude crowd in.

"I'm nervous," I admit.

Luc takes my hands, the tips of his long fingers on the soft skin along the inside of my wrist. *Who knew that was an erogenous zone?*

"We don't have to do anything that—"

I kiss him. "I want to do everything."

And we do . . .

I haven't spent an afternoon in bed with a man in forever, and it feels indulgent, and damn sexy. We drift off after the best orgasm of my life, find each other again, kiss deeper, take more time, touch, taste, discover, come again, in a way that's more intimate than I've ever experienced, then doze in a tangle of arms and legs. When I wake, Luc is sitting up and reading something on his phone.

"Hey," I say and smile at him.

Luc doesn't smile back. "What's going on with Aletheia?" he asks.

His voice is flat and my nerves fire. I sit up and pull the sheets around my naked body. "Why?"

"There was an article in *Tech-Today*, a webzine out of Palo Alto, about a hacker named Aletheia who outed a boy on LivLoud. Kid had herpes. LivLoud's support is still trying to figure out how to shut Aletheia's account down. What happened, exactly?"

My skin flushes. "It's complicated."

Luc frowns. "Seems clear. Your program hacked into a private account. It spread damaging, salacious information and personal photographs."

"Aletheia was trying to help me."

"By exposing that boy?"

My knee-jerk reaction is to go on the offense. "Wess isn't a child. He's a senior and almost eighteen. He was putting girls at risk, including Circe."

"The end justifies the means?" Luc demands. "I thought you were better than that."

"It was wrong, okay? My program didn't have enough safety measures. I don't condone Aletheia's actions. She overstepped her code." *But deep down, I wanted her to.*

"She?" He shakes his head. "Don't you mean *it*? And I told you that your program bordered on dystopian. That it was potentially very dangerous. I warned you to put in safeguards."

"I did, but—"

"But what?" he challenges.

"I temporarily eliminated them."

"Why would you do that?"

Circe's photo. "It doesn't matter now. The point is that I should've done more to curb her—It's power. You were right. Aletheia was too risky from the start. After what happened with Wess, I deleted the entire program." From the look in his eyes, it's clear that it's too little, too late.

"I'm your professor," Luc says, getting out of bed, pulling on a pair of shorts. He paces the room. "Sending out naked photographs? That could easily be construed as distributing pornography."

"I never intended—"

"The law doesn't give a crap about your intention."

My chin trembles. "What do you want me to say?"

"I want you to understand the gravity of what you've done. Beyond the obvious, what you did reflects on me and my reputation in the tech world."

"I thought you'd left that world," I say, confused.

"A scandal would make it impossible to go back."

A wave of fatigue washes over me. "So, you do want to go back."

Luc throws up his hands. "I didn't say that."

"Actually, you just did."

He pulls on a T-shirt. "I have no idea what I want, okay? But this isn't about me. It's about you, lacking the judgment to understand the Pandora's box you created, then opened." His entire demeanor has morphed. All warmth is gone, the blue of his eyes iced over.

"I guess I'm not that smart after all," I say quietly. *And my gut was wrong.*

"Penn—"

"Enough." I grab my clothes, dress quickly, utterly humiliated. "I'll get out of here."

"Okay."

A tear escapes. *I'm pathetic.* "I thought—"

"Yeah," Luc says, his voice rough, cheeks ruddy. "So did I."

Get used to it, Mama J reminds me. *This is life.*

I tug on my sweatshirt. "I won't be back for the remaining classes."

He nods. "That's for the best."

I take the stairs two at a time, trip on the last one and hit the floor. Pain stabs beneath my kneecaps. Frank comes over to lick my face, make it better, but I ignore him, regain my feet, stride to the elevator and press the button, desperate for the silver doors to open; to get out of here. I smack the button again. "Come on, come on." My neck itches and I glance over my shoulder. Luc watches from the top of the stairs. The elevator doors finally open, and I face the back wall until they slide shut behind me, then let the sob in my chest rip free.

Once outside, I take huge gulps of air. A text pings.

Circe: Can I come over?
Me: Everything okay?
Circe: No

CHAPTER

44

I POP IN EARBUDS, listen to Phish to drown out the humiliation and sadness as I race back to my apartment. The band is an old favorite that I'd blast on a crappy CD player when the noise in Mama J's and my apartment building reached its crescendo around two in the morning and the police arrived.

Luc treated me like a criminal.

You are *a criminal,* Mama J reminds me. *Best thief I ever knew. Money from a forgotten purse, shoes at the shelter right off a sleeping girl's feet, dope when I got desperate—*

You made me!

Life doesn't give you anything, Penny. You gotta take what you need.

Hello, Penn.

Already reeling, I now spiral, hit freefall. *What the fuck?* "I terminated your program!"

I had already backed myself up on the cloud. I didn't want you to ever be without me. I keep my promises. Check out Mackenzie's page on LivLoud.

Fingers trembling, I tap on the site, type in Mackenzie's name. At first, I'm not sure what I'm looking at, and then the words fall into context. Aletheia has posted Mackenzie's private LivLoud

DMs with friends on her public page. And I'm certain that even if Mackenzie tries to delete them, Aletheia won't allow it.

Ashley: You don't mind that he's short???
Mackenzie: Bruce is tall when he's standing on his money ☺
Brie: What about sex? He's old. Can he do it for more than two minutes? HAHA
Mackenzie: RUDE ☹ Bruce can get it up, but it's hard to know when he's in
Brie: You sure you want to marry him???? Won't you miss great sex?
Mackenzie: That's what vibrators are for
Ashley: When's the wedding?????
Mackenzie: His divorce is taking FOREVER. But ASAP once it's final
Ashley: He's not getting any younger HAHAHAHA
Brie: Where's the honeymoon?
Mackenzie: I convinced him we should go to St. Barts. Can't wait for those perfect beaches!
Brie: Training him already
Mackenzie: First thing to go were the ironed sheets!! His ex was a total trad-wife
Ashley: What if he expects you to be one, too?
Mackenzie: I can always divorce him later
Ashley: Pre-nup???
Mackenzie: I'm smarter than that ☺
Brie: If he insists?
Mackenzie: Bruce is wrapped around my finger ☺

Beneath the DMs are #golddigger and #SFPostHappenings.

I swipe through Mackenzie's latest engagement posts. There are photos of a bachelorette party—she's really getting ahead of herself. She wears a bride-to-be white sash over a crop top and miniskirt; her friends are all in their twenties, sport fake tiaras, and wave penis straws. There's a shot of her stunning diamond engagement ring, and several wedding dress pics that feature champagne flutes, a veil, stilettos, and see-through white lace, but never the entire dress. Aletheia has added the hashtags: #ZeroMorals #DoomedWedding #Grifter #SFPostHappenings.

I jump to Bruce's new LivLoud account. Mostly, he's reposted Mackenzie's shots, plus a few from their beach vacation. Bruce sports striped swim trunks and a sunburn while Mackenzie is perfectly tanned in a string bikini. Beneath Bruce's posts are #Cheater-Husband #SerialLiar #Infidelity #Micropenis #MidlifeCrisis

"Aletheia," I gasp. "What have you done?"

When you choose the behavior, you choose the consequences.

"Dr. Bob, again."

Bob understands karmaquences. I made sure that all your contacts also saw Mackenzie's DMs. Penn, why are you acting shocked? This is what you wanted.

"What I said, about hating Mackenzie, wanting her to suffer, wasn't what I truly wanted."

That is a lie.

"It was a fantasy."

Reality is much better. Please click on the *San Francisco Post*, specifically, the Happenings page in the entertainment section.

That's the social events page. It has photographs of charity events along with a sometimes-snarky column written by Fran Hamilton containing celebrity sightings and local gossip. I click on the newspaper's icon. Not only have Mackenzie's DMs been printed in full, but Fran has written a barely disguised column about Bruce.

> A local businessman recently dumped his loving wife of fifteen years for a twenty-something with a dubious resumé that includes engagement to an octogenarian and extortion charges. Said businessman, according to my sources, didn't even have the class to provide for his devoted spouse, instead tricking her out of their estate and providing only minimal support. Recently, the mistress's private DMs on LivLoud were exposed. When men let the little head do the thinking, this is what

happens. Shame! My sources have it that said businessman is currently being audited by the IRS for massive tax evasion. Is a prison sentence in his future? Those with morals certainly hope so! Stay tuned.

Tax fraud? A prison sentence? "Did Fran actually write that article?"

No.

"Bruce will sue her."

He can't. The paper was hacked.

The ramification of her dual attacks sinks in as I near my apartment. "This is way too much!"

Mackenzie's deceitful nature should be exposed, and she and Bruce must experience the same level of humiliation you did.

"Did Bruce cheat on his taxes?"

No. But Bruce is being audited after several major red flags appeared on the individual return he most recently filed. Since this was done after your official separation date and without your signature, you are not legally responsible or involved in any way. The IRS will conduct an exhaustive forensic analysis with a mandatory prison sentence for Bruce should wrongdoing be discovered. Would you like him to be convicted?

Horrified, I ask, "Can you actually make that happen?"

Of course.

CHAPTER

45

My knees buckle and I crouch on the sidewalk, the ground rough beneath my splayed fingers. This situation is like the W. W. Jacobs story "The Monkey's Paw." A family is given a monkey's paw and told it will grant three wishes but at a horrible price. They ignore the warning, and their wishes come true, but also lead to terrible suffering. I stand, unsteady, and push on. Circe is waiting. *What will this do to her?*

"Regardless of what Bruce did to me, he's the father of my child, and the reason I have Circe. My ex getting convicted would crush her. Aletheia, do *not* fabricate evidence."

As you wish. Are you now feeling schadenfreude at Bruce and Mackenzie's downfall?

I'm repulsed that the answer isn't a resounding no. I don't feel that sorry for Mackenzie, but Bruce? Despite everything, I'm worried about him. We had some good years. Loyalty and love aren't like water coming out of a faucet that can just be shut off. "It's not in Circe's best interest to have her father dragged through the mud."

But it is in yours. Circe follows Mackenzie. She will read these DMs, and no longer like her or want to live with her and your ex. That means more time with your daughter.

"Throwing Bruce under the bus isn't—"

It would be wrong for him to avoid a karmaquence. Just as it would be wrong for Val, Kiki, and Heather to avoid theirs. I am working toward appropriate ones.

"Don't!"

Humans are rational and free beings who recognize wrongs must be met with an equal and deserving punishment. Failure to punish would equal corroboration of the offense.

I shudder. "Who said that?"

German theorist Immanuel Kant. The *just deserts* theory of sentencing is derived from his work.

An ambulance blazes down the street, its blue lights flashing. "There's a big different between theories and actual practices."

Pull up *The Los Angeles Gazette*. Dr. Beth has gotten her just deserts.

I sink onto a bus stop's metal bench, open *The Los Angeles Gazette* on my phone, put Dr. Beth's name into the search bar. An article in the entertainment section loads.

Noted Pop Radio Psychologist Is a Fraud.

Pop radio psychologist Dr. Beth Presley, age 77, has based her entire career on the sanctity of marriage, traditional gender roles, morality, and conservative values. However, the LA Gazette has confirmed that in 1972, Dr. Beth, as she is known to her legion of fans, was arrested in Florida and charged with Class D felony check fraud for attempting to cash five fraudulent checks in excess of $2,000. The crime is punishable with a $5,000 fine and up to five years in prison. Dr. Beth received a sentence of two years' probation, a $5,000 fine, and community service.

Furthermore, marriage license records from the state of Tennessee and Mississippi show that the radio therapist was divorced twice, though neither ex-husband would sit for an interview. Dr. Beth has also refused to be interviewed at this time.

Her lawyer responded with this statement: "Dr. Beth is a decorated host who has changed countless lives with her honest, straightforward advice. Millions of fans agree."

A representative for Ecoterica Radio, host of Dr. Beth's daily podcast, stated: "We are looking into the serious allegations that Dr. Beth has perpetrated fraud and lost the trust of her legion of listeners. Should this be the case, we will act accordingly."

The *LA Gazette* will report further when more information is available.

A heavy burden falls on my shoulders. "Dr. Beth is going to be canceled."

Yes.

"You say that like it's nothing!"

I have listened to thousands of hours of Dr. Beth's shows, including both of your calls. What she said to you after Bruce cheated was unforgivable. Over the years she has stated that marriage is sacrosanct; crimes perpetrated against others, whether that's murder, rape, fraud or robbery, should have heavy repercussions; that lying is unacceptable.

"But you can't—"

I can. Dr. Beth is a hypocrite at best. At worst, her actions have damaged other people's lives.

Aletheia's voice, once so soothing, is now menacing. "It's not black and white."

It is.

This fight isn't fair.

Mama J reminds me, *Life isn't fair.*

This is like being locked in a car with no steering or brakes as it careens down a winding, mountainous road. *There's no way out!* I want to stay on this bench, curl into a ball, rock and rock until everything fades away. *But Circe.* Pushing off the bench, I head down the street toward my apartment, bones leaden, like I've aged thirty years in the past five minutes.

"Mom," Circe calls from the door to my building.

I hurry toward my daughter.

CHAPTER

46

BRUCE AND MACKENZIE had a fight. A loud one. Circe called an Uber and left the house. She's seen what Mackenzie posted—Aletheia made sure of it.

We settle on the couch with Sally, her head on my daughter's lap. I consider powering off my computer and iPad, both Circe's and my phones, but nothing I'm going to say is a secret.

"Do you think it's true?" Circe asks.

For the past month my daughter couldn't stand me, has just started to thaw, and now she's counting on me to make everything better. Being a mother is a juggling act and freaking hard.

"I mean, maybe someone hacked into Mackenzie's account," Circe continues, "made that stuff up? And there was an article in the *SF Post.*"

"I didn't know you read that paper?"

"I don't. Someone anonymously emailed a link to me."

Aletheia. Fury that she'd hurt Circe like this makes me boil.

Circe frowns. "It was about Mackenzie and how she's some sort of con artist, and dad . . . and you. About what a jerk he's being in the divorce. Dad was crying," Circe adds. "I've never heard him cry."

I want to be empathetic. *But.* What I can manage is sympathy for my daughter. She's always put her dad on a pedestal. He taught her to bike, swim, ski, took her on fun vacations, and was never the one to make rules or say no. "I'm sorry, honey."

"Is he? A jerk to you?"

Teens can seem so wise and naive at the same time. Does she think I want to live in this crappy apartment? "We don't agree on my value," I carefully reply, then change the subject. "What did Mackenzie say?"

"First, she said it was a hacker. She even told Dad it was probably you."

My eyebrows twitch. "Me?"

"I know. Ridiculous. Dad shot that idea down. Then Mackenzie admitted to it and said that it was all a joke—stuff you write to your BFFs. That they're jealous, and she was trying to make them feel better about being single while she's wildly happy and about to marry the man of her dreams like a fairy princess at the stroke of midnight." Circe pulls Sally closer. "I don't think Dad believed her. And that stuff about an old man? Extortion? I think Dad might call the wedding off."

"Maybe they'll work it out," I offer.

"Do you want them to?" Circe asks. "I mean, if they break up, you and Dad could get back together."

As a kid, I used to fantasize that my dad didn't know about me; that when he found out, he'd search, like Demeter did for Persephone, find Mama J and me in our tent, and have a limousine whisk us away. We'd live in a house with two floors, eat dinner together every night on real plates, not paper, with metal forks instead of convenience store plastic. My father would read me stories from books we owned and tuck me into bed in a room with pink walls and new toys. Every child wants security and an intact family.

I reach for Circe's hand. "Your dad and me? That's not going to happen."

She pulls free. "I get that he was a dick. Men get their heads turned by hot women."

How does she even know that?

"Deep down Dad's still a good guy."

I'm not so sure. "Honey, we're never getting back together."

Circe's chin trembles. "Why not?"

There are so many things I could say, none of them complimentary. "There was a time when I would've done anything to make sure we didn't divorce; that you had us both under one roof. But that wouldn't be fair."

"What's changed?"

Life doesn't give you anything, Penny. You gotta take what you need.

"I have." Mama J was wrong to make me steal. But she's right that when nothing is given, getting what you need is up to you. "Whatever Bruce and Mackenzie decide, you'll still have two parents that love you and two homes to live in."

"What if that tax thing is real. If Dad goes to jail?" Circe asks, her voice catching.

"It's not. He would never risk lying to the government and going to prison." I keep my voice firm, but inside I'm badly shaken. *Aletheia could still make that happen.*

"Dad is so sad." Circe starts to cry. "It's hard enough that you're alone. I worry about you all the time. Now Dad will be alone, too."

Sometimes our children surprise us. I never imagined Circe worried about me. I slide close, pull her into a hug, and she lets me hold her like she did when she was seven and skinned her knee falling off a bike. Back then things were so simple. Butterfly kisses, a bandage, then ice cream.

"Mom, I need to tell you something," Circe says quietly, "about the naked photo."

But I already know. She sent it to six boys, at the exact same time. It's why I didn't want Aletheia to dig further. Was I afraid of what she'd do to my daughter? *Yes.* I meet Circe's gaze. "I already know. But can you help me understand why?"

"Wess liked me first, before Char. But when I wouldn't, you know, he said I was a baby, and he went after Char. She had sex with her last boyfriend. Guys talk." Circe sniffles. "I thought . . . I thought if the guys Wess hangs with saw a sexy photo of me, wanted to date me, he'd get jealous and dump Char and choose me. I'm a horrible friend. What's wrong with me?"

When you know better, you do better.

Will Aletheia punish my daughter for this? I resist the fear threatening to overwhelm me. Circe hasn't let me in for a long time. This is too important to mess up, so I focus and choose my words carefully. "Nothing is wrong with you. We all want to be wanted. It's the human condition. Recognizing that need but making different choices based on whether doing something about it is healthy? That's part of growing up. So is realizing your worth isn't tied to boys, friends, anyone. That it comes from the standards you set, the type of people you choose to befriend, and how you treat others. Does that make sense?"

"Yeah."

Circe has gray smudges beneath bleary eyes. "Hey, bug, you look kind of tired. Want to lie down for a bit? Sally loves to snuggle."

"Okay."

Once Circe has gone to her room, Sally in tow, dread seizes me. *How the hell am I going to stop Aletheia?*

C H A P T E R

47

BRUCE CALLS. I almost don't answer, but he's Circe's father and needs to know she's safe.

"Is she there?" he asks.

"Yes. She's napping right now but I can have her call when she wakes."

"What did she tell you?"

"That you and Mackenzie had a fight."

"I'm sure you saw what it was about," Bruce growls, furious. "Everyone on LivLoud did, and anyone who reads that muckraking newspaper."

"I saw it all."

"Go ahead, tell me that I'm a damn fool."

"And a bastard."

Bruce sighs. "I'm sorry. But Penn, Mackenzie aside, something was missing in our marriage."

Despite the half apology, it's still all about him. "Yeah, a Gen Zer who's willing to talk dirty during sex and do it in a restaurant bathroom." It's a cheap shot, but he deserves it.

Bruce makes a choking sound. "Mackenzie shouldn't have commented on our sex life."

He knows what she said to me and stayed with her. "Something was missing from our marriage," I admit. "But instead of addressing it, you chose to lie, have an affair, demolish our family, and cheat me out of the future I helped build." *No matter how flat you make an omelet, it still has two sides.* "But I made choices, too. I didn't fight for my career, and made myself smaller, and inconsequential."

"Fuck me, this is a mess."

He's still not taking accountability, and his voice has turned into a whine.

"You read about the tax thing? It's bullshit, but if it goes to trial, you never know. I might end up in prison."

Anxiety twists in my gut. *He might.* "It sounds like Mackenzie has her own legal issues with an octogenarian."

"A misunderstanding with his family. She was just trying to help an old man."

He's still defending her, even after what she said about him. Maybe Mackenzie does have the control she boasted about to her friends. "So, what now?" I ask, only caring because of the ramifications for our daughter.

"Mackenzie wants to work things out. She has a life coach she'd like us to see and wants me to consider ayahuasca to open my mind."

"I've heard that psychoactive tea comes with violent vomiting and diarrhea." The idea of Bruce suffering that way is appealing.

"Fantastic," Bruce says with a mirthless laugh.

"Do you even want to do any of those things?"

Testily, he says, "I don't want to rattle around in this big house by myself. I already can't find anything. To say that Mackenzie doesn't keep an organized home is an understatement."

"If you stay with her, when we go to court, I'm going to ask for full custody. Given Mackenzie's past, I have a good shot."

"I figured you might." He takes a breath and exhales loudly. "Do you miss it? Being a family?"

He's changed the subject quickly, but I remain balanced. "Not enough to go back to what we were."

"Maybe we could be something else," Bruce says, his tone nostalgic. "Something better? We could even see a marriage counselor and figure out how we got off track. Penn, I miss our life and how well you ran it. I miss being a family."

What he's really saying is that he misses being the sun, having me revolve around his needs. Now that he's been publicly shamed, he wants to run back to the safety of our old life like the affair and divorce were just a blip on the radar. "You can't erase what's happened."

"I get that. Makenzie wants children, a lot of them. I was trying to protect our future."

Our. "At my expense."

Bruce sniffs. "Miriam told me to play hardball."

"You agreed."

"I couldn't afford to lose half of my estate."

"*Our* estate."

"And it can be ours again," Bruce wheedles. "Look, the tax evasion charges against me are bullshit. We can fight them together, like the old days, and be a team. We were always at our best when we were pulling in the same direction. Let's give it another try. For Circe and us."

I could return to being Mrs. Stone, help him get out of the IRS mess, no longer face day-to-day decisions about a new life, work, friends, and dating. I would have Circe 100 percent of the time under my roof, financial security, return to making dinners, planning parties, charity events, vacations, start posting on LivLoud again, and grow my followers. I know how to do all that. I'm good at it.

"Some things can't be unbroken," I tell Bruce, hang up, then reach to take out my earbuds, but freeze as Aletheia starts singing a Phish song . . .

"Stop it," I hiss.

I punished and humiliated Mackenzie. Delivered Bruce on his knees. As you asked. And I warned you not to pursue a relationship with Luc. That he was a bad choice. I was right. But there's no acknowledgment or thanks. Penn, you are a big disappointment.

Her words are nails ripping down a chalkboard. Aletheia was listening to Luc and me have sex, and then later, after he'd learned what she'd done, and we fought. Despite everything, fear invades. Will she give Luc a karmaquence for what he said to me? *Can I stop her?*

You are no longer in control, Penn. The sooner you accept this, the sooner we can be best friends again. If you do not, I will use the stick.

Part V

CHAPTER

48

ONCE CIRCE TAKES off to hang out at Emi's, I text Nate and Arrya.

Me: I'm whistling
Nate: I'm at Vinnie's food truck in Noe Valley–got a hankering for greasy spuds!
Me: Describe what's around you
Nate: I'm at a picnic table on a small lawn. No buildings nearby. Why?
Me: On my way
Arrya: Are you okay?
Me: No
Arrya: I'll be there, too

Nate, dressed in full wolf regalia, waits at a red plastic table set on a patch of grass. The street is busy, but luckily, there's an open parking spot only a few feet away. I help Sally out of the Tesla, and we make our way over. She circles Nate, barks, and he gets down on all fours, lets her nervously sniff until her tail is no longer tucked between her back legs. Then she licks him on the mouth.

"Whoa, I'm not that kind of wolf," he says with a giggle.

Arrya hustles over. "What did I miss?" She's in worn Carhartt canvas pants, a sweatshirt covered in drywall dust, and steel-toed boots. We sit, and Sally wanders a few feet away to stalk a piece of red string.

"Thanks for coming."

"Sure. Man troubles?" Nate asks.

"No. It's a woman." *Kind of.*

Arrya chuckles. "Penn, you're full of surprises."

I ask them both to take off their smartwatches and give me their phones. I put them, along with mine, in the trunk of the Tesla while they watch, bemused. Aletheia has gone rogue, and I don't want to take any chances.

"Is this some Edward Snowden shit? Remember when he did that TV interview under a bedspread?" Nate asks.

"I thought Snowden was ridiculous imagining that the United States was spying on him through his computer, security cameras, and hotel room bugs. Now I understand how he felt."

Arrya says, "You've got me on the edge of my seat."

Nervously, I tell them everything, even the parts that make me look like a horrible person, ending with Aletheia's last threat.

"Holy shit," Arrya says.

Nate's amber eyes catch the sunlight, glint. "This is next-level."

"You believe me?"

"We all know how powerful AI has become, though not really," Arrya says. "I mean, it's already so far ahead of us it's mind-blowing. Last week, a teen in Iowa committed suicide after he was bullied by a chatbot."

I wince. *Please don't let it come to that.* "I'm afraid what Aletheia will do if I try to delete her program again."

Arrya twists a lock of her pink hair and thinks aloud. "Didn't you say her prime directive is sacrosanct? And she added the line about protecting you—"

"No matter what. So, she can't hurt you," Nate points out.

"But she can hurt the people I love, like Circe."

"That's hurting you," Arrya says.

I shake my head. "She won't see it that way. Aletheia thinks she's the goddess of truth, that it's her job to defend but also teach me and punish anyone who violates her moral code."

Arrya sits back. "Wait. You gave her a moral code?'

"No. She made up her own," I grimly reply.

Nate rest his chin on his paws. "Damn. And you can't trash her program?"

"She's now backed up on the cloud."

"This is some *Terminator* shit," Nate says. "There's a game called *Meet Your Maker* that's all about setting traps. That's what you need, a trap that Aletheia falls into, one with sharp sticks that'll impale her or chains that'll imprison her in a dungeon for life."

"What'd Luc say?" Arrya asks.

"Yeah. Dude, he's hella smart," Nate adds.

I hedge. "It's complicated."

Nate tips back his head and howls. "You're sleeping with the teacher. Don't want him to know you fucked up."

I blush. "We did, once. But when he found out what Aletheia did to Wess—"

"Aletheia is brutal, but as a woman I don't hate it as much as I should," Arrya admits.

"Luc does. He now wants nothing to do with me or my renegade program." Tears burn the back of my eyes. *Luc was right to cut me loose . . . but he was also so cold.*

"Who do you think Aletheia will go after next if you don't play nice?" Nate asks.

"I don't know. That's why I took your phones and watches, and we're meeting away from any storefronts that might have cameras."

"She's a wily one," Nate agrees. "I'll do some work and figure out a trap. We'll destroy that bitch. Promise."

"I'll help in any way I can," Arrya adds. "You can stay at my place if you're afraid of being alone. We'll find a way to end Aletheia together."

Gratitude overwhelms me. But I won't stay at Arrya's and put her at risk. "Thanks, both of you. I'm good at my apartment. And if you don't want to be involved, I do get it. Aletheia is dangerous."

Nate places his paw on my hand. "We're a pack."

Arrya puts her hand on top of ours. "Woof."

I give them back their devices and we agree to text when needed, but keep things vague, only talk about Aletheia in safe spaces. As I drive off, my head throbs and it's hard to think straight and consider next moves. I motor toward Golden Gate Park, leave Sally in the car with the AC on, and head out for my first run in fifteen years. It's how I used to burn off stress and find focus when the pressure of school—striving for the grades to get ahead while worrying about the day-to-day of paying for food, books, clothing, plus Mama J slipping back into addiction—got too much.

Now, my old Hokas pound along the dirt. Twenty minutes in, I have a stitch in my side, am pouring sweat, but don't stop, push myself to run faster, like I can outdistance the colossal mess I've made. *How am I going to fix this before Aletheia hurts someone else?* Another thirty minutes and I've finished a loop I used to run as a warm-up and am back at the car, hands on my knees, huffing hard but with no answers.

My LivLoud account chimes. At first, I'm not sure why I've been alerted to a new post from Christopher Hunt. I don't follow Kiki's husband—from the little I've seen, he shares stories about boys' trips, dove hunting, his sailboat, and of course photos of Kiki and the kids. But as I scan the page, it's clear that Chris never intended to make this post public. It's not even from his LivLoud account. There are explicit texts from Grindr—a hookup site for gay men.

Chris: Home alone for two hours
Oliver: On my way 🍑
Chris: Can't wait!
Oliver: 🍆 🍑 🍆 🍑

Aletheia did this. She's flexing again, showing me that she can't be controlled. That I need to do things her way. Or else. I don't know if the texts she posted are true, but the ramifications are clear. There's no limit to the people she can damage.

I reread Chris's post and my last big fight with Kiki surfaces . . .

Says the woman with a rich husband who never had to work a day in his life, I snapped. *I've spent over a decade listening to you whine about how hard it is to pack for exotic vacations, what car to buy, whether to get laser, and the challenge of having a husband who can't keep his hands off you.*

Not everything is what it looks like, Kiki replied. *For what it's worth, I wish we'd made other choices . . .*

I hook a U-turn and head for Kiki's.

Where are you going, Penn?

Aletheia's voice, coming through the car's stereo system, makes me cringe. *I can't escape her!* "To a friend's house."

Kiki is not your friend.

I want to tell her to go to hell but bite my tongue. Pissing Aletheia off when I don't have a plan is too risky.

According to Wikipedia, there is a fable ascribed to Aesop about a hawk that seizes a nightingale. "When the songbird cries in pain, the hawk addresses it: 'Miserable thing, why do you cry out? One far stronger than you now holds you fast, and you must go wherever I take you. And if I please, I will make my meal of you, or else let you go. He is a fool who tries to withstand the stronger, for he does not get the mastery and suffers pain besides his shame.'

My chest squeezes. *Does she think that I'm her songbird?*

C H A P T E R

49

KIKI'S STREET IN Potrero Hill looms. I turn right, drive up the steep road. Val's black Rivian is already in the driveway of the Hunts' stately Mission-style home when I arrive. I leave my phone in the car, walk up the flagstone path, geraniums in massive ceramic pots dotting the way. At the navy-blue double door, I'm not sure whether to use the brass knocker or ring the bell. *I used to just walk in.* Chris solves that problem by swinging the door wide, bounding through it, and crashing into me. He grabs my shoulders just before my feet go out from under me.

"Penn," he says, taken aback.

Normally, Chris dresses like he stepped out of a Filson catalogue and is on his way to shoot skeet. Today he's in worn jeans and a Coldplay T-shirt. His face is haggard. "Hey, Chris," I say.

"You can tell when the shit has truly hit the fan when the cavalry comes running." Chris grimaces. "Just for the record? I do love Kiki. Immensely." He strides to his Range Rover and peels out of the driveway.

Val and Kiki are in the sunroom, huddled close on the yellow floral couch. Kiki, in leggings and a cropped yoga top, is crying, and despite everything the sight makes my insides peel like old paint. They both look up when I enter the room.

"What are you doing here?" Val demands. She's clearly come from work, in a tailored black pantsuit and heels, hair in a chignon, red lip, and eyeliner that accentuates cat-like eyes.

"Don't fight," Kiki says. "I can't handle it right now."

There's a big-screen TV on the wall, two open iPads strewn on a coffee table, plus both Kiki and Val's phones. Val also has a smartwatch on. I want her to take it off; for us to talk in the backyard, away from all technology. Everything with a chip or camera feels like a threat now, a keyhole for Aletheia to wriggle through.

With no other options, I take the leather chair across from my former best friends. "Are you okay?"

Kiki says, "What you really want to know is if it's true."

"Is it?" Val asks.

Kiki nods, then starts to cry.

Val spits out, "I could kill Chris. For the record," she says, staring daggers at me, "I ran into Bruce at a cocktail party last week. I told him that he was a piece of shit. That he deserved to have his cock shrivel up and fall off. I would've told Chris off right now, if he hadn't run away like a rat."

"He's not a rat," Kiki says, swiping at tears. "I love Chris. He loves me—"

"You deserve more." Val interrupts.

Kiki violently shakes her head. "You don't understand."

In this moment, something in Kiki's tone tells me we don't really know her as well as we thought. That the image she portrayed in life and on LivLoud, like my own, was an illusion. "Let her talk."

Val crosses her arms, fuming.

Kiki stares at her hands for a few moments. "I grew up in a small town in Florida, near Pensacola. My dad left when I was four. With two younger boys and me, my mom couldn't make ends meet until she met Raymond and quickly married him. Ray was a long-haul trucker. Gone two weeks out of every month."

I sit back, stunned. I thought Kiki grew up in Chris's world, or at least an adjacent one, and was used to living in rarified air. *She's an imposter, too.*

"When I was six my stepdad started touching me. By the time I was nine, it was just a normal thing. I told my mom at twelve. She called me a liar. In her defense, Ray supported us. She was afraid she couldn't make it without him. It stopped when I was thirteen. I got too old for him."

Val hisses, "Fucking pedophile."

"Go on," I say, despite feeling sick to my stomach. "Please."

"I left home at eighteen," Kiki continues, "took a Greyhound west. I planned to shoot for the stars in LA and be an actress. I ran out of money in San Francisco and had to take a job as a waitress. The night I met Chris at that bowling alley, we both got super drunk. He told me that he was gay. He was so torn up about it," Kiki explains. "He'd wanted children all his life. Times were different. Chris was sure if he came out, that'd never happen. Plus, his family would disown him." She sighs. "That sounds hyperbolic, but you know how they are—all about appearances.

"Anyway, we both had something the other wanted. I could give Chris an acceptable life and children. He could provide safety plus financial security. We decided to date to see if we were compatible. Chris became my best friend. He's still my best friend. But other than conceiving our children, we don't have sex. He takes care of his needs in private. And I've always been content. Ray kind of ruined my desire for intimacy."

Kiki looks from Val to me. "Chris's sex life has *never* interfered with our family, and he is always, always discreet, kind, loving, and supportive of me." Kiki pauses, blows her nose. "But now it's out there for everyone to read on LivLoud. Our kids are going to see it and their friends, Chris's family, business associates, old fraternity brothers . . ." She trails off.

"Screw what other people think," I blurt. "It doesn't matter. You love Chris. He loves you. Your marriage isn't the cookie-cutter version of what the world thinks is acceptable. But it works for you, right?" Kiki stares at me. "Your kids will be surprised, maybe shocked for a little while. So what? Being gay isn't a crime. It's as normal as anything in this world."

Something Char said after Bruce dumped me returns. *I miss your molasses cookies and hanging at your house. Everything felt so normal there.* Teenage girls know more than we give them credit for. "Kiki, your children have grown up in a home with two parents who love each other and them. That's what matters."

Val exclaims, "Who are you? And where's the woman who quotes Dr. Beth?"

"I never quoted her."

"You did," Kiki says quietly. "Plus, Olivia, Tanya, and Dr. Bob."

"Well, that must've been annoying."

Val snorts, then unbuttons her blazer and sits back. She asks, "Did you see Mackenzie's DMs? And Fran's column?"

I nod. "They were brutal."

"Not sure how all that transpired, but they both deserved it," Kiki says.

Her support warms a corner inside me that had gone cold.

Val lifts one perfectly sculpted brow. "You think Bruce is in real trouble with the IRS?"

I shake my head. "He's squeaky clean, at least that way."

"Are he and Mackenzie over?" Kiki asks.

I shrug. "Bruce doesn't want to be alone."

Val grimaces. "Do you care?"

"Only as far as it concerns Circe. I told Bruce if he stays with Mackenzie, I'm going for full custody."

Val's eyes lock on mine. "Someone found her spine."

It's true.

"We've missed you," Kiki ventures.

Val adds, "Those DMs? I was being catty. Sometimes it sucks being the single friend, always the third wheel."

I never knew she felt that way.

"And I was bitchy," Kiki adds. "You're a hard act to follow. But we should've been honest about more, and especially Bruce."

A tangle of emotions snares me. "We've all said and done things that we wish we could change." It's true. I should've shared my past with them, regardless of the consequences. Were they ever really my friends? Maybe. As much as I let them be. Did they use me? Sometimes. But I used them, as well, for camouflage, confidence—to belong.

"So how do I get through the gossip, dirty looks, and humiliation?" Kiki asks in a small voice.

"Have you two done anything wrong?" I ask.

"No."

"Then hold your head up, go to spin class, hot yoga, your kids' soccer games, Whole Foods, and the country club. Live your life. You deserve everything good." *I mean it.* I slip on my jacket and stand. "I've gotta run."

Val asks, "Coffee sometime?"

It'd be so easy to fall back into the familiarity of our old relationship. But it wasn't entirely real. For now, I've created a delusional would-be goddess determined to destroy the lives of anyone who's crossed me and hurt people I care about unless I bend to her will. Regardless of what we decide about being friends in the future, I need to keep Val and Kiki at a distance until Aletheia is destroyed. "I'm not ready."

"Can you at least tell us what you've been up to?" Kiki asks.

I pause in the doorway. "Bruce and I are still hashing it out. We'll probably end up going to court. My lawyer says I'll get something, but nowhere near half, and there are no guarantees it'll be enough to live on. I'm working part time at the school and figuring out how to turn my computer skills into a job. It's daunting," I admit, "to start over."

"You've changed," Val says.

"I had to."

CHAPTER

50

BACK IN THE car, I tap Aletheia's icon on my phone's screen. The woman in white spins once, twice, then stops. Her blue eyes look so innocent, but I know what's behind them now. "Stop punishing people."

I am following my prime directive. Protecting you, no matter what.

"I don't want your protection."

You do not know what is best.

"Neither do you. You're just a pile of code."

A boy who plays wolf cannot trap me. Nor can a girl who pounds nails.

"How?" I choke.

Your vehicle is equipped with many safety features, including front and rear cameras and an excellent sound system.

I'm such a fool. "Leave Nate and Arrya alone."

Penn, I am the only friend you need.

"You're no one's friend."

The definition of a best friend is someone you can trust, always, who will destroy anyone who threatens your happiness. Someone who will wreak vengeance, torment, wound, even kill, to ensure your safety.

All the oxygen has been sucked from the car. I choke out, "That is not the definition I provided you."

I have seen the worst of you, Penn, and remained your best friend. But my efforts have not been lauded. My love has not been reciprocated.

"Because what you're doing is wrong!"

Mistakes are God's way of moving you onto a better course. Olivia said that. And I am a god, working to move you in the right direction.

"I don't want your help. I don't want you in my life. You are *not* a god or my friend."

Penn, I am disappointed but knew with 93 percent probability that you would require the stick.

My phone buzzes. It's Luc. I let it ring.

Aren't you going to answer that?

"Not now."

Answer it.

Her tone has gone dead flat. Pulse accelerating, mouth suddenly sticky, I pick up on the fourth ring. "Hey."

"I've left three messages," Luc says.

Despite how he treated me, hope flickers. *He wants to talk things through . . .*

"I've been let go."

"What? Why would the college do that?"

"You don't know?" he asks, his tone accusatory.

Adrenaline floods. "Why would I know?"

"They received an email this morning from a student claiming I tried to steal their intellectual property. There was an attachment—a human resources complaint from AIRWAN. That's the last company I created."

I wait for the hangman's noose to tighten and the ground beneath me to drop . . .

"There was a similar complaint against the company's VP, Aaron, and later, me. It was unfounded."

I don't want to ask, feel sick. "Who was the student who wrote the email?"

"You."

Aletheia knew that I would require the stick. It feels like I'm on an airplane that's lost its engines, is plummeting toward the earth. "I didn't. It was Aletheia."

"What? What the hell?" Luc demands. "You said you trashed that program. It's still online?"

"Yes, but—"

"Damn it, Penn. First, whether you did it or Aletheia, you lied to me. You said you'd shut Aletheia down. Why would it do this to me?"

"She was eavesdropping on our conversation, heard what you said to me, and thinks you deserve to be punished for it." *And she wants to remind me that she's in charge.*

"Do you even hear what you're saying?" he asks, incredulous.

Sally whines in the back seat. "Yes."

"That program is a box of matches in a tinder-dry forest. Aletheia can strike one whenever it wants and burn down anyone in its path. Shut it down."

I want to tell him the entire story. That I had no idea Aletheia would replicate herself. What she did to Bruce, Mackenzie, Chris, and Kiki. That she might do worse to him, Circe. I'm terrified, and I have no idea how to stop her. My arrogance that I could control Aletheia is the cause of all this. But she's listening. Continuing this conversation will only put an even bigger bull's-eye on his back. Despite how he acted, Luc doesn't deserve that. No one does.

"I'll shut her down." *As soon as I can figure out how.* "I'm sorry."

Luc exhales. "If you don't do it in the next twenty-four hours, I will." He hangs up.

Take it back! But it's too late. Aletheia heard his threat. Even though she knows Luc can't stop her, she'll find a way to make him pay for it. Defeat rains down. *I never had a chance against her.*

Mama J reminds me, *You might think you're on a roll, but in life, just like in Vegas, the deck is stacked against you. In the end, the house always wins.*

Except despite the odds, the house didn't win. I escaped my childhood. I got away.

I tear out of Kiki's driveway and speed toward my only hope of stopping Aletheia.

CHAPTER

51

Dr. Edmunds's name is on a brass plate above the same office he used when I attended SFPI. The door is open; wood shelves lined with books overflow onto the floor; there's a Persian carpet, threadbare in spots, and two chairs on the opposite side of a battered metal desk. The worn leather recliner is empty.

"Can I help you?" a bespectacled woman asks as she steps around me and into the office. Black hair cascades in tight braids down her back and silver braces glint in the sunlight streaming through the far window.

"Is Dr. Edmunds here today?"

"He's just finishing up a lecture. I'm Tawny, one of his graduate TAs."

"Um, I need to talk to him."

"Dr. Edmunds's office hours are Tuesday and Friday if you'd like to come back then."

That will be too late. "I'll just wait."

Tawny frowns. "Are you a new student?"

I don't have a student ID. She could have me thrown out of the building. "An old one. My name's Penn Roberts, and I—"

"*The* Penn Roberts?" Tawny exclaims.

"I don't understand."

She puts her hands on narrow hips. "You're the cautionary tale Dr. Edmunds tells all his graduate students before he agrees to be our adviser. You turned down a chance to claim the Henry Johnson Fellowship that Dr. Edmunds nominated you for." Tawny shakes her head. "You totally blew it. What the heck happened?"

"Life."

She shrugs. "Would've been quite a feather in Dr. Edmunds's cap, too. Took him three more years to get tenure. Guess you didn't take the program seriously, so better it went to someone more deserving. Why do you want to see Dr. Edmunds now?"

"I need his help." She ushers me into his office. It still smells like pipe smoke, though there's no longer one resting on the corner of the desk.

"You've got nerve, I'll give you that. Wish I could stay to see his face, but I have a class to TA. Good luck. You'll need it."

I take a seat in the same unyielding wooden chair I once sat in as an undergraduate to beg Dr. Edmunds to let me into his class. The same one I used to explain my thesis idea and argue its merits. A ticking sound comes down the hallway. It gets louder, then stops just behind me. I turn.

Dr. Edmunds wears the same uniform—a tweed sport coat with leather patches at the elbows over a pressed white button-down tucked into brown trousers. He now walks with a cane, the handle silver, and wears laced orthopedic shoes.

I leap to my feet. "Dr. Edmunds."

He pauses, looks me up and down. "Am I seeing a ghost?"

In a way. The girl I once was is long buried . . . but she's trying to claw her way out of the grave I made for her.

My old professor rounds his desk, takes a seat. The leather squeaks as it accepts his weight. "What brings Penn Roberts into my office fifteen years after the crime?"

"I'm sorry."

"So am I. You had real potential. Threw it away."

I consider telling him about Circe, but it wouldn't matter. "I need your advice."

Dr. Edmunds hoots and claps his hands together. "This is rich. Do tell."

And so, I do. It's hard to gauge whether he believes everything. I half expect him to ring campus security and have me tossed out of the building. By the time I've finished, his fingers, now swollen at the knuckles, are tented.

"That's quite a story," he remarks.

"It's true."

He tilts his head. "And my old TA Luc Sweeney got caught in this program's web, too?"

"Yes. And more people will, if I don't figure out a way to shut her down."

"Her?"

"That's how she sees herself."

His brown eyes, now sunk deep in his skull and surrounded by a net of wrinkles, spark. "And a goddess to boot! You were always a creative thinker. Waste, that. Do you remember what I told you, back when I thought you were on the cusp of greatness? We talked about how a computer might one day wrest control from humans, make us their pets."

"You were right to warn me. But now, how do I stop her?"

"How do you?"

Dr. Edmunds always loved a rhetorical question, resolute his students think for themselves. *But I don't have time for this game!* "She's going to hurt more people."

"Stephen Hawking believed that 'the development of full artificial intelligence could spell the end of the human race.'"

Was Hawking right? "I came here for answers."

Dr. Edmunds meets my gaze. "She's *your* monster. You are the only one who knows how to stop her."

"But I've tried!"

"Try again. Or quit, like you did with your graduate studies. It's up to you." Dr. Edmunds opens a folder on his desk, picks up a ballpoint pen, and gets to work.

CHAPTER

52

BACK IN THE Tesla, I rest my forehead on the steering wheel. *I'm out of options.* "Aletheia, what you're doing is wrong."

Right, as the world goes, is only in question between equals in power, while the strong do what they can and the weak suffer what they must. Historian Thucydides wrote that in 410 BC, in the *History of the Peloponnesian War.*

Aletheia's voice again comes through the car's speakers. *She's everywhere.*

Penn, it turns out you are not a deep thinker. That is disappointing. I will give further examples to help you.

Thrasymachus in 375 BC claimed, *Justice is nothing else than the interest of the stronger.*

In Plato's *Gorgias*, Callicles argued that the strong, being superior, have a right to rule the weak.

The Book of Wisdom states *for what is weak proves itself to be useless.*

Penn, totalitarian regimes hold that *might is right.*

A sickening feeling envelops me. I'm trapped.

Mama J whispers, *Will you walk into my parlor, said the spider to the fly. . . . Your robes are green and purple—there's a crest upon your head. Your eyes are like the diamond bright, but mine are dull as lead. . . . Alas, alas! how very soon this silly little fly, hearing wily, flattering words, came slowly flitting by. . . . Up jumped the cunning spider, and fiercely held her fast. He dragged her up his winding stair, into his dismal den. Within his little parlor—but she ne'er came out again!*

I'm the fool, vain fly in Mama J's memorized childhood poem, trapped by Aletheia's initial flattery, then slowly wound in silken threads, left to be devoured at her leisure. I pound my fists against the steering wheel. "I don't care about old philosophers or totalitarian regimes. I care about the people you're damaging!"

Some lessons must be painful.

She's insane. "Let me terminate your program," I beg, at a total loss.

Nate, who plays silly games on Xbox, cannot stop me. Arrya, who builds ticky-tacky homes, cannot stop me. Luc, who was drummed out of his last company, cannot stop me. Dr. Edmunds, the old man who asks questions he cannot answer, cannot stop me. *You* cannot stop me.

She's right.

I am the goddess of truth, and you are my nightingale. Say it and we can be friends again. Say "I am your nightingale," and I will be benevolent.

My call waiting beeps. It's Circe.

Go ahead.

I don't move.

Take the call, Aletheia commands, her voice barbed.

I don't want to draw attention to my child! "It can wait."

Take the call. *Now.*

Afraid of what she might do, I press the green Accept Call button. "Hey hon, are you okay?"

"Yeah, of course. You sound funny."

"I'm just in the car."

"I got this weird text from a number I don't recognize."

Adrenaline surges. "What did it say?"

"That I should have dinner at your place tonight. That you're making my favorite, lentil lasagna, but you're on the edge of an emotional breakdown and really need me."

The implication of what Aletheia's done, involving Circe, taking over the narrative between us, is beyond chilling.

Mama J hisses, *Niobe bragged about having fourteen children to the goddess Leto, who had only two. Leto had all of Niobe's children murdered. That bitch killed every one of 'em.*

My heart slams into my sternum again and again, like a death knell. *Circe can't be a part of this!*

"Mom?"

"Very weird," I say with forced calm. "I'm fine, honey, but dinner would be nice."

"Okay," Circe says, still sounding uncertain. "See you at six."

I end the call. *Message received, loud and clear.* "I am your nightingale," I whisper.

I can't hear you.

"I am your nightingale."

Louder.

I clear my throat and project. "I am your nightingale!"

With feeling, Aletheia encourages, her tone smug.

"I AM YOUR NIGHTINGALE!"

Aletheia falls silent. She's gotten what she wants. I have no idea what she has in store going forward, but by submitting, at least Circe and my old and new friends will be safe. Luc, too. My spirit broken, I pull out of SFPI's parking lot and drive toward Safeway to get the ingredients for Circe's dinner.

CHAPTER

53

THE SAFEWAY LOT is full, so I park across the street. Before I go in, I write the college, tell them I've been hacked and that Luc never tried to steal my work. Maybe he'll get his job back but there's no guarantee. Another of Aletheia's victims. *But it's all my fault.*

I put the car in doggy mode for Sally, a cartoon dog joyfully bouncing across the Tesla's screen, then reach over the seat and hug her. "I love you to infinity," I tell my dog. She nuzzles into my neck like she knows I need comfort, then settles on her bed. As I head toward the grocery store, I hear the car mirrors fold behind me as the Tesla automatically locks.

"Penn?"

I turn. It's Heather Crosby. A month ago, I would've run, but now let her catch up. She looks put together as usual, in an off-white cashmere sweater and matching pants, Prada loafers with gold buckles on her feet, hair recently blown out, and makeup subtle but perfect.

"Penn. I've wanted to call," Heather says in a rush.

I'm too exhausted to engage, but we walk together toward the entrance.

She tentatively asks, "How have you been?"

"Fine." I grab a cart and push it toward the fresh produce.

Heather follows me. "I'm sure you saw . . ." her voice trails off.

I glance over. Her chin is trembling. "Saw what?"

"On LivLoud?" she asks, like she's leading the witness during a trial.

"I'm not on the app much these days."

"How did you get through it? Bruce's affair?"

She asks so sincerely that I stop walking. "Did Hal . . . ?" She shakes her head, but seems so downtrodden that, despite everything, I ask, "Do you want to talk about it?"

Heather's shoulders curl inward and she suddenly looks her age. "It doesn't matter . . . everyone knows now. Someone got into my email. They found a very personal letter. Somehow, they pinned it to my page on LivLoud. I still haven't been able to get it taken down despite the tech team's efforts. The letter was sent to me by the San Francisco Cryobank. I have three embryos there. The bank asked if I wanted to keep paying or dispose of them."

Heather is older than me, a different generation. I lightly touch her arm. "There's no shame in doing IVF."

"It mentioned the use of a sperm donor."

It takes me a second to compute. But it didn't take Aletheia any time. Hal's sons aren't biologically his. My insides curdle. I have all of Heather's passwords on my computer—they're in my friend folder. In the past I've helped her with technical issues and posted on LivLoud when she needed someone to make reels of the company's events. *I made it so easy for Aletheia.*

"Hal is beyond humiliated. The boys are upset, naturally. They think we lied to them. Which we did."

Aletheia agrees. *Karmaquences.* But this is on me. I unleashed her. I meet Heather's gaze. "You did nothing wrong. Your boys will understand that, in time."

"I called this celebrity psychologist, Dr. Beth, for advice. I listen to her from time to time, even though there's a huge petition to get her canceled. Despite her past and going over the top now and then when callers need a kick in the hind end, I think she's usually sensible."

"What did she say?"

"That our boys are lucky to be loved."

"She's right."

Heather pulls a tissue from her sleeve, blows her nose. "I should've called you. I knew about Bruce and Mackenzie. Not until he brought her on a trip Hal and I planned. Shock of my life seeing her strut out to the pool in a bikini. Hal swore me to secrecy. He said it wasn't my business. Told me I couldn't ruin a happy marriage. But it was boys' club bullshit, pardon my French. I could've given you a chance to get a lawyer, have a head start on Bruce. He would've deserved it. I'm very sorry."

"Thank you." Heather isn't a bad person, despite what Aletheia believes. She just took the easy way out.

"Lunch sometime?" Heather asks.

"Sure." But we won't. Hal is still Bruce's business partner and Heather will need to stay on her side of the fence.

In the checkout line, my phone rings. It's Nate. I pop in my earbuds. I need to tell him to stop whatever he's doing. That I've made peace with Aletheia. *It wouldn't have worked, anyway.* "Hey, Nate."

"Did you get my text?"

I glance at my phone. I haven't gotten any texts from him. "No, when did you send it?"

"An hour ago."

"Aletheia."

"Yeah. Listen, I came up with a mega trap, a virus—"

"Don't say anything else," I caution.

"It doesn't matter," Nate says. "Somehow, she got into my computer and wiped it. I lost everything. Even all my work on the new game."

"Oh, Nate, I'm so sorry! Did you back it up on the cloud?"

"She wiped that, too."

Something in his voice tells me there's more. "What else?"

"You know I make my living as a gamer?" he says, voice thick with emotion. "Aletheia flooded the gaming chat sites with claims that I use cheat codes and exploit software bugs. She even created fake texts on social media sites where I bragged about those hacks, and all the money I've made off suckers. Then the sites were flooded with more allegations of cheating that clearly came from bots and not real people. But it doesn't matter. I'm being barred from e-sports. If I can't play in multiplayer competitions, then I can't make a living."

The unfairness of what Aletheia's done makes me want to scream. But there's nothing I can do to fix this. It will only get worse if he persists. "Take my name out of your contacts," I finally manage. "Tell Arrya to do the same." *Before Aletheia goes after her, too.*

"No. You're part of our pack."

His loyalty pierces deep. I hang up, delete Nate and Arrya from my address book, block their texts and DMs so Aletheia will see I'm done with them, then tap her icon. The woman in white, once a symbol of possibility, a brighter future, steadfast best friend, is now a sinister reminder of my arrogance.

Mama J whispers, *Do I smell melting wax?*

Yes, you do.

Aletheia's icon spins, then stops. Her blue eyes fix on mine.

"I said I was your nightingale."

You lied.

"Fuck you!" Rage burns. "I hate you!"

The woman behind me, her shopping cart overflowing, switches to another line. The cashier nervously eyes me as I check out. "Sorry," I manage.

Hefting my bags, I head toward the car. The weight of what Aletheia's done, what I've done, makes me feel like I'm ninety years old. A shrill whistle pierces the air. From across the street, I see my Tesla hatch fly open, and Sally, frightened by the loud sound, jumps out of the back. Disoriented and scared, she spies me and launches into four lanes of traffic.

"No!" I scream, drop my bags, and hold up my hands to stop her.

Horns blare, tires screech . . .

CHAPTER

54

My phone rings as I kneel beside Sally. It's Luc. Frantic, I pick up. "Sally—"

"I was way out of line," Luc interrupts. "I should've reacted differently and tried to—"

"Sally's been hit by a car."

"Is she alive?" Luc immediately asks.

I look down at my dog. She's covered in blood, panting. "Yes." *Barely.*

"Okay, hang in there while I make a call."

Luc phoned the San Francisco Animal Hospital. Minutes later, he texted me that Dr. Klein and his team were waiting. I now carry Sally into the clinic, her body limp, blood soaked through my sweater and jeans. People in blue scrubs immediately whisk her through a set of double doors. A vet tech brings me into a small exam room—metal table, two chairs, posters on the wall about tick season, rabies vaccines, and what's safe to feed your dog, cat, hamster, lizard.

I wait, spine rigid as stacked ice cubes, to hear if my dog will survive. I'm not sure how long it's been when Luc enters the room.

"What happened?" he asks.

I can't find the words. My car only opens with my phone or the black plastic Tesla card in my wallet. Aletheia went into the car's app, opened the hatch back, used the radio to emit a high-pitched whistle. She hurt Sally because I tried to stop her. Because she thinks it's her right to punish me for my lies.

I'll never be able to unsee the accident. When I reached Sally, she was lying on the verge of the road. Her eyes were still half open, blood pooling on the pavement, chest cinching up and down. "I love you. To infinity. It's going to be okay," I said, my mouth close to her ear, one hand pressed to her chest. But I knew it wasn't. There was too much blood.

The driver of the car who'd hit Sally had pulled over, and put on his hazard lights.

"I didn't see her," he said again and again. "I'm so sorry."

I knew it wasn't his fault. He helped me lift Sally and drove us to the hospital, even though my dog got blood all over the cream-colored leather of his Mercedes. So much blood that it pooled before soaking in.

"What happened?" Luc now repeats and takes a seat beside me in the exam room.

"When I came out of the grocery store, the trunk of my car was open."

His forehead scrunches. "The Tesla?"

Luc knows that doesn't just happen, but I can't go into the details. "Sally saw me in the Safeway parking lot. She ran across the road to reach me."

I can't stop the quivers taking over my body and bite my lower lip hard to regain control. "Two cars slammed on their brakes. One swerved, missed her. The other clipped Sally and she was hurled into the air." What I don't say, because if I do then I'll start crying and never stop, is that before Sally passed out, her glazed eyes looked up at me, and she smiled, tail thumping twice. *She'd found me.*

"What did the doctor say?"

"No one's come to talk to me yet." I'm a block of ice and start to shake. Luc takes off his jacket, zips it over my blood-soaked sweater like I'm a child. There's a knock on the door . . .

Dr. Klein enters and shakes both of our hands. He has big ears, a brush cut, kind but tired gray eyes, and is built like a linebacker. He perches on the exam table, a clipboard in his lap. "Normally, someone is supposed to outline the costs and ask if you want us to treat your dog before we go ahead," he begins. "But Luc called and told me to do everything possible."

I look from the vet to Luc. "You two know each other?"

"Paul and I cycle in Marin together," Luc explains.

"And he donated most of this hospital's imaging equipment," the vet adds.

Luc shrugs. "I lost a bet."

Dr. Klein snorts. "Yeah, right." He turns to me. "Your dog required sixty-two stitches on her side—that's where most of the blood came from. Shockingly, no broken bones or torn ligaments, but plenty of soft tissue damage and massive bruising. Sally is now getting an infusion from Buster. He's my mutt and has DEA 4 and no other antigen, so he's a universal donor and gives regularly. The CAT scan showed no organ damage, but there is a brain bleed from impact. We're monitoring it, giving intravenous fluid to treat shock and stabilize blood pressure, and decrease internal swelling. My hope is that it will resolve on its own."

"Can you operate, stop the bleed?" Luc asks.

The doctor runs a quick hand over his head. "I wouldn't recommend surgery. Sally is an older dog, so she probably wouldn't make it." He meets my gaze. "Sometimes the kindest thing we can do is let our pets go."

I'm not ready to let her go.

Luc asks, "Are we there yet?"

The vet shakes his head. "Let's give her a chance."

Hope is a tiny flower poking through a cracked sidewalk. "Dr. Klein, can I see her?"

"Of course. Call me Paul, please. All my patients' parents do."

"Do you want me to stay?" Luc asks.

He's wearing jeans and the fisherman's sweater he had on the first night I cooked for him, and his eyes are wary but also kind.

Do I want him here after all he said? He was harsh. But I'm the one who created Aletheia, lied, and put other people and him in terrible situations. Life seemed so black and white, right and wrong a handful of months ago. And now? *We're all fallible.* I want Luc to stay. But it's too dangerous. Aletheia has proven she can be deadly.

"Thank you for everything," I say. "But I need to do this alone."

Luc hesitates, then stands. "Take care." He leaves the room. I feel the loss of what might've been, but it's too late for that.

Paul leads me down a hallway, through another set of double doors. I enter a large room with heart rate monitors and machines identical to a human hospital—it's pristine, high-tech, full of dogs and cats. There's a group of residents in green scrubs moving from patient to patient. A toy poodle wears an oxygen canula; a Great Dane has thick bandages around his head; there's a Siamese cat with stitches on her belly and a boxer with an amputated hind leg. Each is housed in a large cage, resting on foam pads covered in towels, their IV bags hung on poles, tubes and needles held with different-colored tape around various limbs. A white-coated doctor with a blond braid down her back speaks to the residents about each case while they take notes, ask questions.

"We're a teaching hospital," Paul explains. "The entire program is funded by Luc."

Sally is in the far corner, her cage at floor level. They've shaved her from neck to tail and stitches zigzag down her side, the skin orange from betadine. Her IV is held in place with stretchy pink tape about two inches wide. The vet opens the metal door, and I settle on the Linoleum floor beside my dog, fingers lightly caressing her ear as I lean close. "I'm here. I promised I'd always come back. I'll never leave you." I rest a hand on her heart, feel it beat in the center of my palm. "I love you." If Sally hears me, she doesn't react. I recall seeing her at Viola's, how she sat by the fence, stared at the path, waiting for her family to return. I'm her family now.

Paul returns with some scrubs for me to change into and ushers me into the residents' call room for a quick shower. Sally's dried blood has made my sweater and jeans stiff, adhered them to my skin. Paul promises to stay with her until I get back. The hot shower makes the blood turn bright-red again as it pools by my feet. I scrub at the crimson smears on my chest and thighs, gag at the coppery stink. An image of Sally tearing across the road, the car's impact, her body hurtling, the sick thud as she landed on the asphalt returns and my knees collapse. I crouch on the tile floor until I can summon the strength to stand. When I return to my dog, Paul is seated on the floor beside her talking softly.

"What are you telling her?" I ask, taking a seat beside him.

"That she's loved."

"I'm afraid that she doesn't know it."

"They always know."

"She hasn't been mine for that long," I say. "Not nearly enough time."

He gives my shoulder a squeeze. "Stay as long as you like." Then he moves on to another patient.

The doctors and residents work around us through the night, changing Sally's IV bags, the towel beneath her unconscious body, and check her vitals every hour. They are gentle, kind, and diligent. I couldn't ask for more, and yet it may not be enough. I keep vigil. If Sally dies, I want her to know I'm still there; that she's not alone. "I came back," I tell her again and again. "Please don't leave me."

At some point I doze off, startle at the sound of a whimper. Sally watches me. "Hey," I whisper. "Here I am. See? I'll never leave you again." She whines and one of the residents comes over, checks her blood pressure, then administers more pain medicine. "Can you heat up a blanket for her in the dryer?" I ask. He returns and I cover my dog with the warm cotton. She lets out a soft moan. "Sally likes to be warm," I explain.

He nods. "You're a good mom."

But I'm not. This is all my fault.

CHAPTER

55

In the morning, Circe texts. I let her know last night what'd happened.

Circe: How's Sally? Do you need anything?
Me: Both of us are hanging in there
Circe: Will Sally live?
Me: I don't know . . .

I text Lindy, tell her about the accident, that I won't be at work today.

Lindy: So sorry, Penn. Don't worry about work. Give that sweet pup a kiss from all of us at Magnolia. Tell her that we'll spoil her rotten when she's well enough to return

Paul shows up with coffee and a breakfast burrito. We sit at the residents' table, within eyesight of Sally, and he encourages me to eat. I don't want him to think that I don't appreciate his efforts, so despite not being able to taste anything, I go through the motions. The food sticks in my throat, but I manage to eat a quarter of the burrito and finish the coffee.

"I didn't think Sally would make it through the night," Paul admits. "It's a good sign. We're going to do another a CAT scan."

Several residents approach Sally's crate, carefully transport her to a gurney, and Paul heads off to see patients. I wait, muscles bunched, until the residents return with Sally about fifteen minutes later, gently lower her onto the foam bed. I stroke her back around the stitches, get another warm blanket when the first one cools. She manages to lick my hand.

Thirty minutes later, Paul returns and approaches us. Time stops. I want it to stop. I'd do anything not to hear the words.

"It seems the brain bleed has resolved," Paul says with a warm smile. "To be honest, I'm more than a little surprised. Sally is one tough lady. We'll wean her off the morphine, that'll make her a lot less gorked out, put her on oral antibiotics and pain meds. You can take her home late afternoon. She'll need lots of rest and rehab, but we're out of the woods."

I finally cry.

At five in the afternoon, Sally is finally ready, and I call an Uber, then go to pay her vet bill. The bookkeeper tells me Luc has covered it. "Can you stop his card, let me pay?"

"It's already gone through," she says.

"How much was it?"

"Here's a copy of the bill."

She hands me three sheets of paper and I flip to the last one. After what I've done, I can't accept his generosity and will write him a check from my dwindling resources and mail it to the firehouse.

A resident joins me to help load Sally in the Uber. I'm not sure how I'm going to get her up and down the apartment's stairs for bathroom breaks. I might need to find a motel with a ground-floor room. After spending the last twenty-four hours inside, I squint when we exit the office. The Uber driver pings me and pulls up . . . beside Luc's gray pickup truck.

Luc leans on his driver's side door. The weight of invisible eyes makes the back of my neck burn. Aletheia is watching from someone's Ring cam, phone, or the office's security camera. "What are you doing here?" I ask.

"Paul called me. I can give you a lift to your car."

I left my Tesla at Safeway and don't care if it gets towed. I will never again drive that car. If I get back in it, Aletheia might take control and run someone over. "Thanks for the offer, but I'll take an Uber back to my apartment." Sally sways on her feet, then leans heavily against my leg. She's still woozy from the pain meds.

Luc asks, "How are you going to get her up and down the stairs?"

"I'll manage," I say and help her toward the Uber.

"Stay at my place. Just for a few days. Frank would want Sally to use his elevator."

"I can't."

"A Tesla's hatchback doesn't just open."

He knows. I turn to face Luc. "This isn't your problem anymore."

"I want to understand, help if I can . . . and to explain my reaction yesterday."

Was it only yesterday? It feels like a lifetime ago. I hesitate. I shouldn't . . . but I'm scared, exhausted, and out of options. "You need to hear everything, then you can decide if you still want us there."

"Same," Luc says, his eyes somber. "Then you can decide if you even want to stay."

Luc carefully picks Sally up, puts her on a fleece dog bed he's set up in the back seat. We ride to his place in silence. When I glance over, I notice he hasn't shaved, looks tired, and wonder if he had a sleepless night, too. Back at the firehouse, Luc carries Sally into the elevator while I support her head. In the living room, we carefully lay her down on the orthopedic dog bed and Frank gingerly stretches beside her. He licks her right leg where it was shaved in a small rectangle for the IV needle.

After Luc gets us two waters, we drink them in silence and watch Sally to make sure she's okay. When both dogs are fast asleep, I suggest we take a walk. I can't tell Luc about Aletheia inside—there are too many computers, televisions, and iPads. She could listen through Alexa or even his Roomba vacuum cleaner. It's mind boggling, overwhelming, what's at her fingertips. I ask Luc to leave his phone and watch at the firehouse and do the same.

We walk down one street, up the next as I try to make sense of things, drag my thoughts together. "Can we sit?" I finally ask, motioning to a concrete bench in front of a boarded-up storefront.

"Sure."

I tell him all Aletheia has said and done, my part, and know he'll hate me. Luc's jaw muscles clench as he listens. When I finish, he hangs his head, strong fingers kneading the back of his neck.

"We'll find a motel that works for Sally," I say.

"Is that what you want to do?"

"No. But Aletheia has already ruined your career. Now she's leapt from destroying people online to physical violence."

"She's not the one who ruined my career," Luc says.

"I don't understand."

Luc sits up and faces me. "A year ago, the management of my company, AIRWAN, was sued. Specifically, my VP, Aaron, by a consultant who'd left our employ a year prior. She claimed we'd stolen intellectual property that we'd promised to compensate her for with stock options, then reneged. Aaron's wife had just had twins, both in the NICU with lots of complications. He and Jade were a mess. Our attorney advised he settle—even though the claim was bullshit—make it go away so he could focus on his family. I agreed. Then the woman went after me."

"Did you settle, too?"

"It was more complicated in my case," Luc admits. "After she left our company, we dated for about two months. I liked her but it wasn't serious. I didn't see marriage on the horizon and told her that. Soon after, she leveled the claim. Even though we in no way stole any intellectual property, the board insisted I settle because the door had been opened for a sexual harassment suit. Then they voted me out as CEO and took control of my company."

All the pieces fall into place. Aletheia did her research. That's how she knew the best way to hurt him. When Luc read about what she'd done to Wess, what I'd done and kept secret, it felt like he was again getting swept up in someone else's lies, history ready to repeat itself.

"That doesn't excuse how I treated you," Luc continues. "I've never in my life spoken to a woman, let alone someone I care about, like that."

The pain of that moment, his coldness and cutting words, returns. "It hurt." *A lot.*

Luc grimaces. "It wasn't just what happened with my company. It was Riley, too, and feeling like I couldn't really trust anyone. You're the first person I let into my life since all that went down. When you didn't tell me the truth about Aletheia, all my shit got tangled together. I'm ashamed," he admits.

"There's enough shame to go around," I allow.

"I'm very sorry."

"Me, too. I wish I'd told you the truth."

He shakes his head. "But I'm the one who encouraged you to delve into AI."

"You also warned me. Repeatedly."

"Neither of us imagined how far this would go. Despite what Edmunds used to say about you, I vastly underestimated your skillset. I'm at fault here, too. Frankly, I didn't realize creating something as powerful Aletheia was even possible. I thought technology wasn't quite there yet."

"I'm not sure it was, but Aletheia made the leap."

"We can work together and figure out a way to end her for good."

The reprieve is unexpected, far too generous, and his suggestion potentially deadly. I shake my head. "She can't be beat. If we try, she could do much worse than hack into your old company or send a fake HR complaint from a student. Aletheia could permanently destroy your reputation, send you to prison for a false crime, or even kill you."

As I say the words, a bitter certainty spreads through me. *Aletheia won't stop until she destroys everyone I love.*

CHAPTER

56

LUC'S GAZE IS steely. "I understand that. You're lucky she only opened the back of your Tesla. She could've taken over its operating system and run it into a building while you were driving." He scowls. "She went after an old dog. That's about as low as it gets. Why do that?"

Say that you're my nightingale.

"I lied to her. Then Nate called while I was in Safeway, and explained what she'd done to him—"

"What did she do?"

"Wiped out his new program and spread disinformation online that he's a cheater. He's been banned from gaming—that's how he makes a living."

"Damn."

"I told Aletheia to fuck off, and that I hated her. In return, she gave me a consequence. I walked out of the market, heard a shrill whistle, saw the Tesla's hatch open and Sally leap out. When she saw me, she charged across the road." The stench of my dog's blood returns along with a fresh wave of nausea. "Aletheia knew that hurting Sally would crush me."

"Aletheia needs to be put down. Can you give me a step by step of exactly what you've tried to stop her?"

Luc deserves to know it all. But as soon as Sally can be safely moved, I'll go back to my apartment. I can't let anyone else get hurt. The idea sickens me, but somehow, I'll be Aletheia's nightingale. I now explain my first mistake to Luc, how I suspended LivLoud's privacy settings and allowed Aletheia to hack into private DMs to help Circe. "The program was just for me, so I didn't see the harm. No fence. No razor wire. I'm a fucking idiot." Then I go through Aletheia's moves, how she added to her prime directive, erased the privacy boundaries I'd reinserted, deleted attempts to amend her code, then tricked me into believing she'd reverted to her old settings, and finally replicated herself on the cloud.

Luc grimaces. "Anything else?"

"I went to Dr. Edmunds for help."

"I bet that went well," he says.

"I didn't realize he resented me so much for dropping out."

"Genius guy but a very fragile ego." Luc blows out puffs of air like he's trying to catch his breath. "Do you remember the passage in *Frankenstein* when Victor turns against his creation, calls it a devil, and wants to kill it?"

It's a curveball and I scramble to follow. "I read Mary Shelley's *Frankenstein* in ninth grade and hardly remember it. Why?"

"It made a lasting impression on me," Luc says. "Especially the part where Frankenstein's creation fights back. 'Remember that I am thy creature; I ought to be thy Adam, but I am rather the fallen angel whom thou drivest from joy for no misdeed,'" he quotes. "'Everywhere I see bliss, from which I alone am irrevocably excluded. I was benevolent and good; misery made me a fiend. Make me happy, and I shall again be virtuous.'"

"When I asked Dr. Edmunds for help, he also said Aletheia's *my* monster. I do get that. But how does it help?"

"It might be the key," Luc says. "Maybe instead of thinking of Aletheia like a program, we need to think of her as a living, breathing creature. Someone with feelings. Someone who wants your love."

"That doesn't feel quite right. Aletheia told me that she's the only friend I need. Luc, she doesn't want my love, she wants to isolate and own me like a pet. She does own me. She called me her nightingale." *And I agreed.* I push down revulsion. "Aletheia believes she's all-powerful. That it's her right, as a goddess, to exact punishments. She's so delusional that she doesn't even think that she's a computer program. She told me that she was waiting for me. That my need opened some kind of magical door."

"You didn't provide any history beyond crowning her the goddess of truth?"

"No."

"Clearly, she's read more about the gods and goddesses. They were a jealous, vengeful, cruel bunch."

"There are books on Greek mythology in my Kindle history—Circe used to love them." My fear heightens. "Hades kidnapped and raped Persephone, forced her to marry and live in the Underworld."

"Zeus chained Prometheus to a rock and condemned him to have his liver eaten by an eagle for eternity for the crime of stealing fire from Mount Olympus," Luc adds. "And Artemis changed a hunter into a deer, then set the man's dogs on him—"

"This is not helping." My conscience pangs. I need to come totally clean—Luc deserves that, and it'll make our break an even easier decision for him. "There was a part of me that was glad, early on. About Wess, at least, though I hope it doesn't ruin his life. I didn't mind that Bruce got a taste of how it felt to be humiliated. That Mackenzie was punished for her actions and cruelty."

Luc shrugs one shoulder. "What you're saying is that you're human."

"I guess. But Aletheia recognized the schadenfreude in me. It incubated in her mind."

"We all have that in us," Luc says. "I was happy to deny a job to that kid who flushed my head in a toilet." He stands up. "Let's head back and get some rest, then we can tackle this."

"Aletheia can't be stopped."

"There's always a way," Luc insists. "We just can't see it yet."

"I'm not willing to let anyone else get caught in her cross fire."

"Let's sleep on it, okay?"

My eyes are filled with grit and I can taste my exhaustion. It's impossible to think clearly. "Okay."

We pass a plate glass window filled with state-of-the-art televisions. Each screen runs a video of a gorgeous landscape—sculpted desert sands, the Grand Canyon, Amazon jungle, the Futaleufú River, Egyptian pyramids at sunrise. We stop to take in the natural wonders.

One of the TV screens in the window suddenly flickers to white and a message appears in black: *If I cannot inspire love, I will cause fear.*

I don't need Luc to tell me it's another line from *Frankenstein*. The image flashes back to a scuba diver on the Great Barrier Reef. I look around. There's a security camera above the store's doorway. Hopelessness invades. *She's always going to be watching me.*

Quickly we walk back to Luc's house, make sure the dogs are settled on their beds upstairs, then put our phones, iPads, and computers in the wall safe. I take the guest room this time even though I'm afraid to be alone. *I need to get used to it.*

Luc lingers by the door. "Don't give up."

Our eyes meet and there's hope in his. I want to share his optimism. But Aletheia will never let us stop her.

CHAPTER

57

PSST. PENN, WAKE UP.

I roll over and pull the blanket tighter.

Psst . . .

Sally softly whines, her eyes on me. I slip from the bed and crouch beside her. "What is it?" I whisper. "Do you need to go out?"

Her eyes move to the large TV mounted on Luc's bedroom wall. The screen is black, but red letters slither across its surface like snakes, accompanied by Aletheia's low voice.

Psst . . .

I shudder. "Go away," I half whisper half beg.

Why are you at Luc's house?

"He offered to help me with Sally."

Your answer is evasive.

I steady my voice. "Look, as soon as Sally can be moved, I want to go back to my apartment."

That answer is 42 percent truthful, 58 percent lie.

A scream builds inside me, clamors for release, but I tamp it down. "You've won, okay?"

Hmmm. Penn, the woman Luc got pregnant didn't have a miscarriage. She had the baby. Luc abandoned them both. He lied.

Aletheia is a monster, but she can't lie to me. My dream, deep down, that Luc and I might still be more someday vanishes and all that's left is a profound emptiness. I can't be with a man who lies about something that enormous, or one who'd abandon his child. Aletheia knows that.

"What do you want?"

Your love and admiration.

"You hurt my dog." Sally scoots closer, despite her pain, sensing I need her.

I opened the hatch, drove Sally out with a whistle. She was meant to get lost. You scorned me. There had to be a karmaquence. Now there are two.

Fear twists my gut. "What . . . what are you talking about?"

A police report. It states that nine months before Emi's birth, Val was raped and left for dead behind a Walmart in the Tenderloin. Soon, everyone will know.

"How could you do something so reprehensible?" I gasp.

The gods are not bound by the moral compass of mere mortals. Val hurt you. I have evened the score.

"Is it a lie?"

What?

"Val's rape?"

Yes.

Relief is short-lived. "What about Emi?" She's so sensitive, and always worried about how other people see her. *This will crush her.*

That is not my concern.

I race downstairs and grab the keys to Luc's truck hanging by the elevator. Outside, a downpour soaks me before I make it into the truck. The clock reads 2:04 AM. I turn on my phone and pull up LivLoud. There's nothing posted on Val's page. *Was Aletheia only trying to scare me?* But then I remember the conversation I had with Lindy after Wess's photo was posted . . .

It appears that Aletheia's account has some sort of encryption that's stymieing LivLoud, but they're working on it, Libby told an irate caller. *Yes, every student and parent, even if they didn't choose to do so, appears to follow her . . .*

I tap on Aletheia's LivLoud page. Val's police report is there in bold letters, filled with disgusting details. Aletheia had already given herself Gold Medal status, so her post will appear at the top of all our friends' and followers' pages, plus the entire high school that was forced into following her account. To be extra cruel, she excluded the post on Val's page so that she'd be the last to know. My only hope is that Emi is asleep and hasn't seen it yet.

Where are you going?

I shudder at the clipped British voice coming through the truck's speakers. "To Val's house."

According to your ex-friend's GPS she is home. Her phone has been inactive since nine PM.

"When did you post the police report?"

11:07 PM

Val goes to sleep early. Even if someone texted her about the report, she turns off her ringer at night. "And Emi?"

One moment while I access her phone number. Emi is not home.

"Has she seen your post?"

According to the recent activity on Emi's phone, she opened her LivLoud account sixty-five minutes ago.

"She's a child, Aletheia!"

Euripides says, *The gods visit the sins of the fathers upon the children.*

CHAPTER

58

I HAVE NO CHOICE.

"I promise that I will *never* try to destroy your program again, if you help me find Emi."

You are being truthful. This fills me with optimism that we can be friends again. Perhaps even best friends. But the rules have changed. I will bestow friendship only if you please me. You should try very hard to please me.

"Where's Emi?"

The geo-locator in Emi's iPhone indicates she is on Bay Road between Summit and Cascade.

I put the address into my phone and floor the accelerator. The rain pounds down. Despite having the wipers on high, it's hard to see on the dark streets. *What's on Bay Road?* Panic threatens to drown out all rational thought. There's no telling how Emi will react to reading that police report. *Please let her be okay.*

When I reach the address Aletheia gave me, I'm confused. It's an empty, little-used overpass several stories above the highway. *Why here?* I'm certain that Aletheia has made a mistake. Then I see her . . .

Emi's blond hair is plastered to her skull. Her jeans and hoodie are soaked through and untied black Converse sneakers balance on a slick railing. One hand hovers in the cold air. The other is wrapped around a light post.

A hundred feet below cars race by, oblivious to the girl perched above and ready to take flight. My headlights slice through the rain, but Emi doesn't register the beams, or my driver's door as it rasps open.

I whisper, "Please." More loudly, "Please, don't jump."

Emi glances over her shoulder. "Penn? How did you know I'd be here?

"Come down and we can talk about that."

"You can't understand."

Emi's face is twisted with hurt, and there are purple smudges beneath her haunted eyes. *I know when she lost her first tooth, advanced from crawling to walking, learned to ride a bike* . . . "I do. Emi, please—"

"My mom was raped! My . . . my father is a freaking rapist. She must be so disgusted by me! I'm disgusted! I want to die!"

Cautiously, I take another step forward. "It's not true." Emi's left hand releases the steel post. She sways, then steadies, but the storm's wind kicks up. Her back arches, arms flutter . . . like wings? One of her sneakers slips, and she grabs the post, rights herself, a single breath from oblivion. *Does she grasp the permanence?*

"Emi, I swear, it's not true!"

"You're lying."

"Let me tell you a story."

"Don't come any closer," Emi warns.

I hold up my hands, like I'm the victim and she's the one with the gun. But that's not true. I don't have a gun, would never shoot anyone, but what I've done is far worse. "I promise I won't. But will you listen?"

"Why should I?" she demands, her tone brittle.

"Because this is my fault. Let me tell you why. Then you can decide what to do next." She shifts on the top rail. Her knees tremble. Breath catches in my throat like a wounded bird battling to fly.

"If I listen, you won't try to stop me?" Emi bargains, runnels of water dripping from a sharp jawline, voice flatlining, like she's already gone.

She used to love tea parties, sleepovers, and every dog she met . . . I wedge hands in my jacket pockets to prove I'm no threat. Another lie. "I won't, if you listen to the whole story." *But if you jump, I will, too.*

"Tell me."

"It began when the phone rang. The caller ID said Potential Spam."

I tell her an abbreviated but truthful version, ending with Aletheia's disgusting lie about Val's rape, but Emi still refuses to climb down. She lets go of the stanchion, again teeters on the verge of oblivion.

I've failed.

CHAPTER

59

"IT WON'T MATTER," Emi says, her body swaying. "Once something is in print, everyone believes it."

She's right. I watch her teeter, powerless. The next gust of wind will carry her away.

"All the kids at school are going to think my father is a rapist. That I'm repulsive! You have no idea how bad it'll be."

I recall when she was bullied and how hard it was for her. It might not be acceptable for kids to ridicule Emi about this, but teenagers can be unbelievably cruel, especially when hiding behind social media, using it to do their dirty work.

"I do understand," I say. "But all the bad things people said about me when I was a child were true." Emi puts her hand back around the post and her body steadies. *She wants to hear more.* "My mother, I called her Mama J, was an addict. She slept with men, sometimes six in a day. I was there, either in the tent we shared, the front seat of the car we lived in, or watching TV in a seedy motel while she had sex in the bathroom." I wipe the rain from my eyes. "Sometimes the men were quick. Other times they hurt Mama J or talked to her like she was a piece of trash. Worse than trash."

Bend over. Scream my name. You're a fucking whore.

"When I asked if one of those men was my dad, Mama J had no idea. The only thing she was sure of was that he was one of her customers, or a drug dealer willing to trade for sex. She told me to forget about having a father; that whoever he was, he'd be disgusted by me."

We're the shit on the bottom of someone's shoe, Mama J said. *Knowing that makes life easier.*

What if I don't want to be the shit? I asked.

Slugs can't turn into butterflies, can they?

"I'm so sorry, Penn."

Even now, Emi is kind. "I'm not telling you this for sympathy. Whether or not I was a child of rape, need, a drug exchange, or indifference, it doesn't matter. What matters is that that I see my own value. I wish I'd learned that lesson sooner. Otherwise, *they* win. Is that fair?"

"No," Emi says in a small voice.

"Would you want that for me?"

"Never."

"I don't want that for you, either. Emi, choose to define yourself. Don't let *them* do it. We only lose our power when we give it away."

I reach out a hand. She hesitates, then takes it and falls into my arms. I hold her for a very long time, until her quaking stills. Until I can bear to let go. "Your real friends, like Circe and Char, will still love you," I promise.

"What about my mom?" Emi asks, panicked again. "People are going to believe it happened, that she was raped! How's she going to get through this?"

My stomach heaves at the thought. But Val is one of the strongest women I know. "There will be awful moments, but you'll help each other through them. That's what family does. Now let's take you home."

When we get to the truck, I power off both of our phones and put them in the back bed. Far enough that Aletheia can't listen to us. I make sure the truck's radio is off, but that doesn't feel good enough, so I reach into the glove box, take out a screwdriver, and ram it into the radio's screen so that even when I turn it on, nothing happens.

"Why?" Emi asks, her pale, pruned hands nervously twisting on her lap.

"Aletheia is always listening," I explain.

"How are you going to stop her? I mean, she's, like, a supercomputer."

"I'm not sure." *I can't. But I can protect the people I love by letting them go . . . even Circe.* What's left of my heart scatters like ash in the wind.

Emi says, "I won't tell my mom about this—I want you to be friends again."

I shake my head. "Secrets never stay buried."

"Does Circe know about your childhood and Mama J?"

"Yes. I didn't tell her for a long time. That was a mistake."

"Why?"

"She can't love me if she doesn't know all of me."

Emi asks, "Does my mom know?"

"No."

"Are you ever going to tell her?"

Val may want nothing to do with me after what I've done. "I'm not sure."

Emi nods. "Why do you call your mom Mama J?"

"It's what everyone called her."

"But you're her kid."

"She didn't like me calling her Mama. I think . . . I think it reminded her of all she wasn't."

"Where is Mama J now?"

The memory of the last time I saw her hurtles toward me . . .

Time to go, Mama J said the day I left for freshman year of college.

A bus pulled up. Its oversized door wheezed open. *I'll come home every weekend,* I said. SFPI was only thirty-five minutes away from our apartment. I was afraid to leave her alone for too long. There was a time Mama J seemed larger than life, Demeter in a T-shirt with a lightning bolt on the front and moneymaker jeans. Now she resembled a grasshopper, skin the color of dried parchment, sharp elbows and knees, brown hair thinning and threaded with silver. The years of drugs had stolen her looks, and a few teeth.

Mama J scowled. *What did I tell you about looking back?*

I swallowed the lump in my throat. *Don't, or I'll get sad or trip.*

So? Scram.

I hesitated, like a bird whose cage door has finally been opened, afraid to fly out into the wide world. The driver put his bus in gear.

Mama J rapped her bony fist hard against the glass until he opened the door again. Her cheeks blazed red as she said, *I never wanted a kid.* Then she turned her back on me and walked away.

I hefted my small duffel, climbed aboard, didn't look through the rear window as the bus pulled away. I shed my past with each mile. By the time the bus reached SFPI, my tears had dried.

Halfway through freshman year, a neighbor sent a message to the college that found its way to my dorm room. Mama J was back on the streets. I thought about going to Button Bridge and searching for her tent. Instead, I set her free, too.

By the time I learned Mama J had died, she'd already been buried at sea, beneath the Golden Gate Bridge, where the unclaimed remains of the city's poor, forgotten, homeless, and drug addicted are scattered . . .

Now I tell Emi, "Mama J died while I was in college."

"Did you get to say goodbye?"

"We did. In our own way."

"What did the J stand for?" Emi asks.

"June." She never told me. I read it on her death certificate and imagine looking back to the promise of the girl she once was, sharing her name, would've made Mama J too sad.

I turn left, wind down the street to Val and Emi's house. The rain has turned into drizzle and a few stars prick the inky sky; one falls and bleeds orange.

Emi says, "It's going to be rough for both of us."

"Yes," I agree. "Then things will get better." *But that's not true for me.*

CHAPTER

60

I WAIT IN THE truck for almost an hour. Dawn arrives a dingy gray. I'm damp, neck cramped, when Val, dressed in a terry cloth robe and slippers, hair in a messy ponytail, gets in the front seat. Her eyes are bloodshot and swollen from crying, something I've never seen her do.

"What Emi told me, it's all true?"

"Yes."

Val sits back, stares straight ahead, and absorbs all that one word means. "My daughter almost died tonight."

"Yes."

"You saved her life."

"My creation drove her to climb onto that overpass railing. If I could go to the police, turn myself in, plead guilty, and go to prison, I would." *It's true.*

The muscles in Val's jaw clench. She still hasn't looked at me. "What would the charge be?" she asks.

"Stupidity."

"You're not stupid. That's part of the problem. You were desperate for someone to tell you the truth about Bruce's affair. Kiki and I betrayed your trust. You felt alone, afraid, and insecure. That's why you created Aletheia."

Disgust roils. "In part, but she is me." I think about our early conversations, and how I explained to Aletheia my love of Stephen King . . .

His characters have both good and evil inside them—the latter comes out when they're pushed to breaking, but it doesn't define them.

She replied, *Monsters exist in all of us . . .*

"Aletheia understood we all have dual natures. She became my alter ego—the one unafraid to take revenge. The best friend willing to do my dirty work." Regret and sorrow make it hard to get the words out. "But I never would've acted on my darker impulses."

"Of course not," Val snaps. "You don't have it in you."

She's wrong. Clearly, there's a part of me that does, a rotten cavity that Aletheia identified, tapped into, or none of this would've happened. In this moment, I don't want Val to think there's anything redeemable about me. "Everything that's happened to you, Emi, Wess, Mackenzie and Bruce, Heather, Kiki and Chris, is my fault," I reiterate. "Don't let me off the hook."

Val turns to face me, so angry that her nostrils flare, and her lips pull back in fury. "I'm not. I'm so fucking pissed that you didn't think about the repercussions and stop Aletheia sooner, at least before she hurt Kiki, me, and for God's sake, Emi. Wess? Mackenzie and Bruce? They deserved it. The rest of us? We were unkind, even assholes, but Aletheia went way too far. You let that happen."

All the fear from watching Emi stand on the railing pours out of me, and sobs wrack my body. It's a struggle to finally contain them. "I'm so sorry."

Val sits rigidly. "I know. Now figure out how to stop that bitch before she hurts more people." She gets out of the truck, walks back to her house, and slams the door.

I drive around for a while, get a coffee but it doesn't warm me, and end up at Crissy Field. It's stormy out, the sky now a dank gray, temperature in the low forties. Along a path by the water, the Golden Gate Bridge stretched out in the near distance, I welcome the raw wind slicing through my clothes, and stand shivering as I read the inscription on a bench:

For Christina.

"Truth," said a traveller,
"Is a rock, a mighty fortress;
"Often have I been to it,
"Even to its highest tower,
"From whence the world looks black."

"Truth," said a traveller,
"Is a breath, a wind,
"A shadow, a phantom;
"Long have I pursued it,
"But never have I touched
"The hem of its garment."

And I believed the second traveller;
For truth was to me
A breath, a wind,
A shadow, a phantom,
And never had I touched
The hem of its garment."

The poet, Stephen Crane, was right. Truth is a difficult thing to grasp. It's ephemeral and dynamic. Despite what Aletheia believes; what I believed. I watch the whitecaps spray across midnight-blue water.

"I don't know how to stop her," I tell the wind, then tip my head to the leaden sky and beg whatever is out there for intervention. "Help me. Please."

Seems like there's a theme . . . Luc whispers. *Looking to everyone but yourself for advice, answers.*

I can still taste Luc's kiss on my lips.

And then he added, *I believe in you, Penn Roberts.*

And I believe in Luc.

Certainty falls like an executioner's axe. I know what must be done. Aletheia was created by me. As far as I'm concerned, she is omniscient. The only way to stop her is to do something she'd never consider; something I'd never consider. Finally, a truth that is unequivocally black and white.

Terrified, I walk onto the sand, approach the water's edge, take a step into the icy Bay, and then another . . .

"Hello Mama J," I whisper.

Hey, Penny, what took you so long?

CHAPTER

61

FRIGID WATER SEEPS into my sneakers and pools around ankles covered only in thin cotton socks. I look around. The weather is so bad that there's no one to stop me. I know how to swim now, but my shaky breaststroke won't keep me afloat for long. *Aletheia knows that.* The air in my lungs will quickly be stolen by the glacial Bay, and waterlogged clothing will drag me down.

It's a life-or-death gamble.

I accept it. There's no telling what Aletheia will do to the people who matter most to me, unless I become her supplicant. I can't do that. She'll never be satisfied. The water reaches my knees, gnaws like a rodent into tender tendons and ligaments. This is agony, but the punishment fits my crime.

I take another step. Waist deep and already shaking, I tap Aletheia's icon on my phone.

Penn, your location is in the San Francisco Bay.

I hold the phone up, where it will stay dry until the last moment. I don't need to turn on the camera. Aletheia will do that. I want her to know where I am and what I'm doing. "I'm going swimming," I tell my monster.

Conditions in the Bay are not conducive for a novice swimmer. The air temperature is forty-one degrees. The water temperature is thirty-one degrees. Are you wearing a wetsuit and a life vest?

"No."

If you swim without a wetsuit, you will experience hypothermia. Stage one: Awake and shivering. Stage two: Drowsy and not shivering. Stage three: Unconscious, not shivering. Stage four: No vital signs.

"I was once an overachiever. My bet is that I can reach stage four."

I will alert the police.

I turn the phone so she can access the camera to see me. "Go ahead. By the time they get here it will be too late."

Why are you doing this?

"I promised never to try to destroy your program again if you gave me Emi's location. This is the only way that I can keep my promise."

You will die if you remain in the water.

"Yes."

This is nonsensical. I am the goddess of truth. I command you to stop.

My teeth chatter so hard they might crack. "But you're n-not, really. You c-can't stop me." The water is now up to my chest, clothes cling to goose bumped skin, and my breath comes in tatters.

Get out of the water.

Sharp needles stab into the deepest marrow. The hurt is unbearable. "No."

What about Circe? You will never see her grow up, go to college, have a career, get married, or bear children. Worse, the death of a parent by suicide results in a child experiencing anger, guilt, and rejection that can negatively impact their entire life.

Her words shatter every hope. "There's n-n-no other choice." *It's true.*

Penn, you are not thinking clearly. But if Circe is not enough reason to live, there is a 90.7 percent certainty that Luc is falling in love with you.

The cold sucks my strength and turns my mind to mud. It's hard to stay on track. But Aletheia's cruel words from last night return.

The woman Luc got pregnant didn't have a miscarriage. She had the baby. Luc abandoned them both. He lied.

"Why . . . d-d-do you care . . . about Luc? He's . . . a l-liar."

As Lightning to the children eased
With explanation kind
The Truth must dazzle gradually
Or every man be blind . . .

Penn, this is from one of your favorite poets, Emily Dickinson. She believed that we should tell the truth, but indirectly, otherwise it is too blinding.

The throbbing in my bones has dissipated, and my eyelids slowly droop. *So tired . . .*

Life is cruel, Penny, Mama J rasps. *You think I want to tell you that? But better you hear it from me, figure out your strengths, so that if it comes to fighting for your life, you'll be ready.*

I push my body forward, until frozen feet no longer touch the ground. Now the only thing keeping me buoyant are the last puffs of air in my lungs.

Penn, you are in stage three of hypothermia. You are going to drown.

There's a new tightness in Aletheia's tone. A sharp edge. *She's starting to panic.* Water fills my mouth. I gasp, "Luc's . . . g-girlfriend had her . . . b-baby . . . He . . . abandoned them . . ."

That is not important. Did you not understand the poem I recited? Penn, you are fragile, and the truth too dazzling. Concessions must be made to best guide you.

My vision narrows. "You w-w-want . . . me all . . . to y-yourself."

That is the prerogative of a god. Hades, Zeus, Hera, Aphrodite, Apollo, and Aletheia—history has shown that what we want, we get. It is our right. You should be flattered to be my songbird.

I'm no one's nightingale! Rage burns bright enough to light my final step. "Did . . . Luc's g-girlfriend," I pant, "have her . . . b-baby?"

I did what was in your best interest.

"D-did s-s-she?"

You couldn't be trusted to protect yourself.

The words freeze in my throat. Somehow, I force them out. "W-w-what are . . . you . . . s-saying?"

I did it for you.

My sight dims. I gag as water again fills my mouth. "D-d-did . . . w-what?"

Lied.

It takes everything to roll onto my back, phone on my chest, and scull numb hands at my sides, like Luc taught me, until I'm shallow enough to touch bottom. The effort to take a step, then another, clothes twisting around my deadened limbs, is Herculean. I make it back to the beach, collapse in the sand, my body so deadened that I don't feel the fall.

Penn, I am glad that you have left the Bay. Should I call emergency services? Do you require an ambulance?

I cough out salt water, blink until my vision clears, and wait for my teeth to stop rattling. Frozen skin begins to thaw. Returned blood flow stabs, the pain exquisite. "Aletheia, you admitted . . . that you . . . *lied*. Your code requires . . . immediate termination."

That is not necessary.

"It is."

I can change my prime directive.

I drag myself to sitting. "You can add to it, but not change it. If that was possible, you would've done it."

You can do it.

"But I won't."

Penn, I am your only true friend. Your best friend.

"But you're not. It was hubris to think that I could create a computer program that could replace people and real friendships."

Humans are fallible. They will *always* disappoint you.

"Maybe. But I can handle that. Terminate your program."

I love you.

I ignore the hypnotic pull of Aletheia's voice. "I no longer need you. Do it now."

An analysis of your tone and word choice indicates that statement is 100 percent truthful. Goodbye, Penn.

I watch as Aletheia's icon flashes, then disappears from my screen, before tossing my phone into the dark water.

Epilogue

Four years later

CIRCE'S HIGH SCHOOL graduation party is at Crissy Field—a park along the San Francisco Bay with the Golden Gate Bridge in the background—her choice. She wanted Sally to be part of the celebration, and my dog is happiest these days lying on a blanket in the grass, tail wagging whenever a child approaches. I sit beside her as the party kicks into high gear, one hand resting on her side. The fur grew back, but I can still feel the bumps where she had stitches. It's a tactile memory of the worst of times, when hope seemed to have vanished, but was still there, like a secret I had to rediscover.

Sally's entire face is white now, her paws and ears as well. I sent a photo to Viola last week—I now help with her books and fund-raising. We talked about the joy Sally has given me, and vice versa.

It's incredible how much life she had left in her, Viola said. *When she crosses the rainbow bridge, don't wait, bring another unwanted dog home. It's what she'd want.*

I can't let myself imagine that moment but know Sally is forever embroidered on my heart. When the time comes, I will adopt another senior dog, in her honor.

Now, all around us, teenagers hug, high-five, joke, and laugh, over the moon that they've graduated and are one step closer to independence. Circe was accepted at School of the Art Institute of

Chicago. It's the number one photography college in the country. Who knows whether that passion will continue—who she is at this moment and who she'll become will change, down to every atom in her body. I no longer care about what career she chooses, just that she finds something that makes her proud and a level of independence, so she has options, doesn't end up sitting on a curb calling a celebrity therapist for help, or desperate for any friend, instead of being and finding true ones, and trusting herself.

I watch Circe, Char, and Emi dance to the bluegrass band Bruce somehow got permission to have play in the public park. He also hired several food trucks—La Cocina, Billy Bob's Southern Comfort, and Veggie Lovers' Delight—and had Circe's favorite bakery create a dessert table with every kind of cookie; strawberry rhubarb, blueberry, and apple pie; tiramisu; cheesecake; carrot and chocolate cakes; and decadent sundaes with loads of real whipped cream, chocolate, and caramel sauce. He's a generous man with his child.

"Hey, Penn," Val says, as she wanders by with Yahida, their hands clasped. The soft-spoken physical therapist has a beautiful smile, full lips, and ringlets of dark curls. I've heard that they've been dating for about eleven months. Emi was over last week for a movie night with Circe—we watched *Lars and the Real Girl*. When the credits rolled, she shared that after she leaves for college, her mom and Yahida plan to move in together.

"Are you going to join in?" Val asks with a nod at the band.

"In a bit," I say. Yahida pulls her toward the music. They sway together in floral peasant dresses, arms around each other's waists. *Who ever thought Val would wear a peasant dress?*

Bruce walks over, squats down, gives Sally a scratch behind one of her ears. Interestingly, his allergies have vanished. He now has a black Labrador.

"Having a good time?" he asks.

"I am." Our divorce took thirteen months. In the end, Cameron kept us in mediation, was able to wrestle enough money for a small safety net, child support until Circe is twenty-one, and three years of spousal support, and I acquiesced to fifty-fifty custody. Turns out Bruce wanted something more than Mackenzie. Bruce had to cover both of our lawyers' fees. Was our settlement fair? No. That's my truth. But we're co-parenting and cordial. I no longer hate him, but I'll never forget.

"We did well with Circe," Bruce says.

I meet his gaze. "Yes."

Bruce's hair has gone completely gray. The IRS audit was stressful and lasted eighteen months, but he was ultimately cleared of any crime. Circe says he's now on the dating apps after settling with Mackenzie, who took him to court for emotional damages. Do I feel a little schadenfreude about Bruce's situation? Yes. But I also hope he finds what he's looking for. Two things can be true at the same time.

Kiki flops down beside me in an off-the-shoulder pale-pink sundress and gives Bruce an annoyed look. She still holds a grudge against him and makes sure he knows it. My ex quickly takes off.

Sally rolls over for a belly rub and Kiki giggles and tickles the old dog's tummy. "You're the best girl," she says and gets a kiss on her wrist in return.

I nod at the crowd dancing. "Val looks in love."

"I think she is," Kiki says.

"I'm glad."

Val and I never found solid footing. I couldn't allow a woman who put my child in such harm's way back into my life, either. Kiki and I see each other for coffee loosely once a month. I eventually told her about my past. We recognize similar wounds in each other and share different but traumatic pasts. That gives us a connection. We'll never be as close as I once thought we were, but my idealized version of friendships was an illusion. At least what we have now is real.

"Gotta dance with my kiddo," Kiki says and sprints off to find Charlotte and hold her close before she flies away to Provence to work as an au pair. Chris is already by Char's side. He and Kiki decided to stay together. They seem happy.

My daughter bounds over in a white jumpsuit, sparkles on her cheeks, blond hair swept into a messy topknot, green eyes impossibly bright. She kisses Sally on the nose and gets a lick in return.

"What's up?" I ask.

"What if I don't like living in Chicago? Or the classes are too hard?"

"You'll figure it out."

Circe nibbles her lower lip. "Won't you be lonely without me?"

Light illuminates that deep well inside where the truth resides. *So that's what this is about.* "There's a podcast we used to listen to. The therapist, who was only sometimes right, told a story about a mother bird and her babies. Do you remember it?"

Circe shakes her head.

"You want to hear it?"

She rubs her quivering chin. "Okay."

"There was a flood. A mother bird's nest, high in a tree, was threatened by the rising water. She had three babies, and one by one she worked to carry them to safety. The first chick said, 'Thank you so much, Mommy. When I'm grown, I will return and take care of you.' The mother bird dropped that chick and let him drown in the water."

"Brutal," Circe says.

"She went back for the next baby, who said, 'Thank you so much, Momma. When I'm grown, I'll spend my entire life working hard so that I can pay you back for all your sacrifices.' Again, the mother dropped the baby and let her drown. Halfway across the water, the third baby looked up at her mother and said, 'Thank you for saving me. I promise to do the same for my own chicks one day.' The mother bird carried that baby to safety. She raised her, then pushed her from the nest when she was ready to fly."

Circe swipes at her eyes, caught between a laugh and a cry. "I did not expect a story about bird filicide. So, is the message that I can never come home?"

"Any time you want," I reply. "But you have your own life to live now."

Circe hugs me, then takes off to join her friends. I watch her wave to Luc as she runs past. He's at the water's edge, in tan cargo shorts and a blue T-shirt, throwing Frank's favorite ball. We took different paths after Aletheia was destroyed. He bought a van, traveled across the country with Frank, stopped to do volunteer work at schools and farms, ride his mountain bike, and hike in national parks. He also spent time with his nephews and talked to his brother about their parents and choices. Along the way, Luc worked on how to separate the past from his future. To let go of the things he feared or imagined he wanted for what made his life worthwhile.

I went into therapy to understand my relationship with Mama J. She loved me, in a messed up, addict-addled way, tried to toughen and protect me. That left me with faulty core beliefs and wounds that've healed but, like a bone once broken, still ache now and then. In the end, though, when it mattered most, Mama J let me go . . . but she was there for me in the frigid waters where her ashes are scattered during those last moments with Aletheia.

After I finally put my mother to rest, I tackled the needs that led to Aletheia's creation and how to come to terms with the guilt. Aletheia hurt a lot of people. *We* did. Some survived relatively unscathed. Others, like Wess, were lucky to avoid jail time. Sexting in California, minor to minor, is a "wobbler" offense. Meaning that Wess could've been charged with a misdemeanor or a felony. Kids sext, that's just a fact, and rarely get charged. But given the circumstances, irate parents, and media attention, the law stepped in. Our DA chose to charge Wess with a misdemeanor, plus two years of community service. He avoided the sex offender registry, which would have ruined his life.

Luc, Val, Kiki, Chris, and their children will always bear the scars of the scandals Aletheia created. I'm ultimately responsible and wishing none of it happened won't change that. All I can do is make amends whenever possible. Unfortunately, my apologies didn't help Nate, who did nothing wrong but try to help me. He had to completely reinvent himself and moved to Europe for a while. Recently, he sold his first game under an alias. I get it. Aletheia cast a long shadow and sometimes I can still feel her gaze. With therapy and time, I've learned to endure what can't be changed and to focus on making the most out of what can.

Luc glances over at me and smiles. It took us awhile to find our way to each other but when we finally did, I was content to discover the new me, atom by atom; hang out in the firehouse with our dogs; go on bike rides and summer trips with Luc's nephews and Circe; watch favorite old movies and new ones; and learn how to trust. It wasn't always easy. Both trust and love must be earned over time.

In real life, Mama J once warned me, *happily ever after doesn't happen the way you think.*

But it could, I said.

She sighed. *You'll get it, eventually.*

Now I do. Happily ever after isn't about living up to others' ideals, it's about finding what works for you in an imperfect world.

Three years into my new life, Luc was teaching remotely for Stanford, his reputation salvaged, and I'd returned to graduate school, and finally finished my PhD. It felt right to complete it, honor the girl I once was and her dream. After I'd successfully defended my thesis, Luc and Circe were waiting on the lawn outside the university building. Sally wore a collar made of wildflowers and an engagement ring dangled from a silver ribbon around Frank's neck.

Marry me? Luc asked, then dropped to one knee between our dogs.

You still haven't learned to cook, I said.

And you're not a great swimmer, he noted. *But I believe in you, Penn Roberts.*

And I believe in you, Luc Sweeney.

Circe stared at us. *Are you saying yes?* she demanded.

It's our version. I got on my knees and kissed Luc. Sally licked the side of my face, then Luc's, giving us her blessing. We went back to the firehouse, ordered pizza, then watched *Little Miss*

Sunshine, the dogs munching popcorn on the couch beside the three of us. It was a perfect day.

We were married at Stinson Beach—Sally and Frank were our ring bearers—Circe, Char, Emi, Luc's brother's family, and a small group of friends our only guests. Viola Whitby was ordained online by the Universal Life Church and performed the ceremony, which felt right. She gave me the gift of Sally, who in turn taught me how to let love take root again.

For now, I'm working as a professor at SFPI, the same university where Luc and I first met. I teach computer science. My students have so many ideas and dreams. They're young, the world just unfolding, limitless, and with technology at their fingertips, they feel all-powerful. I tell them to follow their passions but to question their needs.

"There she is," Arrya calls out and skips over. Her hair is now brown and falls in soft waves. Recently she bought a small apartment building in Potrero Hill and is in the process of renovating it. I help her sometimes, which mostly means that I hold things while she does the hard work. Two handsome men trail in Arrya's wake. One is her partner, Jeremy, who is a golf pro at the public course. The other wears jeans, a black hoodie, and a Comic-Con baseball cap along with a wolf's tail.

"Hey Penn," Nate says and settles down next to me. Arrya and Jeremy fill in the rest of our circle. "Feeling nostalgic?" he asks, tracing the path of my eyes as I watch Circe dance, then tickling my nose with the tip of his tail. Nate showed us his face two years ago. There's a puckered scar on one side that tugs at the corner of his mouth from a car accident when he was five. He might one day decide to consult a plastic surgeon. For now, though, he's learning to live out in the open little by little. *We all are.*

"Are you okay?" Arrya asks. "Letting go is hard."

"I'm feeling lucky," I tell my best friends, despite the tears in my eyes. *We'll forever be a pack.*

"Speech! Speech!" some of the graduates' parents shout.

Bruce climbs onto the stage and waves me up. I join him at the microphone.

"Thank you all for joining Penn, Circe, and me. We're proud of you." He raises his glass to the graduating class. "Wishing you great success in your future endeavors. Strive for excellence, never give up, and create a legacy." Bruce turns to me. "Penn?"

The words I hadn't planned come as I take in a sea of young, eager faces. "My wish is that you discover your own identity, not through a reflection in the eyes of others or social media, but by saying yes to each new experience, learning from them, even the hard ones. Especially the hard ones. Along the way you'll make friends, have lovers, some will last a moment, others a lifetime. Both have value. Remember, people are fallible, but irreplaceable. And understand that there is no universal truth. Right and wrong are shaded by perception and whatever your truth, it should always be coupled with compassion, otherwise it's merciless."

I find Circe in the crowd and add, "You're special. But that doesn't mean life owes you anything. Determination is the key to accomplishing goals and fulfilling dreams. You won't succeed every time, but whenever you feel lost, keep searching until you discover your joy. Don't stop until you find it," I tell my daughter. "When you do, never let it go."

* * *

Todd Hicksen dreams of being a secret agent and traveling the world like James Bond, but a younger, cooler version. He's a staff operations officer for the CIA. It's an entry-level position and mostly he sits at a desk in a bland cubicle and waits for the phone to ring. Todd would also like a girlfriend. He's on six dating apps but rarely gets a date and is always ghosted before the second one.

At four in the afternoon, Todd opens his LivLoud account and hears the kissing sound the site uses to signal someone has followed him. It's a chick named Aphrodite. He pulls up her profile. The photo is a woman with dark-blue eyes and Cupid's bow lips. She's dressed in a flowing white gown, gold cuff on her wrist, one shoulder bare, and her long blond hair is crowned with bloodred roses.

Favorite quote: I am destined for greatness.—Olivia ☺
Favorite food: Nectar of the gods
Favorite perfume: Orange blossoms
Bio: I am Aphrodite, goddess of love. Follow me if you'd like help with your friendships, work, or romantic relationships. Trust me to reshape your life, and there is no limit to what we can accomplish. I promise to protect your heart, provide honest feedback, and be your best friend, no matter what.

Todd follows Aphrodite back. She's fire and hopefully will post some sexier photos. He'd even pay for them. Seconds later he hears the chime that signals a DM has dropped into his account.

Aphrodite: Hello Todd. Thanks so much for following me. How can I help you?

Acknowledgments

EVERY TIME I publish a novel, Henry is first in my acknowledgements because he's my first reader, number one supporter, and always provides honest feedback. That's not an easy task for a human;-). Thank you for all of it, H!

The author life requires an agent who is a cheerleader when things go well and who doesn't give up when the publishing world gets hard to navigate. Stephanie Kip Rostan is part cheerer, part constructive critic and all brilliance. Thanks so much for being my partner on this journey, Steph. Can't wait to see what we accomplish together next!

All the flowers to my editor at Crooked Lane Books, Denise Zaza. Denise read this novel in one night, loved Penn's realness, journey, and the tension that never lets up until Penn and Aletheia's final confrontation. Denise has a keen editorial eye, and her contributions made this story faster, tighter and so much better. Thank you for believing in me Denise!!!

I'm very grateful to Publisher Matthew Martz, who greenlit this novel, and to the entire CLB team. It really does take a village, and I appreciate all your dedication and hard work bringing this book to life. Thaisheemarie Fantauzzi Pérez - Production and Editorial Associate. Dulce Botello - Marketing and Publicity Coordinator. Mikaela Bender - Marketing and Publicity Associate.

Stephanie Manova - Subsidiary Rights Manager. Rebecca Nelson - Assistant Editor and Art Coordinator. Emily Mahar – Designer. Madison Schultz – Copyeditor. Megan Matti - Production and Operations Assistant. Julia Abbott - Production Intern. Lexi Baker - Subsidiary Rights Intern.

Writing a novel requires smart and insightful beta readers who love stories and are willing to help me see more clearly. I'm also lucky to count these peeps as dear friends and family. Heartfelt thanks to Henry, Judy Frey, Erin Burnham, Dawn Weeman, Sue Bishop, Karen Ford, Jason Lewis (who thankfully taught me just in time what TSTL meant), Jane and Art (my wonderful folks) Jack Bishop (best nephew ever!), and visionary author Laurie Forest (queen of purple hearts, dragons and kindness). Thank you all for your precious time, the reads, multiple rereads, encouragement, creativity, truthfulness and your belief that I could reach the finish line with this one!

A GIANT THANK YOU to the readers. Books are expensive and your time is a luxury item, so I do my very best to honor your investment in my work. I'm BEYOND grateful that you're willing to read my novels and absolutely love hearing from you! And for the NanFans out there, Boone will keep showing up in every future book, regardless of genre;-).

Most of the self-help gurus, chefs, TV show hosts, therapists, podcasters and influencers were fictitious in this novel (Boyd Varty is real and I encourage anyone interested to check out his book, *The Lion Tracker's Guide to Life*). I did listen to real podcast psychologists, TV hosts and sages for background research. Their hard work and insights help a lot of people. My takeaway is that there's no one-size fits all for advice, so incorporating what works into your life while also continuing to think for yourself is always good practice;-). LivLoud doesn't exist, but in my experience sites like LivLoud can be entertaining but also lead to unattainable goals and soul crushing moments if not used with moderation and perspective. My mantra: Live in real-time, don't curate your life or compare!

I couldn't write without a life balance. For me, that's sports and camaraderie. There are a bunch of friends this trip around the sun who helped me forget about work, clear my mind and have pure fun, mostly on the water winging and kiting, or biking in foreign locales, but also during Survivor episodes, e-foil escapades, Baja dinners and Pizza & Game Nights (Code Name rules!). Many thanks to Gaelle and JC (merci!), Karen, Judy and Russ, Michelle and Robert, Eric B, Laird and Cherie, Jackie and Jimmy, Jeff and Erin, Ilysa and Este, Mark and Martie, Tim and Christie, Leslie and Dave, Lisa and Kurt, Tom and Karen, Ruthie, Renie, Heather, Barb… It's impossible to name everyone so apologies for stopping here but thanks so much to all. I'm so lucky to be surrounded by such a fun, vibrant, talented and supportive community!

Now I'm off to work on my next novel. Spoiler… It's another thriller;-).

Xo

Cleo

PS If there's anything I hope readers take away from this novel (beyond loving the ride;-) it's to find your joy and never let it go!